Writing Therapy

by

Tim Atkinson

Acknowledgements

My thanks go to Revd. Richard Coles, Jill Pepper, Jeannette Elwood and Sarah Chant, all of whom read and commented on the text at various stages of development, and to my father, David Atkinson, for his technical assistance.

Thanks also to Matt Clifford, for taking the cover photo of my own 'Imperial Model T' typewriter.

For Sarah

'For, lo, the winter is past, the rain is over and gone.'

CHAPTER ONE

This is not a real book; not really. A real book tells a story. A real book starts at the beginning and it has a middle and an end, and I should know - I've read enough of them. I read so many books that one day I woke up as a character in one. I'm there now, trapped between the pages in the story of a young girl who drops out of school, who reads more than is good for her and ends up in the loony-bin. And she is not the only one here stuck between the covers: there are other characters, like the nurses for example: Ted and Monica; and there are other patients too, like Debbie and Jason and Lizzie. And, of course, there's Dr Grimshaw, my psychiatrist.

'So we're all just characters in a book then, are we?

That's him now, *psychiatrising* me. He asks me questions that he thinks he knows the answer to, and I sit here and tell him what he thinks he already knows. That's our therapy; that's the treatment. That is what we do. That, and take the tablets that he gives us.

'Yes we are,' I told him.

'That's interesting' he said. 'So who is the narrator?'

'Me, of course.'

'And you're the author?'

'Yes.'

'And we're now in the middle of the story?'

'Absolutely! Yes. I know exactly what to do, you know.'

'Of course you do.'

'Yes. First of all you start off with a plot hook, and then begin the story in the middle – *in medias res*, it's called. You can use time-shift; write habitual behaviour; slowly build your characters. I know all the tricks, you know – tricks used in a proper book, a book that's written by a proper author.'

'But you're not a proper author, are you Frances?'

'No,' I said. 'One day, though – maybe? I would like to be, if only everyone would let me.'

'I'm sure you would' he said, and smiled. 'But first of all you must complete your therapy.'

Of course he didn't mean *my* therapy at all, oh no. He meant *his* therapy: his talking, tablet-giving, asking questions-type of therapy; the sitting-in-the-silence-wondering-what-to-say-next type of therapy.

'And in order to do that,' he went on, 'you must start at the beginning, Frances. Not 'in medias res' as you put it. You should know that well enough by now. If you're ever going to make a full recovery we must go right back to...' and he gave a little snort '... the *first* page of your story.'

I sat and scowled at him.

'It all makes sense you know,' he added, smiling like a vicar.

Sense. It all made *sense*; it was the *sensible* thing to do. But no, it didn't and it wasn't. I can see that now. Why should it make more sense to do things his way? Whose story was this, anyway? Mine. So why wouldn't it make sense to do things my way? Yes, that's right - there was another, better way of understanding what had happened to me. There was a different kind of therapy: research therapy. That was it! My life to date – the mess I'd made of everything, the dropping out of school and all of that – well, it was all just research for a book. It had to be; it was. Either

6

I was just a loony in the loony-bin like all the rest of them, or this was part of an enormous literary plan: my plot, my writing therapy.

'Look, Frances,' he continued, 'don't misunderstand me. This is *quite* a good idea.' He lifted up the blue school exercise book that I'd been writing in. 'Will means well, I know, but...'

'Yes, I know. He's just the *student* nurse...'

And you, of course, are the *psychiatrist* - the boss, the fat consultant, the enormous ego. But he wasn't. To be honest Dr Grimshaw had been something of a disappointment. For a start there'd been no couch for me to lie on, or even a comfy chair to sit in. And he didn't wear a three piece suit or have a gold watch on a watch-chain stretched across an ample stomach. He didn't have a stomach. Or a waistcoat. He wore brightly coloured jumpers. His consulting room was bare - a desk, two chairs; a plastic box of toys – no more. I had expected so much more of a psychiatrist. I thought at least he'd have a tiny beard. And I'd expected him to make me to lie down on a couch while he read out random words and I responded with whatever came into my head: you know, like 'school – *teacher'*, 'book – *story'*, 'fantasy – *reality'* etc. I'd expected him to do all sorts of things. And most of all I had expected him to cure me. But here we were, months later, doing all the same things that we'd done so many times before.

'Will means well,' he went on. 'But he's got some strange ideas. And anyway, he won't be here for long.'

'He doesn't need to be,' I said. 'He's already done much more than anyone to help me. Look there – see that? See - those comments in the margin? Marginalia. *Nota Benes*. That's him writing in the white space of my story. He's more like my editor, really. He helps me get the words down on the paper. But I'm still the author. I am the omniscient narrator. And I'm the central character.'

'Ok then,' Dr Grimshaw sighed, deciding to indulge me. 'Tell me what kind of character you are.'

He looked down at the file of notes that he'd been making and he started reading: *Frances Nolan* – that's me - *is a girl who's done more reading than is good for her, and now she thinks that she's an author. She's really just a schoolgirl - a sixth-former – studying literature, or at least she should be. But she hasn't been to school for months. She left one day, quite suddenly, for reasons that are as yet unclear. At first she hid the fact that she'd been sent home, from her mother. She got up every day as normal, got dressed, left the house, and went off the public library. There she spent the day behind the stacks, reading fiction alphabetically, until...*

'Until? What happened then?' he asked.

'I got as far as *J'* I said.

'Ah yes.'

'And that was when you found me.'

That was the day that everything had ended, or the day that everything had started – I don't know. Who does? Some things can be hidden, even from the author. Some days, for example, Dr Grim could ask me questions and I'd know the answer. But at other times we'd simply sit in silence listening to each other breathing, listening to the typists typing in the typing pool next door, or listening to cars and buses driving past the door; the church clock chiming.

'Look,' he said eventually. 'I'm not sure that this is working.'

I could have told him that before. I knew all about the problem – conflicting narratives: there was creative tension lying like a snake between us. He wanted me to write a different kind of book but I resisted. In his narrative I was just a girl refusing to face up to what was wrong with her. I wasn't co-operating with him; I was withholding information, even from myself.

'Why don't you want to talk to me?' he said. He looked hurt.

'It's not just you,' I told him, 'I don't want to talk to anyone. The characters in my book are all more interesting. It's their conversations that I'm listening to.'

'Maybe,' he replied and sighed. 'Although I really think it's time we knew now what was happening. There has to be some action soon or else people will stop reading.'

'Perhaps,' I said, 'but I not just yet – we're only on page six,' I told him. 'If I get to it too soon then it will spoil the surprise.'

'Perhaps,' he muttered, turning back to his untidy pile of notes. 'Although I think I might have one for you.'

There. He'd done it now: he'd stopped the story right there in its graphite tracks. And I had no idea where to go from here. I had to hand it to him. I suppose I should have seen it coming. As we sat there on that late December afternoon I should have known he would demand a new, dramatic twist: some action, progress, resolution – at the very least a change of setting. Even I knew that we couldn't simply stay in his consulting room forever. Every Thursday he would meet me at the big front door of the town's Child Guidance Clinic. He would smile and turn and lead me down a corridor, past the typing pool and into the converted kitchen at the back where we sat scowling at each other for an hour. On the wooden desk were photographs of smiling, blond-haired children. His, I thought they must be, even though his hair was dark and wavy, trailing slightly on his open collar.

'You are taking all the tablets I'm prescribing Frances, aren't you?' he would always start by asking me.

Yes, I was. And then we'd sit in silence for a while.

'You do want to get better don't you, Frances?'

Actually, I don't. I like being depressed. It's good fun hurting all the time. I like not being able to get out of bed each morning. And I love the constant washing – can't you smell how clean I am? That smell - like bleach without the fumes? Can you smell it? Can you? No. Of course he couldn't. I just nodded.

On the wall behind him was a poster that I used to look at. The Psychiatrist is... IN, the sign said. Charlie Brown was sitting looking glum: 'Sure you're depressed' sneered the girl, Lucy. 'We're all depressed. Get over it.'

I sat and watched him breathe; I heard his wristwatch whisper. Along the corridor the typists might observe a brief ceasefire. If I strained hard I could just catch fragments of their conversation: boyfriends, diets, new contraceptive methods. How come they found this so easy? How come they could talk about it all so openly? And then I realised they were reading from the script – the letters they sat typing, typing, typing, all the words dictated through those stethoscope things that they plugged in to Dr Grimshaw's Dictaphone. But there was no script for me here in the consulting room; no prompt; no words; no clue. And I didn't have the confidence or the experience to ad-lib.

'Look Frances. Talking therapy is successful in over 80% of cases. It's how we do things nowadays. It is how you and I will gradually discover what is wrong with you. It's how you will get better.'

I nodded, even though I disagreed.

'This isn't really helping,' he went on.

'No,' I said. 'It isn't.'

'We're going nowhere. You've been seeing me for over three months and we're still no nearer finding out what all this means.'

'All what?'

'All this...' he held the manuscript for me to see. 'All the writing that you're doing and the washing – everything. The Health Authority is making cuts, you know. I might not have as long as I would wish to go on sorting out your story. We need to get things into order. And I need you to co-operate. We've got to get to the bottom of what's troubling you, Frances – and to do that you will have to talk - to me; to someone; anyone.'

I suppose deep down I knew that, too. But there was nothing more that I could tell him. Nothing that I'd not already told him. I had told him everything; I'd taken everything that he'd prescribed. I had been coming here and seeing him for three months and the pain was still there buried deep inside, impossible to ignore.

'Of course, at first you would only have to be a voluntary patient.'

I looked up and I saw that smile again.

'That would have to be the basis on which you would be admitted.'

What had I admitted? What had I volunteered?

'I think time as an in-patient would be useful at this stage' he went on. 'At Lowood Lodge, I mean...'

I stood up suddenly. This wasn't in the script.

'Isn't that... you know... ISN'T THAT THE LOONY-BIN; THE FUNNY-FARM; THE SPASTIC FACTORY?'

Silence.

'Does that worry you?' he asked, and put his hands together. Outside, the late December sky grew dark; cold air hissed like gas through small gaps in the window frame. The Venetian blinds were buzzing for an answer.

'Lowood Lodge is not the same as Cranford Hospital, you know. It's in the *grounds* of the hospital, of course...' he went on, shifting slightly in his chair. The working day was coming to a close. Soon, those typists would be going home. For once, he didn't want a long discussion. He wanted a solution. What he wanted was a happy ending. He wasn't satisfied with the resolution I'd provided for him.

'Yes - it's in the *grounds*...' he went on 'but it isn't really part of Cranford Hospital at all. It's different. It's a place for young adults like you, you know, who need to spend some time away from family and school, away from all the stress of everyday life. That's all. It won't need to be for long. You just need a little time to sort things out, that's all'.

Time? To sort things out? I had the narrative worked out by now; I knew the characters and the plot. The details

11

might have needed more work, sure - but the basic structure was already sliding into place, or so I thought.

'Oh, I know exactly what you're thinking,' he was interrupting.

Oh God, I thought. Is that true? Can he see inside my head? Does he know what I've been thinking all along? Is that what psychiatrists can do?

'You're worried, aren't you?'

That was true. I was.

'You think that everyone who goes there must be mad,' he said.

I did.

'You think that if you go there, it must mean all the things that people have been telling you, and all the names that people have been calling you at school – it's all true: that you belong there; that you're like them – that you're mad, too.'

True. Perhaps he *did* know everything that I was thinking? That would be exciting - suddenly, an independent character emerging - someone capable of taking the story in a new direction.

'I'm going to tell you something now,' he told me 'and I think you'll be surprised.' He leaned towards me confidentially, and beckoned me to come a little closer; then he put his mouth close to my ear. I felt him take a breath, and then he spoke.

'You know,' he whispered followed by a pause. 'There's no such word as mad.' He smiled at me – a small, triumphant smile - and sat back in his swivel chair.

'I know' I said. 'I read that in a book somewhere when I was in the library - the word was *a*mad, then we lost the *a*.'

'What? That isn't what I meant,' he said.

'It isn't?'

'No. I mean – there's no such *thing* as *madness*' and he drew quotation marks around the m-word with his fingers.

12

'What?'

'There's no such thing as madness' he repeated.

'But that's crazy.'

'Maybe,' he replied. 'But true.'

And then we had another silence. Someone shouted 'see you tomorrow' and the front door closed.

'So?'

'So?'

'So what do you think of what I've said?'

'Well,' I started. 'Well - ok, then: if that's true, and if you're right and if there's no such thing as madness... well, I don't know...well - what is there, then?'

'No Frances, what I meant was...'

Yes I know, I know, I thought. I know exactly what you meant. I know what you were thinking. I could read him like a book.

'Will you come to Lowood Lodge?' he asked again. 'After Christmas, I mean.'

I didn't bother answering. It didn't really matter. By then, another story was already being written. Nothing ever happens till it's written down, I once remember reading. In a moment Dr Grim would have the words all safely typed out on the paper in a letter to my mother:

Dear Mrs Nolan

Further to our earlier discussion I now feel it would be useful to admit your daughter Frances to the Adolescent Unit. This will allow her treatment to continue more intensively. Although, of course, the final decision rests with both yourself and Frances I would add that – in my clinical opinion – her admission to Cranford Hospital needs to be done as a matter of urgency...

And that was it. So simple; so straightforward - an opening, a conflict, and some exposition. Now for the setting.

CHAPTER TWO

'So they've caught up with you at last,' the wicked witch hissed once she'd read the opening chapter. Actually, she didn't. Or she wasn't. That was just my mother, laughing when she got the Grimshaw letter. But every story needs a baddie – an antagonist - and at first I thought it might be her. There has to be some rivalry; someone has to thwart the hero's plan in order to create dramatic tension. But my mother couldn't even play the villain. Sometimes she was barking like a mad Alsatian; at others she was whining like a kitten.

'I wish I was depressed,' she was opining. (*That's* a good word!). 'I wish that I could lie in bed all day not bothering with anything...'

It was cold, early in the dark January morning. I'd spent Christmas and New Year in bed. I lay there for a moment now while trying desperately to work out who I was and what to do. But I was tired; I hadn't slept. Pretending to be somebody from fiction was exhausting.

'I'm not going,' I mumbled to my pillow.

'Yes you are my girl,' my mother shouted, pulling back the duvet. 'Come on - get up, now. It's time to pack.'

Cold air washed across from all directions. Still I didn't move. I couldn't. Once I'd realised that the ache was still inside, I froze.

'Come on – get up. Get dressed. They'll all be waiting for you – all your loony friends.'

'I can't.'

'What do you mean, you can't?' she snapped. 'You won't, more like. You're lazy, that's your trouble. All that sitting, reading...'

But I wasn't listening. I was somewhere else already. I was always somewhere else. I always had been. Mostly somewhere else had been a place of meadows, flowers and sunshine; nice things happened there, things I wanted to happen, things I had decided. Now though, it was different: the sun had gone, and I was deep within a forest far away from anywhere; things I didn't want were happening. It felt like there was something growing, leaking poison through my body. It was more than just a pain; it was alive. It was a living thing, this thing inside me; it was more alive than I was - a memory of something terrible, maybe; a memory of something bad and horrible; a memory I couldn't...what? Remember! That was it. So should I tell her? Should I try describing it to her?

Of course not, no. Why bother? Anyway, she thought she knew already; so did Dr Grimshaw; so did everybody. They all thought that they knew, even though it was only chapter two. And they thought I was hiding it from them. They thought that once they'd got me diagnosed they'd cracked the case (the head case – get it?). They thought that once they'd done their tests and handed out the pills they'd solved the problem. But the name 'depression' is no more than a red herring. Diagnosis – that's just the start of it; that's only the beginning of the story.

Let's take Lizzie for example, or take Debbie: both patients at the adolescent unit, both of them depressed in different ways - both paralysed by what they've done and both of them unable to remember what it is, to face it and move on. That's what depression is, you know - paralysis. Depression is erosion, slow erosion, wearing you to nothing. Depression leaves you nothing but a shell - not even ill. It's not an illness – can't be. If you're ill then there's a 'you' that is ill. But when depression strikes you haven't got a chance. There is no 'you'. You're dead already: finished; empty. No-one knows that - nobody.

'I do,' said someone suddenly. It was Dr Grimshaw once again, and we were in his surgery.

'I understand. Why don't you talk to me?'

'I can't,' I told him. 'You're not in this chapter: this is just between me and my mother.'

'Well tell her then.'

Tell her. Tell her! As if. But if I tell him then he'll ask me why and I can't tell him that. And then he'll think that I'm denying something or refusing to face up to it. He doesn't understand about the plot. He already has the ending written. He knows what is going to happen, or he thinks he does.

'But shouldn't you know too?' he'll ask me. 'You're the author.'

Yes I am. And I know where I'm going.

'No,' he'll say, 'you mustn't, Frances. Don't do that.'

But why not? Not yet obviously. It's only chapter two. But why not take the most dramatic ending, ending everything forever?

'Look' he says 'I don't think that's a very good idea. There are so many other ways for you to take control, like...'

'Write a book?' I say to him.

But he won't answer.

'And then if I do,' I go on, 'I will have to introduce a little drama. Lots of authors do – and think of what it does for sales. It'll guarantee my immortality. Think of Sylvia Plath.'

'But you're not Sylvia Plath – you're Frances Nolan.'

'Yes. You've heard of her, no doubt?'

But no, he hadn't. So we sit in silence once again and slowly in the cloying heat of his consulting room, my eyes begin to close and I feel tired. My head is getting very heavy...

'Are you sleeping, Frances? At night I mean, instead of in the middle of my consultations.'

Finally, a question I could answer.

'No.'

The tricyclics Dr Grimshaw had prescribed weren't working any more. And now I'd started writing it was more difficult than ever just to do a simple thing like sleeping. Sometimes at night I'd lie awake for hours just staring at the ceiling, thinking, plotting, planning. In the distance I would hear the church clock chiming, counting down the hours until the morning. Then at other times I'd fall asleep so quickly that I'd hardly know my head had touched the pillow. But an hour later I would be awake again and lying in the darkness listening to the many voices of my characters. I could see their words and conversations swirling round the room like mother's cigarette smoke. I would lie and watch them as they twirled and twisted into words and shapes and sentences and statements. Then I'd have to get up out of bed and write them down before forgetting. Didn't want to – *had* to. They would make me; they would never leave me. They are there now in the darkness; they're what makes this happen, they're what makes me get up and get out of bed and take a pencil and a piece of paper and start writing. They dictate to me. They're doing it right now; they're writing this, not me. It is not my doing. They insist; the words insist I write them down. The words don't rest; they never let me sleep. I'm just their channel; I'm their secretary. So what does that make me? As mad as them perhaps? Perhaps I am. Perhaps that's why I'm here. Perhaps that's why all this is happening? Perhaps my mum was right about me all along.

'Right about what?' he asked.

'About...'

'About what, Frances?'

'That. You know. It. Him. Them. Everyone - the other characters; the minor ones; the people in the book you haven't heard of yet, the ones who don't appear till later, like the people at my school for instance.'

'Who?'

'You know – the teacher, Mr Jones, and Louise Anderson. That's the problem, if you want one. That's what's wrong with all this. They are all still there in spite of all my editing. Each successive draft has pared down their significance to almost nothing. But I can't get rid of them. They're there now hiding in the margins, lurking in between the text like ghosts.'

'What have you done to remove them, Frances?'

'Everything,' I told him. I wanted to destroy all traces of them, to expunge them.

'That was when you started your self-harming? The compulsive washing?'

'Yes, but that was just the skin. Once that was clean I still had all my clothes to sort out.'

'And how did you do that? More washing?'

'No – I burnt them.'

'What?'

'Set fire to them.'

'What – all of them.'

'No – only my school uniform. Anything I'd worn when I was with him.'

'Why?'

'I told you – to get rid of him. Get rid of them. To rid the story of all traces of them.'

'But that can't work,' he said.

'I know that now,' I told him. He was making notes now, writing it all down in his black folder, adding to the growing pile of paper.

'Tell me why you thought that burning your school uniform would help,' he asked.

Ah yes – why! That was the question everyone was asking.

'WHY?' my mum screamed when she got back home from work and saw the mess.

18

'Why?' Miss Nicolson had primly asked next morning as I stood before her desk dressed in a pair of jeans. A tractor-mower moved across the field behind her. Out in the playground, underneath her window, schoolgirls talked about the latest bands, their plans for the weekend, last night's telly. In the wooden panelled room a breeze disturbed some papers, fluttering the yellowing net curtains. The stench of petrol fumes and ash rose from the fat black plastic bag that squatted in the corner.

'Why?' Miss Nicolson enquired again. I didn't answer her. I didn't want to answer. And even if I did I didn't know the answer to her question.

At the end of the empty corridor the school bell rang. There was a silence like the breath before a person starts to speak, and then it started. First a trickle, then a torrent, followed by the whole dam burst as all six hundred schoolgirls flooded through the open doors and filled the building. Seconds later teachers left the staffroom, wading hard against the tide. Half way down the corridor my own class would shoal left into their form room. The big fish, Louise Anderson, would be there sitting at the back. Mandy, Claire and Sharon would be sitting in the middle. On the front row, next to Jane and Helen, there would be an empty chair.

Mr Jones would walk in and then they'd all stand up and smooth their skirts. 'Good morning girls,' he'd call out; they'd reply 'Good Morning Sir,' or most of them would anyway. Louise and her friends would still be talking at the back, pretending that they hadn't heard or hadn't noticed him come in. I noticed, though; I noticed them ignoring him. That's the kind of thing that writers do. I always noticed. So did they. But they ignored him. And I noticed that.

'When you're ready girls,' the teacher would call out more patiently than they deserved. And when they were he'd take the register. And this morning, when he got to my name on the list there'd be no answer.

'I simply do not understand,' Miss Nicolson said at last and slowly shook her small grey head.

'Me neither Mrs Nicolson,' my mum replied.

And Miss Nicolson – Miss - Nicolson in flat black shoes, black stockings, with her black gown hanging off her shoulders like a blackbird's moulting feathers suddenly seemed lost for words. Her hair was scraped into the tightest bun; her skin was wafer thin, so thin that you could see her skull.

'Well,' she sighed at last, 'I think you need professional help, young lady. I'll try and arrange it for you presently.'

'Thank you, Mrs Nicolson, thank you very much!' mum gushed.

'*Miss*...' Miss Nicolson trilled as she got up to see us out before assembly. '*Miss* Nicolson.'

'Oh yes,' my mum had said 'of course... I'm......'

Sorry?

But of course she wasn't.

CHAPTER THREE

So here's the plot: I'm depressed - and I mean really, badly, seriously depressed, not simply sad or miserable or something – and I'm not at school. I should be, but I'm here instead; I'm stuck inside the loony-bin with all the rest of the adolescent patients, trying somehow to get better, which is tricky when you're not sure what the matter is. And that's the story's setting: a large old-style Victorian asylum complete with clock-tower, gothic arches, points and pinnacles and crenulations. It's the kind of hospital you don't see any longer; the kind there used to be in every town; the kind of place where people shuffle round the sprawling grounds in slippers; the kind of place where people would be sent and then forgotten.

That's just the background, though – the scenery. The next thing that I need to do is introduce you to the characters. Character creation is one of the most difficult jobs you have to do when you're an author. Making someone come alive on paper: how to do that? How to make a character seem vivid: real, believable and maybe even likeable? Character creation is the beating heart of fiction, I read somewhere in a book. It takes time and patience. So it's a good job I'm a patient - an in-patient, ha ha ha! But no – it still takes lots and lots of effort. Where do all these people come from? Where do writers find them? Where do I come from, for instance?

Some authors use themselves for inspiration, raiding their past as if they're midnight-snacking from the fridge. A little bit of this, and some of that; some cheese, some soggy lettuce and some limp, left-over cucumber. It's amazing what you can scrape together as a tasty character if you have to. I've heard of other authors seeing faces in the street and just deciding, there and then, that that's the person they are looking for; that's their character - that one there, with freckles and the light brown, almost blond-but-not-quite hair; that person standing over there – yes, her.

Just look at her. She's tall; she's fairly slim: not fat; not yet. If you look hard at her she'll look at you; you'll see her eyes are greeny-blue. Her head is lowered so it seems she's looking up to meet your gaze; she doesn't really want to look you in the eye at all. She's shy, that's why. She doesn't really want herself to be seen. She doesn't like talking and she doesn't like other people looking. She can't stand all the questions they keep asking. But she's happy writing.

Can't you see? That's me you're looking at. I'm that girl. I'm Frances Nolan. Well I'm not, of course. That's just my pseudonym. But I'm the author. I'm also the narrator, I suppose. And I'm the book's main character. This is my story; or rather it's my therapy. I'm sitting here putting all these word down on the paper. That's what I'm doing, now. I'm making up the story, slowly – line by line and page by page; chapter by chapter until eventually the weight of words and pile of paper says there must be something worthwhile just because of all the time and effort that it's taken. As the word count grows there will be something tangible, some record of what happened in my life to put me here, in the Cranford Psychiatric Institution, in the loony-bin, the funny farm, the mad-house. There - you can't see that by looking at me, can you? No. I have to tell you that - explain, one line at a time. How else would you ever know?

'Well you could show us, Frances. That's what writers sometimes do – they show, don't tell.'

But no. I couldn't show you madness, could I? Really? Real madness? Like the kind of illness Dr Grimshaw had suggested did not exist? Well, it did in here. In here there were patients who were really mad, who even *looked* mad - patients who had staring eyes like corpses, patients with twisted and distorted faces; men and women whose gait and features had been warped by this 'imaginary' illness. They all wear their diagnoses on their faces. They don't change. There is no cure for what they've got. They'll not get better; they'll be here forever.

We won't, though. We're all going to recover. Here in the adolescent unit we look different, for a start – we all look *normal*. You can't see what is wrong with us by looking. You won't, for instance, see the razor marks on Debbie's legs until she gets undressed in chapter nine. You can't see the knife marks on my wrists until I've made them later on in chapter five and even then not until the bandages are taken off. The wounds have started healing now, hardening into neat white scars. That's what happens here. Things change in the adolescent unit; narratives develop. Some of the patients here have even been discharged by the end of the story. But you still can't see from looking at us why we're here, apart from Lizzie maybe, and even then you've got to know the signs – the slightly hairy arms and cheeks, the skinny legs and wishbone arms. Her clothes disguise it all so well. You can't see them hanging off her bones like so much surplus skin. But that's from the outside looking in; that's not what she sees when she looks into the mirror. No. But what she sees isn't really there at all. In her head she sees a fatter, bigger version of herself; she sees somebody to be tortured into being thinner, someone who must suffer. And we all think we should suffer in some way. That's the one thing that we've got in common: pain. Pain on the inside; pain we try to hide. And how could I 'show' that as all the writing schools would say? How can I show anyone what's happening inside Lizzie's head? I've got to tell you, in the same way that I'm telling you what's going on inside my own. Except I'm not at present, because there's nothing there to tell. I mean, there *is* something obviously, but I've forgotten what it is and now it's there, but like a black hole - empty. I can feel it, and it hurts. But what I can't do yet is think it. When you think about it that could be exciting. Is it some dark and heinous crime that I've committed but I can't remember? Is it a horrendous murder? Whatever, it has not forgotten me; I'm being punished for it now – indefinitely. Definitely. That's why they have sent me here. That's why mum is shouting in my ear right now and bawling at me, telling me to wake up, to get out of bed, yelling that it's time to go.

Eventually I struggled out of bed and packed my case. I left the house as quickly as I could. I called out just before I closed the door, and waited in the darkness for an answer. Rain as fine as mist began condensing on my face.

The streets were empty as I dragged my suitcase through the town. When I reached the station the bus was already waiting with its lights on and its engine running. I paid my fare, whispering the destination to the driver. But nobody was listening. The other passengers were staring through the dirty windows. Some read newspapers. No-one looked excited. Not one of them anticipated what was happening. In many stories this would be the start of the adventure. Even in my book I was leaving home forever. We could be out at sea or on an epic journey, maybe. This could be the Nautilus. It wasn't, though. It was the service bus.

'Cranford Hospital,' the driver called out as the bus slowed down.

I didn't move.

'This is it love,' he repeated. 'Journey's end.'

'I'm sorry?'

'Better not be late for work,' he smiled.

As the bus pulled off in clouds of fumes the countryside returned to silence. The rooks began to caw.

Light was slowly making tangled silhouettes of naked branches, black against a empty sky. Across the road small fragments of the hospital assembled like a jigsaw picture of a castle. There was nobody around. No-one knew that I was here. I was alone, a mile outside the town. I screwed my eyes up trying to make sense of the faded bus timetable. I fumbled in my purse to count the change. Suddenly, the ache inside intensified. The hospital reared up through the trees like an approaching liner. A dog barked somewhere in the darkness. A light went on in the little cottage by the entrance, and I heard the sound of footsteps on a gravel path.

'Bye love,' a voice called out. I hid behind a bush. A garden gate clicked shut as someone turned and started down the long drive to the hospital.

'Excuse me,' I was saying, as I hurried after him. 'Please...'

But he had gone and I was suddenly surrounded by enormous black trees, closing round me like a cage. The early morning sun was starting to dilute the darkness, outlining gothic spires and crenulated walls. Here and there small bright lights shone out from the asylum windows. There were people watching. I kept walking, getting faster, until the grounds began to open like a flower. And there, in the middle of a tiny crossroads, was a sign with arrows and a list of ward names - Manderley, Pemberley, Thornfield, Misselthwaite and Skeldale. At the bottom was a name that was familiar from the letter I was turning over in my pocket. In the farthest corner of the grounds I could just make out a large house end-on to the main road. There was a steeply pointed roof like praying hands and two shallow sloping wings on either side like nave aisles in a church. As I approached I could see there was a smaller, flat-roofed building turning black and green from the sap and damp of overhanging trees. Hedges screened the lower windows of the house; the lights were on upstairs. I walked up to the door and rang the bell and took the crumpled letter from my pocket like an introduction.

...The adolescent unit is a small therapeutic community in the grounds of the Cranford psychiatric hospital. There are usually no more than half a dozen patients resident at any one time. This ensures that staff can work intensively with each patient on an individual level, thereby considerably speeding up the process of recovery...

'Hi! I'm Jane,' a voice called from the open doorway. As my eyes adjusted to the naked bulb behind her I began to see her features: an open face; large eyes, and long brown hair cascading down onto her shoulders.

'You must be keen: we weren't expecting you until oh… at least nine.' She offered me her hand.

'I'm sorry...' I replied and wiped my palm against my thigh.

'That's ok,' she smiled. 'Come in. We're having breakfast. Have you eaten yet?'

I hadn't.

'Yes,' I said.

'Ok, then. Come in anyway; I'll introduce you to the others.'

She was wearing jeans and had a loose, hand-knitted, light-blue sweater. The trainers on her feet were white and clean.

'Hey listen everyone,' she called out as we walked into the breakfast room. The noise subsided for a moment. 'This is Frances – Frances Nolan.'

People looked up from their cereals and nodded briefly, then the sound of spoons being scraped around the breakfast bowls resumed.

'You're lucky, Frances. It's quiet at the moment. They're all still half asleep.'

'Hello,' I said to no-one in particular. No-one seemed to notice and I suddenly felt hot. This wasn't going well. Introducing characters should be dramatic; memorable in some way. Each one should make an impact on the reader. I was failing miserably.

Jane led me by the hand across the room.

'This is Lizzie,' she began. 'She's about the same age as you, I think – how old are you now?' she asked.

'Sixteen,' we both replied, together.

'Jinx!' spluttered Lizzie, spraying cereal across the table.

'Well that's a start,' said Jane. 'Sit here,' she said to me 'while I go into the kitchen. Lizzie will you introduce Frances to the others?'

'Mmm,' Lizzie nodded through an overflowing mouth of yellow mush.

'Hi!' I said again. The girl looked up and smiled. Stray whiskers were extending from her hair line to her jaw. Her spoon-arm flapped the loose folds of her sleeve like a broken wing as she chased the cereal around the bowl. I turned away. A boy looked up and leered. I blushed. I waited for Lizzie to speak but her mouth was full. Soggy scraps of food were falling on the table every time she shovelled in another spoonful.

'What you here for, then?' she asked eventually, picking up the bowl and slurping down the milk.

'I don't know,' I told her.

'I mean – what's your problem?'

'I still don't know,' I said. 'What's yours?'

She squeezed another spoonful in her cheeks and started chewing frantically. 'Him,' she said, and pointed to the corner of the room.

'That's Ted,' said Jane following the direction of Lizzie's spoon. 'He's in charge.'

'He thinks he is,' muttered Lizzie. In the corner Ted presided over breakfast like a judge. He was tall, with a fringe of grey hair round a pale bald head. He stood up straight, arms folded tight across his chest, eyes like chocolate raisins at the bottom of a glass. I looked away before he caught me staring.

'And *this*,' said Lizzie, nodding at the woman sitting down beside me, 'is Monica.' Monica was sitting down and opening up a large manila folder.

'I'm in charge of new admissions Frances.'

'Sorry?'

'I'll do all the paperwork Ted,' the woman was calling out across the room. And Ted, without changing his expression, was laughing. Monica clicked a ball-point into action.

'Name?' she started.

I looked across at Lizzie.

'Sorry?'

'Please confirm your name Miss Nolan,' she continued.

'Frances Nolan,' I replied.

'Address?' It sounded Irish. The voice, I mean. The question. Everything.

I told her my address, my date of birth, my doctor, school and everything. She wrote it all down with her biro on a green form headed 'Cranford Hospital: Admissions'. So much for Dr Grimshaw's fiction.

'What does that bit mean?' I asked her, pointing to the entry under 'Status'. A rubber stamp had printed – VOLUNTARY – across the cover.

'That means you're here because you want to be,' she told me.

'Do I?'

'Yes, of course you do, my dear. You're here because you've chosen to come here, haven't you? You're here to get better, aren't you?'

'I...'

'Of course you are,' she went on. 'And that process starts in half-an-hour, Miss Nolan.'

'What begins in half-an-hour?' I hissed across the table as Monica got up and left the room. A low growl rumbled from the corner.

'Steady on Lizzie,' grumbled Ted, as more food sprayed across the table. 'Frances will assume you've got no manners'.

28

'Community Therapy,' said Lizzie, ignoring Ted completely. 'Happens every morning.'

'What?'

'A meeting. Talking. Arguing. Discussing. Lasts about an hour.'

'And does that happen every Monday?'

'Every Monday, Tuesday, Wednesday, Thursday, Friday,' she went on, giving a snort. 'Every morning after breakfast we all sit around and talk about each other.'

'What do you mean?' I asked. 'What do you say?'

'Well, people ask each other questions I suppose – you know: about their problems and all that. And you have to answer. We all take turns to be the chairman and anyone can talk as long as no-one's interrupting. And you can say anything. Nothing is off-limits – we can all say we you want about each other. And you can't complain about it or refuse to answer, either. If it's in the meeting then it's all supposed to make us better.'

'But what about our... you know - privacy?' I whispered to her.

'The only privacy you get in here is in your head,' she laughed. 'There aren't even any locks on the loo doors, Fran. Start getting used to it,' she added.

'I won't,' I said as much to me as her.

'You will,' she said. 'We all do. You'll get used to it in time.'

I won't, I thought. But I was wrong.

CHAPTER FOUR

Readers always want an explanation. There are so many questions that an author has to answer, like, for instance - where do your ideas come from? How much research did you do? Which bits of this are based on real-life? How much of what we read is true? Well, you should know. You're asking me. And you're all there, you know. That means you must be in the book – you must be as real as me. So you must know. Go on, then – ask! What is it that you want to know?

Patrick, for example; let's start off with you. You're smug and look self-satisfied. You sit there with that slight smirk on your face. You think that you're so clever, and you are. But we know what you're up to. We know you're not really writing all the silly little games on that computer-thingy you and Jason play with. We know why you want to keep it all a secret. Anyway you're not interested in me. You should be. You're an important part of the story later, just you wait and see. But at present you're just sitting in that tatty arm-chair sneaking sideways glances to where Debbie's sitting, hoping no-one's looking. You won't ask me any awkward questions. You'll just sit there like you always do, pretending you've got better things to do.

What will Debbie do while he is ogling her? Will she even notice? No. She'll sit there with her feet tucked underneath her and her hair tied back in bunches, picking at her fingernails. And if she does look up and find him watching her she'll be surprised. That smile she flashes at him will be genuine. But she won't be deceived by him. *He doesn't love you, Debbie and you need to know.* I'll make sure you know the truth. But you don't seem to care. You sit in your enormous chair, your eyes red and your face puffed up from crying and from lack of sleep. Did you even notice last night I was missing? Was it you that told them? Say you didn't; say it wasn't you. And please don't ask me any awkward questions.

What about the baby of the unit, though? What name shall we give to him? It's Jason, surely – got to be - and he is *desperate* to ask a question but he's never quite sure what to say.

'I'd like...' he starts, 'I'd like to know...' He's thinking; you can see it happening, see slow ideas stirring from behind his inch-thick specs. 'What I mean is....' and he's struggling. He doesn't know what to say next. And I feel sorry for him. After all, it's me that's making him so tongue-tied. I'm the one not giving him the words to say. Why won't he look at me, though? Why can't he see me smiling at him, encouraging him, willing him to go on?

As usual Lizzie will sit scowling in the corner, knees tucked underneath her chin and sighing, waiting for the meeting to be over. But by then her breakfast will have left her stomach. Besides, there'd not be time to vomit. Once this thing is finished we've got school to go to: lessons in the adolescent unit classroom, with our teacher. That was our routine, you see. Breakfast – Meeting – Lessons, work sent from our schools. And the meeting was as Lizzie had described it. Once the washing up was done and all the morning chores had been completed, we slouched to the day room for group therapy. There was no choice. Lizzie had been right. It was the way they did things here.

'No secrets,' Ted would murmur, making sure he got the picture.

'I declare this meeting open,' Debbie suddenly announced. This morning it was her turn to be chairman. That was ironic. I looked at her as she sat curled up in the chair. She looked as if she hadn't brushed her hair. Her cheeks were red and tear-stained. She'd slept alone in the little room last night. I had seen to that. The whole thing had been my fault. But I didn't mean to hurt her. She knew what was what: she understood the plot. At least, I thought she did. She'd seen what I had written and she'd promised not to tell where I was going or what I was doing.

But Debbie hadn't even been there at the beginning of the story. She arrived quite suddenly one evening near the start of chapter four. That's quite late for someone as important to the plot as she was going to prove to be.

'Can't we wait a few days before admitting her?' Jane was asking.

'No,' I overheard Ted saying. 'She needs to be admitted urgently - tonight, in fact. It's an emergency.'

'But we've got no room. You know that, Ted.'

'Girls are your department, Jane. You know I wouldn't dream of interfering!' And he laughed a low, catarrhal laugh, like dirty water bubbling down a drain.

'The girls' room is already overcrowded,' Jane continued. 'If she must come in tonight we'll have to put her in the little bedroom.'

'We can't let her go in there,' he said. 'It's terrible. It'll give her nightmares.'

'There's nowhere else,' said Jane. 'It's either there or not at all.'

There was silence for a moment. I could see them clearly through the little gap between the open door and door frame: Ted was sitting on his swivel chair and Jane was perched before him on the corner of his desk, her feet together and her skirt stretched tight across her thighs. Then he put his hand on her bare knee. I saw it. But she didn't move. She just looked at him until he looked away.

'It's all a mess,' he sighed, and shook his head.

He was right. It was a mess. The room was dark, like a cave; the enormous trees outside the window cut the light in half. Dark things had happened there. A former patient had once, well... no-one quite knew what had happened in that dingy room. But now the wood-chip paper was all torn and hanging from the walls in strips. Graffiti had been daubed on every surface. It was like an adolescent Lascaux: pictures, drawings – toilet wall stuff; horrible. Since that night the room had been left empty. The boys were all squeezed into a single dorm. Girls too, when I had first arrived.

'Besides,' Ted added 'if we put her there then she'll be all on her own.'

'I'll go in there with her,' I heard myself announcing as I stepped into the nurses' office.

Ted spun round. Oh God! Perhaps I should have knocked or coughed or something? This was confidential. They assumed that I'd been listening. I turned to go, embarrassed; frightened, even. But then Jane made a move towards me.

'That's very thoughtful Frances,' she had said, and put her arm around my shoulder.

That night as Debbie lay in the bed beside me in the darkness, I could hear her crying softly. Hardly breathing I lay in the darkness, listening to her sobbing late into the night. I forced myself to stay awake until the noise gradually subsided into sleep. Then once I heard her breathing softly, I offered up a little prayer for her as she lay sleeping.

'A prayer?' asked Dr Grimshaw suddenly. 'Why? Are you religious, Frances?'

I hadn't really thought of it before.

'You said you offered up a prayer.'

I did. That's true. Because that's what it felt like with her there breathing softly, lying in the bed beside me. There was nothing in the world that I could do for her. I couldn't help her, solve her problems, cure her. You can only cure yourself, I know that now. And you can only do that when

33

you know what's wrong. And as we lay there in the darkness I had no idea what her problems were or why she was in here. What else could I have done but think about her? What else but concentrate my hearing on her breathing, listening as it started rolling forwards like small waves breaking on the beach? I could think about the next day. In my head I could write down the words that I might say to her next morning: me and her; just me and this fragile human being lying in the darkness just an arms length from my bed. But at that moment, she was all that I was thinking.

'That's like praying, isn't it?' I asked him.

'I don't know,' Dr Grimshaw said.

'Well, it is if there's no God' I said. 'And if there's nothing you can do. That's all prayer is anyway – something to do when you can't do anything to help; something that's designed to make us feel less helpless. Why pray at all if there's nobody to pray to anymore?'

'And isn't there?' he asked me gently.

'No,' I said. 'Of course not.' Silly question. 'If God existed why would he have done all this to me?'

'All what to you?'

'All this,' I said and pointed to below my ribs.

'So tell me what it is,' he asked me. 'Tell me when it started.'

It was all a trap. He wasn't interested in her at all. He didn't care what I was saying. He didn't care about what we'd been doing. Just when I felt I might be on the very edge of something, somewhere. I might be on the verge of saying something, knowing something, realising something that could be important. Just when there were words emerging – just when I could see them in the distance gathering like fluffy clouds on the horizon – just when things were happening, he went and asked another stupid question. Now, because of him, I couldn't write a thing. Damn him! How am I supposed to write a book with all these fucking interruptions?

Each afternoon at Lowood Lodge was set aside for psychiatric consultations. Two floors below the attic room where we were seen there would be noise, activity. The boys might kick a ball about outside; the girls watch Crown Court on the telly. Up here in the narrow roof-space it was dark; the ceilings steeply sloped. Sounds from down below would drift up lazily like the smell of something cooking. The narrow window showed the tops of the tall trees slowly coming into leaf. A soft green haze glowed like a halo round the branches.

'Ok,' he said at last. 'Don't think about that, now. Let's get back to Debbie, shall we? You were telling me that you loved her.'

'Was I?'

'Yes, you were – quite definitely.'

I wasn't sure. How could I be?

'Just have a look,' he told me.

So I did. I turned the pages back and there it was – in black and white: 'I think I fell in love with her,' it said.

'I didn't write that,' I said.

'You did,' he told me.

'How? When?'

'I don't know. Don't let it worry you. Continue with it. Carry on. Keep talking to me. Tell me when it happened,' he was saying.

But I don't know when it happened, really. Probably at about the same time that I found the knife, I thought, although I'm not about to tell him that. That was the first time for ages that I'd ever felt anything other than the heavy ache that I'd been carrying for months.

We had both gone for a long walk in the grounds. *A little exercise is just as good as all this medication* Monica used to tell us as she handed out our pills.

Of course, we always went for walks in pairs. We had to, just like we had to sign out in the nurses' office. It seemed only natural that Debbie and I should go together. We were room-mates; we were friends. And yet we were so unlike each other. But it didn't matter. She had something that I needed. I could learn from her, I thought. I could learn to be like her. I could become her and at the same time finally become myself. She had something that I wanted. She was something that I wanted. And I hadn't realised I wanted it until we met.

One afternoon we'd left the road that ran around the back of the asylum. The grounds here in this dark, forgotten corner of the hospital were overgrown and long neglected. The grass was long and yellow; flower-beds choked high with last year's weeds. The paths were overgrown, so overgrown we didn't even see the little summer house at first. But then it started raining, and we sprinted for the nearest shelter. There in the corner, almost hidden by the long grass was a large flat shed with a low-pitched overhanging roof and small veranda.

'Frances... the door's unlocked,' Debbie panted. 'Let's go inside.'

The door was stiff. Inside, the single room was dark. Against the walls were propped what looked like old, abandoned gardening tools. Thick dusty cobwebs hung down from the roof like rotting gonfalons suspended in the school chapel.

'I wonder what it used to be.'

'Dunno,' said Debbie as she slumped down in an unwinding wicker chair. Outside, the rain was getting heavier, washing down the dirty windows in a waterfall. Sudden gusts were picking up whole fists of rain and throwing them like gravel at the glass. Debbie looked at me. A crash of thunder trembled through the timber. I walked over to where she was sitting and sat down on the chair arm next to her. Then I put my arms around her and I held her tightly.

'How did that feel?' Dr Grimshaw asked.

I didn't know. It wasn't like a feeling I had had before. It was just me, and her – together. Nothing else mattered.

'Describe her to me.'

'What?'

'Describe her to me.'

'But you know her! She's your patient,' I replied.

'I know.'

'You know exactly what she looks like.'

'Yes, I do.'

'So why should I describe her to you?'

'I'd just like you to, that's all. You'll see why. Now go on...'

'But I don't know where to start.'

'Start anywhere,' he told me. 'Picture her. What do you see when you close your eyes and think of her?' he asked.

'I see her face,' I started.

'Yes?'

'And then I see her eyes: her clear eyes. Are they green or are they blue? Do you know, I don't know. Both, I think. Sometimes they look blue and sometimes green. I see her pale skin, too: not white or pasty - smooth and healthy, pale with freckles sprinkled on her cheeks and nose like little grains of sand. Her lips are slightly pursed, as if she is about to speak or maybe smile. Except she doesn't speak or smile: she looks at me as if she's questioning or waiting or expecting something. Her auburn hair is longer now than when she first arrived. It's sleek and shiny like a pony, washed back from her face as if she's dived into a lake then broken through the surface of the water, coming up for air. It's held in place with a small pink elastic band. Her eyelids and eye-lashes, every strand of hair is strong and auburn-brown, like autumn leaves. I couldn't look at her for long. I felt a lump swell in my throat. Tears began to prick the corner of my eyes. The wider she smiled that smile, the more a different sort of ache inside my heart intensified. I didn't need to make her up. I didn't need to invent her hair and eyes, her youthful beauty. She was there in front of me. And she was beautiful. She was. But she was magical, too:

magical as well as beautiful. She was doing magic too me. There was something in her eyes that seemed to ask me such important questions.

'And did you have an answer to them?'

'Maybe,' I replied. 'But not an answer I could ever put into words.'

Even as I said it though, I knew it wasn't true. What we had done together, and what Debbie did for me reminded me of words I'd read once, things I might have said, and thoughts; reminded me of where in the story I now was, where I was going and where I had been when...

'When?'

When what? When fantasy became reality? When what is written down becomes what happened? When what isn't written hasn't happened; when we've edited, revised what has been written; when we have imposed a structure and a narrative?

'If only you'd have told me this before,' said Dr Grimshaw nodding at my blood-stained, bandaged wrist.

'I couldn't,' I replied. 'I didn't know myself.'

'Ok,' he whispered. 'Tell me where you found the knife.'

The rain had gradually begun to ease. I got up, looking through the window at the grass, now beaten flat and splaying out in all directions. As I stood there watching the rain subside she got up from the chair. I could feel her body getting closer. Even though I wasn't looking at her I could tell precisely – to the nearest millimetre – where she was. It was as if her body had become a part of mine, as if she was attached to me in some way. She put her arm across my shoulders. I turned my head towards her and she moved a little closer. I moved closer; she moved closer; like the seconds of a clock we ticked a little nearer, tick by tick. Then suddenly, the hour chimed and our bodies were together. I pushed my face against her breast. She pulled me closer with her arm, while her right hand started gently stroking my hair.

'There there,' she whispered. 'There there, Francie.' And inside, deep inside, I smiled. Had Debbie read it too, I wondered? Whose words was she quoting?

'It's going to be all right,' she said, and for a moment she was right: it was. With her it always was all right. If I could only stay this close to her I think it might be, just about, all right forever.

We sat down on the dusty floor together. A vague damp smell of wood was rising from the ancient building. It was dirty down there, not that either of us noticed. We lay down; we lay there in each other's arms for ages. Neither of us noticed when the rain stopped falling. Neither of us noticed that the sun had started shining and the whole world had stopped turning.

'We'd best be getting back,' she said at last. 'They'll wonder where we are'.

Of course they would. She turned and climbed to her feet, fastening her jeans as she stood up. The separation of our bodies was an amputation.

Then, as I hauled myself up off the floor my foot caught something, hidden underneath a pile of rough brown sacking.

'Ouch!'

'What is it?'

And as I bent to rub my toe, I saw it lying there in front of me.

'God, Francie,' Debbie shouted. 'Put it down: it's horrible.'

'No way' I said. 'This could be exactly what I'm looking for. This is a discovery.'

'But they'll kill us, Francie' Debbie said. 'And anyway, it's useless.'

She took it from me and she pressed the blade against her arm.

'But I could sharpen it. And anyway, I'll need a knife to cut the pages as I'm reading.'

'Not anymore,' she said. 'Not these days. God - what kind of books have you been studying?'

She turned it over in her hands. It wasn't much - a vegetable knife, blunted after years of cutting cauliflowers and cabbages. The blade was dirty, too, and flaking with corrosion. She ran her thumb along the rust-serrated edge, then tossed it on the floor.

'No, Francie. Let's just leave it here.'

But I could see the possibilities. I knew it could be polished, sharpened to a fine stiletto. I could see how useful it might be to the emerging plot. Stories always need a prop; a special object – a murder weapon, even!

'Look, if they find out about it we'll be for it,' she was saying.

'That's true,' he added. 'You knew the rules: *No knives, no scissors and no mirrors.*'

But I had other plans; I had another book to launch. And so I hid the knife inside my knickers. Flakes of dry rust crumbled off and stained my skin. The blade felt cold against my bum. When we got back to the unit I slid it underneath my pillow. And no-one ever found it. No-one knew that it was there. They didn't know a thing until the evening that I used it.

CHAPTER FIVE

And now I held it right there in my hand. The whole thing was resting in my palm: the plot, the characters, the narrative, the setting and – at last, at last - the ending, the conclusion, the final chapter. I was so sure this would be the last page. This was the denouement, or the resolution – early maybe but then I knew by now my story was only short, a novella maybe. I didn't need it to develop any further.

Outside the open bedroom window, high up in a tree, a thrush had started singing. The evening sun was shining. A gentle breeze was playing through my hair just like the fingers of a secret lover. I'd washed it specially that afternoon – it's all part of the ritual. I'd put on clean clothes and I'd tidied up my few belongings. I'd also tried to write a note for Debbie. I'd sat down with an empty piece of paper and I'd watched as phrases floated round the page in front of me. Trying to get hold of them was futile; it was like trying to swat flies. They were much too quick for me: for me, the writer. None of them would settle on the paper. None of them expressed what I was feeling. No words could possibly describe what I was doing. Nothing I could say could tell them, no words of mine could make them understand. There were simply no words for it. It was beyond all language. And, in a strange way, that was good because beyond words there could be no thoughts and without thoughts there would be no painful memories. Nothing. End of story. Simple, so I thought.

But then, when there are no more words to read, when you've read them all and when they don't mean what they used to; when the books all aren't worth reading; when you've finished writing, when the last page of the book you're working on has just been written, then what? When the words suggest themselves it's natural to write them. That's what writers do. They write. That's what they are. But what are writers when the words aren't coming? What was I now that there was no more writing? I was struggling. Something had to happen. I had to make it happen.

A sudden breath of scented air brought distant sounds into the room. There were shouts and shrieks, the sound of children playing. Somebody was laughing. The trees were coming into leaf, the branches filled with singing birds and fresh green leaves. In a few more days the hospital would once again be cut off from the outside world for the summer. It was now or not at all. I had to get the story to the publishers. I had to let the world know what had happened to me. It was the only way. I read through what I'd written once again, to make certain that I'd told the story accurately. Then I parcelled up the package and started my escape.

The catches were supposed to stop the window opening more than a few inches, but they were old and the metal had been twisted. If I just...pushed...hard...once. Yes! The frame flew open, leaving the catches hanging in mid-air. I tucked the book beneath my arm and climbed onto the window ledge. From there it was a small drop to the flat roof of the kitchen. I threw the package down ahead of me, hung down from the drainpipe at full stretch then dropped onto the ground. And then I was away.

I decided not to walk along the road, where cars and buses would be passing. There was a footpath leading back across the fields, shielded on both sides by a high hedge. That would take me to the town. Once there, I could easily locate his street, or so I thought. And when I did, when I delivered the completed manuscript to his hands and when he read what I had written, surely then, when he had read the final chapter, surely then he'd understand? The words would do my work and I would be somebody. Not a sorry little schoolgirl with a crush on her former teacher – but a writer! He would understand and nod and smile, and then he'd hold me in his arms and tell me I was wonderful, and that he loved me. Surely? He would smile at me and say how much he'd missed me. And? And if he didn't? If he didn't, well - I always had the knife.

But as I walked along the lane dodging brambles and avoiding nettles, I began to have my doubts – doubts about my own ability to write, to tell a story. Did it begin too early? Was the conflict sufficiently dramatic to hold the reader's interest? Was the time-shift too confusing? I had to make him turn the pages. But what if he stopped reading? What if the development went on too long? And what if the denouement wasn't credible?

I sat down and unwrapped the parcel. As I flicked through all the pages there was someone's name in almost every paragraph. There she was at school so effortlessly doing well in everything; there she was getting everything she wanted - the high marks, the praise, the prizes, kisses. We had been in friendly competition for so long. She had been a nice girl in the first form – ribbons in her hair, no make-up, no short skirt - but things had changed. The earrings, lipstick; high school boys all waiting at the school gates for the bell. And there she was, still winning all the prizes even though the game had changed. And I nowhere; I was being left behind. I wasn't even in the background of my own life-story.

That was when I had decided to change tactics. I had noticed there was something that she couldn't get, no matter how she tried, no matter how many buttons on her crisp white blouse she left strategically undone. What she couldn't get was *him*. And she had tried so hard to get him, too. Every time he came towards my desk to help me, every time he spent some time with me, helping me and answering my questions, patiently explaining to me what I should be doing, she would be there with her hand up calling to him, trying to attract his attention. She could do it all so easily: finish early, rock back on her chair and then...

'Sir!'

'What is it Louise?' As he lifted up his head, I got a faint whiff of his aftershave –*Blue Stratos* as I discovered from the testers in the local pharmacy.

'I've finished sir,' she told him. But she hadn't. No, she hadn't even started. Right in the middle of my explanation; right in the middle of *my* time with him - just as I was starting to begin to understand, just when the clouds of literary analysis were at last starting to clear.

'Ok Louise. I'll be with you in a minute,' he would be saying. 'Now, what you've got to ask yourself in this extract is - what's the author's motivation? Why is she doing what she's doing? Why is she behaving in this way, and why do incidents like this – so trivial, so incidental to the plot – why do they *bother* her so much?'

'What shall I do now, sir?' Louise Anderson would call out. He would stand upright and turn to face her now. And I would clench my jaw tight, swallowing the things that I'd be thinking. She *wouldn't* let him be with me; she *would* not. It was as if she were still jealous of me; her – the girl who had the lot, the girl that everybody liked; the girl with boys lined up and waiting by the bus-load for her at three-forty-five. She couldn't bear to see him spending time with me; she couldn't bear to see me getting his attention. And when she called, of course, he'd have to go to the back row, to be with her; to talk to *her*. Instead of me.

By the Lent term I was struggling. Everything that I was writing seemed so clichéd – pupil, teacher, teenage rivalry. The pretty beauty and the school swot. But I wasn't even that. I was in danger of being withdrawn from the 'O' level entry; there was talk of doing CSEs or Sixteen-Plus exams instead.

'You had better pull your socks up then, my girl!' Mum had told me as she read the latest school report.

I didn't argue with her, even though I wanted to. I didn't scream at her and tell her she was so unfair, although I thought about it. She always sounded so damned pleased when things weren't going well for me. She seemed so pleased that something might be standing in the way of what I wanted. I knew what she was thinking. She was thinking that it would do me good to leave the sixth-form, not to go to university – to 'have it easy' as she put it. I didn't tell her that, of course. I never did. It did no good.

'You're right.' I said instead. And then I waited. How long should I leave before it sounded like a new idea, I wondered? How many seconds would it take before it sounded like a plan that I had just that minute thought of?

'Mum,' I started.

'What?' she snapped.

'Mr Jones says I've got a chance of maybe staying on into the sixth-form.'

'What!' she spluttered! 'You?'

She started laughing. Well, her mouth was open and her eyes were closed and she was quacking like a duck, although I knew she didn't find it funny. Once she'd finished I could tell she couldn't quite decide what to say next. Or how to react: whether to tell me I was useless and that Mr Jones was being generous, or to tell me something else, perhaps: that Mr Jones was after something – *you know you're teacher's pet with him* – and that she would put a stop to it.

'You ought to try working in the shop, my girl. You'd never manage it!'

'I know,' I humoured her. 'But Mr Jones mentioned extra lessons after school,' I added.

That was true. He had. *I'll help you*, he had said. He'd offered weeks ago. He'd said that if I ever wanted any extra help he would be more than happy to provide it. And I had thought....What had I thought? I suppose I'd thought it was a golden opportunity. God – if he existed – must be smiling on me. In the end the big denouement seemed to be surprisingly easy.

'I'll want to see some progress,' Mum demanded. 'And I'll want to see it quickly.' Then she announced that she would 'phone the school next day.

'No,' I interrupted, trying not to sound too panicky. 'It's ok Mum. I'll ask around at school tomorrow. Mr Jones sometimes helps me in the lunch-hour: maybe he would do it for me?'

And for once she was too tired to argue. A day on her feet in the shop – as usual – had tired her out. This was always the best time to ask for something controversial. She was just as likely to tell me to get lost or shout at me or storm off in a rage. But this evening she didn't. She swirled the ice around her glass, then drained the gin and closed her eyes – and she agreed.

Next day at school I stayed behind and asked him. I had to get it sorted out before Mum changed her mind, or summoned up the energy to take it on herself.

'Sir!'

'What is it, Francie?' He was putting stacks of books into the cupboard in the corner of the room. When I spoke he had his back to me and turned to look over his shoulder. I felt something move inside me.

'Sir?' In spite of having planned exactly what to say and how to say it, I was struggling.

'Sir - I was wondering…'

'Yes?' He stopped what he was doing and came over to the desk. 'What were you wondering?'

'I need to improve this, sir.' I said to him, and showed him some of my writing. 'I want to be a writer – go to university, maybe even train to be a teacher.'

'Not put you off then?' he said with that broad smile, more like a grin. His pale blue eyes seemed lit from inside – some writers might say 'twinkle' but that sounds so twee. No. The skin at the corners was permanently creased into fine lines. He smiled a lot, especially at the end of the day, after lessons, when I would go back to the form-room to collect my bags. He smiled so much that when he wasn't smiling you could see the skin beneath was white, like a faint ghost of a smile in the corner of his eyes.

'What do you want me for?' he asked me, calmly.

Perfect. Now I didn't need to beat about the bush. I could come straight out with it. Ok, then... But instead of asking him my mouth went dry. The words I had rehearsed stuck somewhere in my throat like biscuit crumbs. I tried again: I took a deep breath, but my voice still quaked a little.

'Will you give me extra lessons, sir? My mum says she can't pay but I can, I will... I mean I think I can and I could always, you know...' I looked down. I felt my face go red.

'I won't need many,' I continued 'just a few to get me sorted. I don't think it will take too long. I just need to get things figured out. Will you think about it, please? Sir, will you?'

By the time I spoke the last word I'd got no more breath for any more. I shut up. And I blushed. I got up from my chair, picked up my bags and made to leave. And then he caught hold of my arm.

'Hey!' he said. I turned. He wasn't smiling. And he looked concerned. Oh God, I'd made it so damned obvious. He was going to refuse; he was going to have to. He was going to ask me what was wrong. He was going to get me transferred to another form. He was never going to teach me anything again.

''Course I will,' he said, and smiled. And suddenly, I smiled too. He let me go. The ache inside me melted and the cold damp patch evaporated. The sun came out: an inner warmth I'd never really felt before and didn't understand - triumph, maybe; after all, I would have him to myself now. I had won. But there was something more. Somewhere in my head there was a voice. Someone was singing: not much, and nothing worthy or profound, but singing all the same – an old song, newly re-done. Madness. This was madness. And it must be love. The rhythm kept me going till I reached the front door, bounded up the stairs, and dived into the safety of my bedroom.

CHAPTER SIX

The lessons at home went well at first. I started writing things, as well as reading things that other authors had created. I sat and I wrote myself a whole new life, a better life – one where I got what I wanted, one where she got nothing. Things got better, as long as they were written down on paper. But in the real world things weren't going well at all. In the classroom it had suddenly become more difficult to concentrate on anything; on everything - except of course what *she* was saying. I always knew what she was doing, even if I couldn't see her doing it. She was sitting on the back row right now watching me, and she was talking to her friends – about me. How did I know? How could I be so sure? Well, let me give you an example.

'Nice shoes Frances,' she would call to me as I walked into the classroom. A compliment, perhaps? A friendly word? No. That's precisely what she wants you to believe. And so you look at her, and maybe smile. You ask her: 'Do you think so?' And then somebody laughs.

'Oh no,' she'd say. 'No, really.' Except that now she would be laughing too. And someone else would then take up the questioning.

'Frances, have you ever – you know... *done* it?' Shrieks of laughter. 'Only... you don't sit with us. Why don't you sit here at the back wi' us, eh Frances? This is where

49

you sit you know, when you've done what boys and girls do; what comes naturally.'

Shut up, oh please shut up: shut u,p SHUT UP! SHUT THE FUCK UP? Why ask all these questions? Why me? Why now and why today? What is it that you want from me? What is it that you want to know?

'Got a boyfriend, Frances?'

''Course she has,' - a different voice now. 'It's Mr Jones ain't it, Frances? Good at it is he? Is he good in bed?'

'Nah. She's not done owt,' someone else says. 'Still a virgin, aren't you Frances?'

'Yeah, no-one'd touch her – ever.'

'Not into lads, eh Frances? Lasses, is it? You a lesbian?'

'Yeah - we've seen you looking at us in the showers.'

As if I would! AS IF I WOULD? Oh fuck!

And then it got to me, you see. It made me angry. Each time I wrote down what they were saying - even though it was me putting words into their mouths and thoughts inside their heads - it got beneath my skin. Writing can be like that sometimes. Dickens wept for Little Nell. And I would seethe like a smouldering volcano at all the accusations and the innuendo. I was bubbling with rage. It made me want to lash out hard – at them, at me, at anyone or anything. But I wouldn't. I would keep it in. I would hold it all inside, slowly simmering through the afternoon and almost boiling over as I marched home on my own with scalding cat-calls spitting in my ear.

When I got back home, I'd close the door; I'd search the bathroom cabinet for something I could use. I found it in a little cardboard envelope that looked as if it hadn't been touched for years. I felt my finger touch my thumb through the row of holes across the centre. I knew exactly what I needed. Something sharp; something capable of drawing blood; something that would cut the skin but not go down too deeply: just far enough to hurt; enough to bleed, enough to mask the boiling pain inside. I'd press as softly as I could...

'And then?'

'And then I'd close my eyes. I'd sigh. I'd be ok.'

'Ok?'

'Yes – but not for long.'

'The trouble is,' Dr Grimshaw went on, 'that the endorphin rush you get from cutting doesn't last for long. Like anything, your body builds up resistance over time.'

'Yes I know,' I said. 'I heard it on the radio.'

'So what would you do next?' he asked.

'I'd clean my wounds and sit and wait for him to come around'.

'And?'

And what? Yes, what? What did I do next? I know; I found the blue school book that I'd been using for my writing. It was carefully hidden. And I started writing. Then, when he arrived I might get round to showing him what I had written. I enjoyed it, being on my own with him; getting his attention; learning things at last. The writing I was doing came on famously. Private lessons started doing for me everything I hoped they would. He was so patient and so kind just like I always knew he would be. I knew beforehand it would be like this; knew he'd want to help me, knew there'd never be a problem. I knew what he was thinking, too. I could tell. He'd talk to me a bit about his life: he had ambitions, just like me, to be a writer. He wasn't happy as a teacher. Well, who would be? And he trusted me. I trusted him. We talked. We talked about the books that I was studying and he introduced me to some extra ones he thought I should be reading, books he thought might help my writing. And we wrote together, sometimes. Fiction, mainly, and some poetry. We were a double-act like Hughes and Plath; we could write anything together.

'Anything?'

'Yes, anything. Except the one thing that I really wanted.'

'Which was?'

'Oh no. No - spoilt it. That's too soon. I can't reveal it now - we're only on page forty-nine. That's far too early.'

'Look - let's be logical about this, Frances' Dr Grimshaw interrupted.

No. Let's not. That didn't work for me. Logic never did. Logic tells you one thing, but emotion says another. It doesn't matter what you think, how hard you rationalise it or whatever. It's what's happens in your heart that matters. I might *tell* myself, for instance, that I didn't care as Louise strutted round the school as if she owned the place. I might *tell* myself all sorts of things. I did. I told myself that she was jealous of me but I knew, deep down, it wasn't true. I told myself I wasn't bothered by her teasing in the showers after games and told myself that I should linger there beneath the tepid water, putting on a show. But no: a quick sprint through the water then a dash back for the safety of the towel. That was me. But never her. She wouldn't hurry; didn't seem to care. She paraded through the changing rooms as if she were a model, showing off her fake tan like the latest Paris fashion. *She* had long blond hair. *She* was tall and slim. *Her* skin was always smooth and clear. *She* never had a single spot. She wore a slightly different shade of navy jumper to the rest of us; one more expensive than the normal stuff that we bought from the schools' suppliers. There was a little white motif embroidered on the left breast. She looked immaculate in her school uniform, and as pretty out of it.

'That's very interesting,' said Dr Grimshaw.

Oh I bet it is. You'd fall for her. They all did. It wasn't any wonder that she had a constant queue of male admirers. Even the teachers liked her. You could tell by the way they spoke to her and looked at her. There was a certain something in their eyes, and there was always lots of laughter when she was around. But it was forced. She made them laugh whether they wanted to or not. Because they wanted her to like them, or even just to notice them. And she was never in any trouble. She could get away with murder.

Just the way she walked through the school, down the corridors; the way she sat in class. She glided in among us like a swan, serene but ready in a moment to turn and hiss, or worse. I studied her. I searched her body for some small, unsightly blemish. Nothing. She was perfect. Her full and rounded breasts were perfect; her long legs were perfect, and her bottom - was it perfect? Was it just a tad too big? Did it wobble just a little? No it didn't. It was perfect.

'Hang on a minute Frances.' Mr Jones was leafing through the blue school book that I'd been writing in. I had finally summoned up the courage to show him my latest work of fiction. I was sure it was exactly what he wanted. As he read I watched his eyes narrow on the text. My handwriting was clear; that was no problem. He was concentrating hard on what I'd written.

'Look Frances, this is all a mess. You've got characters here on this page that you haven't introduced yet. Others are just sketchily presented. And the narrative – look at it – it's everywhere, it meanders like a river. Where are we now, for instance? When is *this* supposed to be happening?'

'Right now of course,' I said to him.

'Right now?'

'Yes.'

'So we're in school then, are we?'

'Yes.'

'And I'm here reading what you've written?'

'Yes.'

'And this is what you want to happen, is it?'

'Well, I...' Now it was my turn to be embarrassed. I'd confided in him, through the story. Now he knew such things about me, I felt vulnerable.

'I'll stop,' I said. 'You're right; it's rubbish anyway. I'll tear it up.'

'No don't,' he told me. 'No – not yet.'

Ah yes – the final act. There was something missing. I wasn't pretty like she was, but I wasn't ugly either. I started looking in the mirror. My hair was darker than it used to be. So one day I dyed it blonde again, just like it used to be. They laughed, of course, but it wasn't meant for them. He didn't comment, but I knew he'd noticed. At school all day he kept his distance: safety, I suppose. But after school, at home – that was when things really started happening.

'What kind of things?'

'Oh, you know.'

'No.'

I suppose it must have been about the fourth or fifth time he came round. He had been coming every Wednesday straight after school had finished. There was just time for him to pack his marking in his little car, then to drive around the corner to my house. I got home just after four and he'd arrive about half-an-hour later. Here. At my house. Mine. And we were on our own. And that was what I really wanted: him - without the interruptions or distractions.

'What happened next?' he asked.

'We worked. He went over what we'd done that day in class. He checked my homework, set some writing exercises; read what I had written for him.'

'And? What had you written for him?'

'You know' he'd say, 'if only you were older'.

And I'd never had a boyfriend, ever. Well, not properly. I'd never wanted one or thought about it or gone looking for one. No boy had ever asked me if I would be his girlfriend. I didn't want to be a girlfriend. I was happy as I was, or so I thought. But somehow, he was different. I might not have boys hanging round for me outside the school gates like she did but I had him - this man. And I knew that she wanted him.

'And you?'

'And I thought it might...I don't know. I thought that it might help me, in some way.'

'You thought that it might help you.'

'Yes.'

'You thought that it might help you to do what?'

'That.'

'What?'

'You know...the thing I wanted.'

'What? What was it that you wanted?'

Somebody to talk to; someone to confide in; someone who might help me with my writing. I didn't want a boyfriend. And he wasn't. He was different. Not a boy - a man. I don't know why I thought it should be him. He was a grown up man, a man who smelt of aftershave, whose shirts were pressed; whose ties were tied correctly and whose fingernails were clean. His hair was combed, and he had money and a car and he could take me out for day-trips if I wanted. But I didn't want him to. I wanted it to be a secret. I knew he loved me. He just couldn't let it show. If anyone found out he'd be in trouble. And I didn't want to get him into trouble. So I didn't want anyone to know. I wanted this to be between us, just us – our secret.

'*What* did you want to be between you, Frances? What was your secret?' Outside the narrow window I could see the tops of the trees beginning to sway gently in the breeze. The wind was strengthening. There was a storm approaching. That night the hospital would crack and shudder. Trees wound bend and break. The ship would slip its anchor.

Of course I didn't tell Dr Grimshaw *who* he was. It didn't matter. Some names have been changed in order to protect the innocent (and the guilty). I only wanted him because I thought that having him might cure me. He thought that the narrative was so straightforward. But it wasn't. There are layers of meaning hidden even from the author. Older, younger, none of that stuff mattered. She was all that mattered.

Outside, along the corridor, in the silence that was forming in the space between his questions and my answers, I could just hear Debbie in the next room talking to her therapist. I thought about the conversation she was having. Was she telling Jane about me? No. She knew the plot, but she was sworn to secrecy. Later, if the sun was shining, we might go out walking and compare our notes. We'd sit together in our secret summer house and analyse our analysts.

'Did you make love to him?' he asked. The question startled me.

But shouldn't that be *with* him? Shouldn't that be 'make love *with* him'? Or even 'Did *he* make love to *you*'? And why is it called 'make love' anyway? What's that supposed to mean? Why do people say that? Why didn't he just ask me if we'd had sex; fucked, shagged, screwed, right there in the kitchen, on the kitchen floor with all my schoolbooks open? Why didn't he ask me *how* we made love, or how we came to make love? How I'd got closer and closer, inch by inch, shuffling my chair across the carpet until our bodies came so near they almost touched; how I'd slowly felt his warm breath brush against my cheek; or how his arm had rested loosely on the chair back and then curled around my back so that suddenly, but naturally, his arm was round me, resting on my shoulders. He was holding me now; his face was close so that I could feel his breathing start to quicken. Everything had worked exactly as I planned. Why didn't Dr Grimshaw ask the kind of questions that would help me tell the story? Why not ask me if he'd turned to look at me, into my eyes, but not said anything? Just looked at me, with clear blue eyes; the whites as clear like a child's, the blue pale with a dark ring round it like a button. And how I'd looked at him? And how then he'd moved his head a little closer? I'd moved mine a little closer, and how I'd closed my eyes?

He even asked me if I was a virgin: whispered, in my ear.

'Yes,' I said. I was a virgin, in a way.

56

CHAPTER SEVEN

It was dark when I reached his little terraced house. The lights were on upstairs. I waited. Maybe if I saw him? Maybe if I caught a glimpse of him? Perhaps he'd see me in the street and open up the front door? Then I would deliver the book into his hands and myself into his open arms. He'd tell me that it was all right. He'd tell me that he hadn't meant to do it, that he'd been manoeuvred into it by her. Of course he had! I could see that now. How foolish I had been.

A car drove past and stopped. A small car; old and cheap; it parked outside his house. And he was at the bedroom window, looking down and smiling at the driver. Then the front door was being opened and a jacket pulled on and the little garden gate was opening and he was walking round the car and getting in the other side and he was leaning in and kissing her, the driver, on the cheek. And then they drove off.

It was half-past twelve before the lights of the patrol car searched the road and found me, underneath the hedge. Back at the hospital my wrist was stitched and bandaged. Heavily sedated, I was carried up to bed in Misselthwaite, a ward high in the adult hospital. In the long night in the old asylum there were strange dreams. There were words and worlds and there were new and different characters; there were people that I knew, and there were incidents and stories. I couldn't get the book out of my head. The characters all came alive; I dreamt new story-lines and plot connections; I figured out solutions to what had seemed to be intractable artistic problems. There was a whole new cast of characters up here. But when I finally awoke and looked around the ward was almost empty: just a few old ladies, staring at me.

I closed my eyes again and tried to get back to the new plot I'd been creating. This time, however, when I fell asleep I was back at school again and sitting in a classroom at my desk. I was trying desperately to make some sense of what was going on in front of me. The lesson was in progress. Mr Jones was standing at the blackboard talking. Then I realised he was telling everyone about me – he was teaching them my story, how I'd wanted him to help me, how he'd tried but couldn't cure me. He was telling them I had been ill – so ill I'd had to go to hospital.

'Which one sir?' Louise was calling out. 'You mean the Cranford don't you sir?' she asked. And everybody laughed.

My skin went hot and cold all over; I had started sweating. I looked down to see fresh beads of perspiration glistening on my skin like tears between my tiny breasts. Why did I have no bra on? And no blouse? Or knickers? I was naked, that's why. I had nothing on, no clothes at all, I was completely nude. I was sitting on the front row too, but nobody had noticed. So I slid low down in my chair. Girls were being called out one by one to draw equations on the board. As each one got it wrong another would be summoned forward. I prayed so hard for my turn not to come. And yet I knew it would. And then I would be there, bare, in front of her, in front of him, in front of everyone. My head was ringing with a rising note of panic like a wine glass just before it shatters in a scream.

Outside the hospital a storm was raging. Branches cracked against the window; rain lashed the glass like a whip. Lights flickered, and the women cowered in their beds. But I had problems of my own to deal with - I would be in trouble in the morning, that's for sure. There would have to be an explanation in the community meeting in front of everybody. Ted would certainly be mad. But that was nothing to what I had seen or what I thought I'd seen or what I might have seen. I couldn't be sure, of course. But if it was, I knew which way this book was going. Oh yes. Things were happening now. Plans would be drawn up and action would occur. The time for musing, dwelling on the story, for meandering development had gone, or so I thought. I fell asleep in a rage as fierce as the storm outside. I slept ferociously, and dreamt up my revenge.

And then, next morning, the elms outside the window were still once more. A few rooks were retching angrily, balanced on the wreckage of their nests, and smaller birds were being blown about like litter. But the sun was shining; yellow clouds were being skimmed like stones along the surface of the sky. And I had been asleep for two days.

'That's good,' he told me later when he'd read the latest chapter. 'Very good –descriptive, too.'

'But who are you?' I asked.

'I'm Will,' the man replied.

'You're not,' I said. 'You can't be Will. I haven't introduced you yet. You don't exist. You haven't been created.'

'Maybe,' he replied and shrugged. 'But I'm here now anyway. And I'm in the story. And now there's no getting rid of me.'

That puzzled me. How could he be? Didn't he understand the sequence of the narrative? I was in control here, wasn't I? I was the omniscient narrator. I thought so anyway, at least until just then. Now I've got my doubts. Maybe the book is writing me.

'Anyway,' he went on. 'As I was saying - there's some realistic dialogue in here: that's sometimes hard for a beginner; and I like the imagery too.'

'The what?' I asked him.

'Imagery... you know: the use of simile and metaphor. Saying what the things are like- the rooks, for instance – instead of just describing or reporting them.'

'Is that important?'

'Yes. It helps the reader understand. It helps us get inside the story.'

'But you *are* inside the story!'

'Am I?'

'Yes you are,' I said. 'You know you are, although you shouldn't be.'

'I shouldn't?'

'No. You don't get written in till chapter ten. You're way too early.'

'But you know that can't be true,' he told me. 'You know why I'm here. You know my function.'

'Do I?'

'You're the author,' he was saying.

'Am I?'

Yes – you know you are. Now, let's get back to the editing. As I was saying...'

'What were you saying?'

'I was giving feedback on your writing. I was helping you, suggesting that you develop further your use of simile and metaphor – you know, saying what something is like; helping people understand by drawing an analogy. That's the kind of thing that makes a real difference to a piece of writing.'

'So you don't like it, then?'

'I didn't say that. But it can be improved. Everything can always be improved. Like your use of simile and metaphor: a lot of the time you just describe things as they are – and you remain detached. It's almost like you don't want things to come alive. You're simply putting down events, one after another, paring down description to a minimum.'

'Is that bad?'

'In a novel, maybe; in therapy, probably not, no. But you could try, perhaps, to be a little more descriptive. Make it come alive for me. Help me understand,' he said. 'Imagine I had never been inside a mental hospital. Tell me what it's like – not here in the adolescent unit. In the hospital. You've been there now. You know what it is like. How does it feel to be lying in an adult ward inside that prison? Interrogate yourself. See what you discover.'

I didn't need to bother. When I woke up I was trapped in someone else's head. All the nightmares about school were over. All the anger and frustration, gone. And I was here at last where I belonged: the mental hospital. Not the adolescent unit on the boundary; not in the *grounds* like Dr Grimshaw had once told me. In the building. In a ward with other women, women who were mad like me. I must be one of them, I thought. I am. I'm now in someone else's skin. I'm being held together by their bones. Their hair is growing on my head. The plan is to keep the big wards open. I am just another victim. I am one of them.

Underneath it all, my mind was still my own. Deep inside the dark skull somewhere there was something that was still 'me'. And that was the problem. It still hurt. I was trapped. 'I' was someone else. Somewhere in the night my body had been utterly transformed; but inside my head I was the same girl that I'd always been. What had happened? What had I just done? I went over the pages again... the arm around my back... the warm breath on my cheek... the knife... then blood...

'AAAARRGGGGHHH!'

'What is it, Bertha? What's the matter, love?'

Oh God. Was that an animal? It was coming from the woman in the next bed. She was trying to get out and pointing straight at me.

'Don't worry love, ' another voice was saying. 'She's not stopping.'

Who's not stopping? What was happening? Who was talking? Where were all the voices coming from?

'The nurses Frances, I expect,' said Will.

'But... the women there; the patients...'

'Yes I know,' he went on. 'If I'd been on nights that evening then it might not have happened.'

'It was frightening Will,' I said to him. 'They all looked so...so...'

'Mad?' he said.

Mad. Yes. That was it. They *looked* insane. Not all the patients looked mad. Some were just admitted for a few weeks then went home again and led a normal life; some of them might not come back here, ever. But the others, like the women in the next beds who looked so frightened – they were here forever, surely?

'Maybe not,' Will told me.

'What do you mean?' I asked him.

'Well, there's a suggestion that these big old hospitals should close,' he said.

'But...'

'And the patients should be cared for somewhere else – in the community.'

'They're mad,' I said.

'Not all of them,' he told me.

'But they even look as though they're mad.'

'I know,' he said. 'And that's their tragedy. Some of those women were sent here as young girls like you.'

'What for?'

'For all sorts of reasons. Some are ill, that's true and they need treatment. Many of them, though, were simply put here because nobody knew what to do with them: single mothers, or sometimes just the daughter of a single mother.'

He was looking at me.

'But they're all so scary.'

'Why, though, Frances? Why are they so scary?'

'I don't know.'

'It's what this place has done to them that's scary. That's the madness. Anyway, back to the story,' he said to me. 'Where were we?'

'I was waking up,' I said. 'Waking up next morning. I was in the hospital.'

'Ah yes.'

Ah yes. The strip-dress they had put me in the night before was rough and scraped my skin. My back felt sore, as if I had been lying out for too long in the sun. I tried opening my eyes, but they had been tightly shut for too long. Slowly I remembered what I'd done.

'Come on, I'll help you to get dressed.'

Jane had appeared beside my bed to take me home. She was pulling back the covers, lifting me into a sitting position.

'Lift your arms up,' she said and then took hold of both my wrists and lifted them up for me. The pain was sharp and sudden – *like a knife.* I sat on the bed like a baby as she pulled the paper dress above my head.

'What's happening to me, Jane? What are you doing?'

'You're getting up,' she said. 'You've slept for long enough. Anyway, the doctor wants to have a look at you and then we're going back.'

'Don't let that doctor near you!' someone shouted. 'It'll do no good!' the woman said.

'I'll close the curtains,' Jane said.

And suddenly I couldn't see them any more. But I could hear, and I could smell their sweaty bodies as they stirred and turned in bed. I felt their odour hanging like a vapour in the ward. I heard them fart.

'Come on,' said Jane and she smiled. I tried to move, but I was stiff. My body ached; my skin felt bruised; my muscles wouldn't work.

'We don't need this anymore now, do we?' she was saying. 'You won't try that again now, will you?' She put some slippers on my feet and helped my hanging arms into a blouse.

'Am I mad?' I said to her, when she had finished dressing me. 'Am I like them? Is that what I'll look like one day?'

'No,' she said and shook her head. 'Noooo,' she said again, stretching out the syllable like the gum that she was chewing.

'How do you know?' I asked her.

'I know,' she told me. 'Trust me. I'm a nurse.' she said. 'Come on now, give me your hand. I'll help you.'

'A ghost,' somebody whispered as we walked out of the ward. 'Frances has become a ghost.'

* * *

The hospital corridors were cold and long and windowless. The wards we passed were almost empty.

'Where have all the people gone?' I asked.

'Home,' said Jane without sounding convincing. Anyway, this *was* their home. We turned into a large white room.

'This is Dr Moir,' she informed me.

The old man in the corner nodded briefly, then began to speak.

'Right now lassie, let's have a wee look at you.'

He grunted at the blood-soaked bandages. 'We'll have a look at those too, while you're here,' he added. The voice was rich and deep; his breath smelt of tobacco smoke. The sound was soothing; reassuring, even. But the words weren't, and I wasn't reassured. He stood there for a moment, narrowing his eyes and looking at me: scrutinising me and saying nothing; staring at me without blinking.

'Now, I'm going to examine ye. Go over there and get undressed for me.'

I looked at Jane. She smiled and so I did as I was told. I walked over to the corner and I sat down on the edge of a large white bed. The old springs groaned.

'Now, just relax and do the things I tell ye,' Dr Moir continued from behind a fabric screen. I slowly started loosening the first few buttons of my blouse, and then I stopped. Nothing happened. I could see his silhouette like the shadow of a ghost behind the screen; I saw him standing, watching; hardly moving: waiting. I could hear him breathing. I saw him catch his foot to stop it tapping. Slowly I undid the remainder of my buttons and I pulled the blouse out from the waistband of my trousers.

'Ready?'

I stood up. I was about to step out from behind the screen when he suddenly appeared. I sat back down, my blouse undone, and turned my head away. He then stepped towards me, eager to get started.

'Sit up straight now lassie,' he demanded.

As I did my blouse fell open and I saw him looking. Oh God! Oh no, please. Not my bra. Don't make me take my bra off. Pleeaaase don't make me take my bra off! I'd once seen Louise Anderson hold pencils underneath her breasts. 'Bet you can't do that!' she said as she showed off to everyone.

I put my hands around my back, towards the clasp and then I stopped. He paused.

'There'll be no need to go that far, young lassie.'

I kept my hands behind me anyway, waiting, fingering the clasp and watching him, expectantly. Are you sure, I wanted him to think. Are you sure that there's no need, I might be saying? It's fine, you know. It's ok. I'm not worried or afraid. I'm not ashamed. I wouldn't mind. I'll do it if you want it.

He stepped towards me. As he did I flinched; I know I did. I didn't think he'd noticed, though. At least I thought he hadn't. Then he put the stethoscope against my chest. I jumped. I took a sharp breath and I almost squealed, it was so cold.

'It's cold,' I said but I was talking to myself.

He wasn't looking. He was listening.

'Breathe in...' he said. 'Breathe out...'

He moved the stethoscope about.

'Breathe in again…'

His voice rose at the end of each phrase just like he was asking me a question. Each breath gave an answer. And each breath I took was getting quicker. I started panicking. Each time he asked me to breathe in or out or in again it got more difficult to move my lungs. I tried to slow down. But the more I tried the harder it became. I was panting, now. I didn't know what was happening. And he would know. He'd hear me panicking. Maybe he could even hear what I was thinking?

'What's matter?' he asked gruffly. 'You're as nervous as a kitten.'

'Sorry.'

'Ok. Lie down on the bed for me, now will ye?'

Lie down on the bed for him. Lie down on the bed for him. Lie down; lie down lie down on the bed for him LIE DOWN, LIE DOWN, ON THE BED, FOR HIM! I forced myself to move. Slowly I undid the waistband of my trousers as instructed. I pushed them down a little bit, below my hips, and bared my tummy. Then I held my breath. I couldn't move. My toes were curled so tightly that my feet were hurting. He reached across and eased my pants down even further – just far enough to reveal the tops strands of my pubic hair. I froze.

'Try to relax,' he told me quietly, almost whispering in my ear. 'I won't hurt – much.'

I stared at the ceiling, trying not to think about the lump now swelling in my throat. He pushed down hard into my groin. His finger-tips were stained. The pressure hurt. If I could have got the breath, I might have screamed. Then with his palms he pressed down flat against my abdomen. He pushed and pressed and prodded here and there. He pressed down harder. And he pressed again, and pressed. What was he searching for? The ache? If so then he was looking in the wrong place. It's not down there, I could have told him.

That's the wrong place, I was saying. But he wasn't listening.

'Ok,' he suddenly announced and stood up straight. 'You can get dressed now.'

As his shadow shrank behind the screen, I sat up on the bed and fumbled with the buttons of my blouse, straining to hear what he was saying. All I caught were tiny fragments, like the words on torn up paper. Even fitting them together didn't help. I couldn't understand.... *otherwise in good... able to withstand.... not my patient, obviously...I'll see what I can do...*

I'll see what I can do. Do what?

'What is he going to try to do?' I whispered as I stepped out from behind the screen.

'Oh he's going to speak to Dr Grimshaw, that's all.' Jane said distractedly.

'What about?'

'You,' she said. 'Your treatment. It might be time for something different.'

'What?' I asked.

'We'll discuss that later,' she replied.

CHAPTER EIGHT

Today I was on telly. That's something that we writers sometimes have to do – to go on TV and be interviewed about our work. I'd done my homework. I was well-prepared. For instance, I'd done research into style and point-of-view. I could justify my choice of narrative perspective. It had to be first-person. Who else could tell the story half as well as I could do? I was prepared for questions about structure, too; and inspiration: I knew where all this stuff had come from. Psychology, astrology, history, mythology: they're all the sources authors use for their ideas. There are many different methods to create a story, and I knew my own – biography - particularly. This is my story. It is based on me.

As I walked into the studio people crowded round me, talking. 'How are you, Frances?' they were asking me. 'What's going to happen to you?' they were all so keen to know. 'Who will you turn into? Which new characters are you writing? What new plot are you inventing?' 'How come your writing is so vivid, Frances? How come your characters are all so real? How come that they're more real than you? How come last night you died and they survived?'

'Five minutes, studio.' I felt my stomach tighten. The lights were hot, like mini suns. People pressed around me on all sides. There were so many questions. Suddenly, I panicked. I didn't know what to say or who to say it as. Should I answer as myself or as my literary persona?

'I declare this meeting open,' someone announced, and that was it - the programme started.

Ted kicked off. This was his show, after all.

'Look, we know this must be very difficult Frances,' he began, almost sympathetically. 'But it's difficult for us as well. We're here to help you to get better, and no-one here had any notion that things had got so bad...'

I could see them all, even though my eyes were closed. I could see them in my head. Ted, opposite, in the place he always sat: in his enormous 'charge-nurse' chair. No-one else sat there. It was his seat. He was in charge. Monica was sitting on the other side, in front of the French windows. Dr Grimshaw next to her, then Laura and then Lizzie; Jason in the corner, sitting with his knees under his chin, and Patrick Randle with his long legs stretched into the middle of the room. And Debbie? Where was Debbie? I slowly separated the upper and the lower lids of both my eyes. The light hurt, even though the room was dark. And suddenly I could see her sitting next to Ted, her head down, hands clasped on her lap. She had been crying. I could see that. She looked so small in the enormous chair, so young and so... betrayed? But no – she couldn't be. That was me.

As I looked at her I felt a tiny stab; a feeling – less, a fragment of a feeling - for a fraction of a second. Something briefly guttered in the darkness, and then suddenly extinguished: something that might once have been a feeling; that might once have been emotion - sympathy or love or guilt or sadness, anything. I don't know. It was gone too quickly. It was what a normal feeling might have been. It was what a feeling was. But there was no fuel left to get it going. No spark, no fire. And no desire. I could have cried, but there were no more tears. There was nothing. I felt emptied out of everything. Inside, it felt empty; hollow. Something had happened. There was something missing.

'No-one's going to laugh at you,' a voice was saying.

But that wasn't what was going through my mind. I felt my shoulders relaxing, slightly.

'We're all here to support you – you can talk to us,' said someone else.

'Go on,' they urged me. 'Tell us. Tell us all about it.'

'But...'

'No buts,' Ted butted in. 'That's the way we do things here. You know that. It's that only way that you'll get better. You do want to get better, don't you Frances?'

I hated Ted. I think that everybody did. Whereas Jane was young and kind and Monica older, colder and superior - Ted was merely loud and mean, aggressive, bullying. He never smiled, or when he did it was because he'd winkled out some new admission or confession out of someone. That was his specialism: making somebody say something they didn't want to say – or didn't want to say in front of everybody. That was his job. He made people talk. He sat there with his hands on each arm of the chair prodding, asking and interrogating, challenging and clarifying. Having him looking at you was like having a bright light pointed in your eyes. Very soon, even though there might be seven, eight or nine people sitting around the room and listening, it became just you and him. No-one stopped him. He just kept on asking questions. 'Till you answered.

'Come on now Frances,' he would say, the engine merely ticking over, 'tell us all about it: tell us what it's like. We want to know.'

I said nothing. I sat looking at the floor. I'd seen this happening to others in the weeks before. Now it was my turn. I knew that there was no escape.

He revved the engine up a little, just to show what power there was to come.

'We're all waiting Frances,' and with his arm he made a sweep around the room.

I looked up and I looked at him. And then I looked away.

No-one spoke. This was his show. He was the charge-nurse. He was in charge. Even Dr Grimshaw sat mute in the corner, looking at me, waiting; wondering: what was it was I was going to have to say?

'We can't begin to help you if you won't talk about it to us, Frances.'

Another, longer revv. Ted thought that silence was denial. He thought not talking was a way of shutting out the pain. He thought I wouldn't talk because I didn't want to. He didn't know I couldn't; that I didn't have the words I needed; didn't have the words he wanted. I couldn't tell them how I felt inside. I didn't know; I only felt it, and it hurt so badly that describing it - I thought - would only make it worse. I suppose that is denying it, or part of it. So maybe he was right about that. But he didn't know what was happening. He was like a reader who wants to see the end before he's finished reading. He was impatient. He was the kind of man who sat at home on Saturday afternoon and watched the wrestling. He wanted action, but he needed words too. That was his dichotomy.

I needed words, as well: words to tell the reader what was happening. But they were sometimes slow in coming. And at other times they wouldn't come at all.

'What about a new perspective?' Will suggested. 'What about another point of view? Think: what would happen if the story was objective, if you were to narrate it in another way, to tell it differently? Maybe that would help in some way.'

'Well, it's worth a try,' I said. 'It might help me get started. Ok, then – that's decided. I will tell you all about my life. I'll write a story. I can do that. I can tell you that. That's easy. Are you ready? Are you listening?'

Once upon a time there was a little girl. Her name was Sophie.

'Sophie? But I thought your name was Frances?'

'It used to be: I've changed it. I'm called Sophie now.'

'But why?' he sighed.

'Because I'm not the same girl now as when the story started; I'm changing; I'm starting to become a different person.'

'But you can't do that,' he said. 'It's far too confusing!'

'Well if you think that's bad,' I said. 'It's nothing – Madame Bovary's eyes change colour half way through the book.'

'Why "Sophie" anyway?' he asked.

'I don't like "Sophia". Sophie's just a bit more modern.'

'What's the similarity?'

'She doesn't want to marry.'

'And?'

'And...Well, she can't have what she wants.'

'Or who.'

'Exactly. So can I carry on with the story?'

'Ok, then. Start at the beginning.'

Once upon a time there was a little girl. Her name was Sophie. She was happy in a way and her mummy and her daddy loved her dearly. Every day was sunny. Sophie played out in the sunshine and she was surrounded by endless fields of flowers. Little animals appeared as she played to see what she was doing. And the animals were magical: they could talk to her and find out things about her; they even knew her future. But they didn't tell her. That would spoil the story.

One day when Sophie woke up in the morning there were clouds on the horizon. Not many, and the sun was still up brightly shining. But when she went into the fields to play the rabbits told her it would soon be raining. Sophie didn't know what rain was, and she stayed out in the fields and played, while all the time the clouds got thicker. Soon they grew so grey and heavy that they blotted out the sun. The rabbits and the birds went in. Sophie looked up at the sky, just as the first dark drops of rain began to fall. In the distance, she could hear the distant sounds of thunder. Sophie went indoors and asked her mother what was happening.

'Nothing,' mummy said. 'Forget about it.' But Sophie saw that she'd been crying.

'Mummy, what's the matter?'

At that moment there was an enormous crash of thunder. The doors and windows rattled as it rumbled on.

'I'm frightened mummy,' Sophie said.

'And so am I,' her mummy then replied.

***

'That's a fascinating story,' Will was telling me.

'But it's not a story,' I replied.

'It is, Sophie. Everything we do is part of a story. It's all part of the fiction you're creating.'

'But this is true,' I told him.

'Yes I know,' he said 'but what does that mean - true? Did it *really* happen? Or is it just a way of understanding something?'

Interesting! So maybe what I'm writing didn't happen to me after all? Maybe, in my writing, the past is something that I've just created or invented? Maybe it – the writing - made me who I am? Perhaps that's what our stories do: the things that happen make us what we are. And, after all, our lives are nothing more than stories, somebody once said.

'That's certainly one theory,' he said to me.

'It's more than that,' I said to him. 'It's true'.

'What happens next?' he asked.

And that was when I owned up. 'I don't know' I said. 'This isn't easy.'

'No-one said it would be though,' he told me.

No, they didn't; that was true. But I was stuck. This was much more difficult than I ever thought it could be. I wasn't sure where I was going anymore. I didn't know what

73

to say. There was something big and heavy in my way. Writers' block, maybe? But what I couldn't understand was how I could go so quickly from elation to despair. Yesterday I knew the plot: the characters; the twists; the setting. I knew precisely what was happening: I knew exactly how the plot developed, how the characters all interacted. I knew how the narrative was moving forward. I knew all about habitual behaviour, what was happening now in the dramatic present. Now where am I? Lost. I don't know where to go. It's hopeless – gone. It's nothing anymore.

'You must be patient Sophie,' he would tell me. 'These things take time.' I was, though – I *was* being patient. I was being a *psychiatric patient*.

'You've used that joke already.'

'Really?'

'Yes, and even then it wasn't funny.'

'Sorry.'

'Look,' he said. 'One thing that people sometimes do when things aren't going well is free-write: write down anything; write the first thing that comes into our heads, write lists of favourite words, write down rubbish, anything - just to keep on writing. No editing or judging what you've written: not even any conscious thinking, just a free association of the words, one after the other, one word leading to another, on and on like a daisy chain until at last you hit a full-stop. Try it. Go on. See what happens.'

So I did. That is what I am doing now: I'm writing for the sake of writing; writing, writing, writing simply to get things going; hitting plastic keys and making words, one letter at a time and making other words and adding words and words and more words, adding words until a paragraph gets written. Sometimes what you write is utter rubbish. Sometimes there is nothing there worth keeping. But sometimes something good comes out of what you write: a thought or an idea – even just a phrase; something you can work on; something you can use. Look at this, for instance:

Sun, warm, calm, dream, smile, happy, dreamy Debbie.

Where did Debbie come from? The freewrite didn't start with her, but ended there. She wasn't there at first but she was there when I had finished. When did the idea of her appear? Where did she come from? Ideas like this just happen. I don't know where they come from. But they appear sometimes unexpectedly, like a line of poetry.

That was good, I thought. It made another chapter. Freewrites were a good idea. And so I tried again, and this time something different happened. It was my mum again, but something very strange was happening. She was visiting me in hospital. She was sitting by my bed but with her outdoor coat on: *I'm not stoppin' long* her body-language was saying. And her handbag – it was sitting on her lap just like a little dog.

'So,' she said, 'you've gone and done it have you?' She wasn't waiting for an answer from me – she was nodding. Somebody had moved the screens around for privacy. Suddenly she looked straight at me. 'Couldn't even get that right, though – could you?'

'Mum!'

'Don't "mum" me. I'm not your mum now, anyway - not really; never wanted to be in the first place. No-one ever asked me, though.'

I tried to, but I couldn't speak.

'Oh no,' she said. 'I didn't want you; never did. If you'd succeeded last night or if they'd not found you lying in the street outside his house, well - you'd have only gone and done what I'd been trying sixteen years ago. Tried everything I could then, to get rid of you: hot baths; gin. We couldn't do it legally, you know; not then. Just two years later and you'd have been a number on a government chart somewhere: abortions, nineteen sixty-seven.'

'But mu..'

'I know, I know - it's hard for you. It's hard for me, too. How do you think that all this makes me feel? But there was nowt else for it - once he'd gone and left me that was that. He left me on me own – with you inside me. How was I supposed to cope? And then when you were born...' she wiped her eyes.

'You're so like him, you know.'

She looked at me. Apart from tears her eyes had something different in them; a light, a memory. For once her face didn't look so angry. Then she suddenly remembered where she was and who it was that she was speaking to.

'I've told doctor that you're not to leave here,' she was saying. 'I said that they could keep you. He tells me they don't do that, not these days. But I've told him that they should. In your case, they should make a general exception.'

'Mum – you can't; there's no such thing as a general exception. Look - it's either...'

'I know, I know. He told me that as well. He said you're only here voluntary. But I've told them, "ok then – this has gone on long enough." It's time that they did summat drastic with your head. It's time you stopped this nonsense, too.' She pointed to my notebook. 'All this writing, love – you'll never be a writer! Face it. You're no good'.

'I am,' I told her. 'Anyway, I must be. If I wasn't any good you wouldn't be here.'

'Oh, wouldn't I?' she said sarcastically. 'Now don't you take that tone with me, my girl!'

'I will take that tone with you if I want to - just because I can. That's what a writer can do - write you, make you real,' I told her. 'And destroy you if I've no longer any need of you.'

'Now look here – NURSE?' she shouted, as if they could do anything to help her. There was no chance. That was that. I closed the speech marks and my mum had gone forever.

CHAPTER NINE

'That's a very interesting approach,' he was telling me.

'Is it?' I replied. I wasn't sure. I wondered if the dialogue assumed too much importance, maybe. Or if the plot had strayed too far from reality? The reader has to be prepared to suspend their disbelief, as Aristotle said. In spite of everything, would the narrative still retain its credibility?

'Oh yes,' he went on. 'Definitely. There's still some work to do, though – some revision. But it's worth it, Sophie.'

'Really?'

'Yes of course it is,' he told me.

How silly of me, though. I haven't even introduced him to you yet. A brand new character appears, as if from nowhere, out of nothing, and you don't even have a clue who he might be. He's new, here; not a patient; not a nurse or doctor: he's a student. His arrival here has changed things quite dramatically: our routines and our therapies; even the dynamics between the other characters. Take Ted, for instance. He still thinks he's in charge. But he starts to lose it in this chapter. Take a look at this: it's the Community Meeting once again, the morning after I'd revealed the murder weapon. I'm sitting in a chair, and they're all talking to me, asking things. They all want me to tell them why. They want me to explain.

'This must be very difficult Sophie,' Ted offered. 'But it's difficult for us, too. We're here to help. But no-one here had any idea that things were so bad.'

You should have done, I thought.

'...not even Debbie.'

I looked across at her. She was sitting tightly folded in the chair opposite. Her knees were drawn up and her head was down. She had been crying. I felt like crying, too, but I was emptied out of tears. Inside, it felt hollow. Something had happened. There was something missing.

'I'd like to say I think we should have seen this coming...' Ted continued. 'We should have known that something like this would have happened. We should have noticed all that anger Sophie bottles up inside. It had to come out somewhere.'

'Do you realise now why it's so important to talk?' asked Monica. 'Do you?'

But I didn't answer. I looked at Ted. But he wasn't looking back at me; this wasn't about me. I was just the... what? What was I? Just the platform, that's what; just Ted's latest opportunity for glory. He was looking at each person in the room in turn, ensuring they had seen him look at them, then moving on. His eyes were dark, so dark it was impossible to see the tiny pin-prick of a pupil in the middle. Or maybe the black dot was so big it *was* his eye, letting in as much light as it could; letting all the light in, trying hard to see the reaction in everybody's faces, staying with them until they had seen him staring at them. As his eyes met theirs, people turned away. Nobody seemed to know what to say. Once the last head turned, he spoke.

'No - we shouldn't be surprised by this at all,' he said addressing the meeting rather than addressing me.

'Suicide is an act of violence,' he went on. 'Yes, everyone - extreme violence: it's homicide – murder – but directed inwards.'

Dr Grimshaw shuffled in his seat.

'There's a lot of anger buried here. This action isn't just about how Sophie feels now, how sad she is or how hopeless she thinks life has become - it's about something buried deep in her past; something she is angry about, so angry that she feels incredibly violent, so violent she can contemplate destroying life - her own life; even other people's lives.'

'But they're only characters in a book,' I said. There were vague murmurs from around the room. But Ted wasn't interested in them. He wasn't listening.

'I want to know why you're so angry, Sophie. Who is it that you're angry with?'

I looked. No-one said a word. Everyone looked first at Ted and then at me.

'I think...' Jane interrupted.

'No...' said Ted, holding up his hand. 'Let's hear her answer...'

Then at last everybody turned their heads and looked at me.

I didn't know what to say. I didn't understand the question. But for the first time I felt compelled to answer, felt I had to think of something. With a rising tide of panic, my mouth opened and I heard myself say something.

'You're hiding something, Sophie. What is it? We know you are.'

Of course I am. And so are you. And so is everyone. We show them what we want to show. We let others know the things we want them to. We control it. I perfected it. Hiding things is what I do the best; telling people – that is something that I don't do. It doesn't take long to learn that telling people what you really think or want or feel can get you nowhere. Hiding things from people, even from yourself, is the way to go.

'That's agreed then,' Ted was saying. 'Sophie will go over to the hospital and we'll start a different kind of therapy.'

'But I think...' a voice was interrupting... 'I'm not sure...'

There was a sudden shuffling of movement and excitement: people sat up higher in their chairs. Heads all turned and looked at Will. He was sitting in one corner of the room. He was waiting for his turn to speak. He had only been here for about two weeks. In that time he'd been watchful, helpful – he had helped at meal-times, for example. But he had chosen not to tell us what he had been thinking. He sat in on the daily community meeting listening carefully to everything that we discussed and talking about it later to the other nurses. He hadn't spoken up before: not publicly. No-one really knew what he would sound like. No-one knew what he would say. No-one knew anything about him.

He had appeared at breakfast time one Monday morning, opening the kitchen door and squinting into the light.

'God,' said Lizzie as he stepped inside. 'The Martians have invaded.'

With his motorcycle helmet off, we could see that he was young – maybe twenty, not much older, and with short brown hair and brown eyes and a close cropped beard.

'Hi!' he said 'I'm Will.' He removed a padded leather glove and held out his hand. Jason was standing at the kitchen sink running a bowl of water for the washing up. He quickly sank both hands beneath the bubbles.

'Oh right. Hi!' he muttered without looking, before noisily clunking plates and cutlery around in the bowl.

Debbie walked in with a pile of dirty plates. She stopped in the doorway, squinting at the newcomer.

'Who are you?' she asked him, screwing up her eyes. That's Debbie for you. Direct; straight to the point.

'Hi! I'm Will,' he repeated, again offering his hand. Debbie wiped her right hand on her jumper and shook hands with him.

The visitor seemed pleased. Then Ted walked in.

'You're late!' he grumbled, 'Earlies start at eight, sharp!'

'Sorry, Te.. er, Mr Rochester. I was...'

But Ted had turned away from him and was looking at us.

'This is Student Nurse Caxton, everyone. He's joining us for a few weeks as part of his training,' Ted announced. 'Make him feel at home,' he added darkly.

Turning back to Will, he ushered him into the nurses' office. When he came out half-an-hour later, he was very quiet. Since then he had hardly said a word to anyone; he sat in silence in the meetings, listening to everything we said. As we ate our meals or read or took our medication, he just watched. If someone spoke to him, he answered. And he asked us questions - ordinary questions: what bands we liked, what books we read – instead of asking how we felt or what we'd done or what our problems were. He helped when it was our turn to wash up. He was just there. We hardly noticed him. And now, for the first time, the morning after I had tried to end it all, here he was, becoming one of them, speaking in their voice, asking their kind of questions. Or so I thought.

'I wonder if I could make an observation,' he began.

Nobody responded. Instead of looking at whoever had spoken as he would normally have done, Ted just turned away, leaving it to someone else. We waited. The student looked at everyone in turn, unsure of what to do. Finally, the silence seemed to grow into an answer, and he cleared his throat.

'There are... other, newer therapies we might try,' he started. 'There are some techniques that I've been studying...'

Ted turned to look at him. The expression of mild irritation now turned to contempt. He began to shift position on his seat. Nobody – not even Will – ever contradicted Ted.

'The community has decided,' Ted interrupted. 'That's the way we do things here – we all decide together, *democratically*. And we have - we're recommending Sophie for a short course of electroconvulsive therapy, aren't we everybody?'

***

No-one wanted to settle down to work that morning, in spite of the teacher's efforts. The boys just messed around at the front of the classroom, throwing scraps of paper at each other. The teacher smiled indulgently and tried to coax them into sitting down.

When the meeting had finished, Will had come along into the classroom with us. After Jane's all-night vigil in the hospital, she had gone off-duty; they needed someone else to be on suicide watch with me.

'I'll stay with her,' he volunteered. I didn't have the strength or the desire to argue.

He sat with me at the back of the classroom for a while, until I started to feel sleepy.

'I'm not surprised,' he said 'with all those drugs inside you'.

He took me upstairs to the bedroom. He looked the other way while I removed my clothes. I still felt weak and drowsy.

'Look – let me help you,' he was saying. I was too weak to worry. He sat me in a chair, and helped me get undressed. And then he tucked me into bed, just like a father would have done. After a while, I fell asleep.

When I awoke a short time later, Will had disappeared. The door was open, though and there were voices. I could hear Ted talking loudly in the corridor.

'What the hell do you think you're doing? What God given right have you to walk in here with... with a bit of training and... and undermine our entire regime with... with these ridiculous ideas? Eh?'

There was a pause.

'Look, Ted. I didn't mean to...' Will began.

'I'M DAMN SURE YOU DIDN'T!' Ted bawled back. 'BUT THE FACT IS THAT YOU *DID* DO, DIDN'T YOU?'

I'd never heard Ted raise his voice before. He didn't have to. Suddenly all the anger that was flickering beneath the surface had exploded. He was out of breath.

'Didn't Freud once say that all great scientific revolutions degrade people in some way?'

'What's that supposed to mean, eh – *Student Nurse?*'

It all went quiet. There were footsteps on the stairs. And then the bedroom door opened. I quickly closed my eyes.

'I suppose you heard all that did you?' Will's voice said.

I smiled.

'Oh well...' he sighed.

'I hope I didn't...'

'No it's not your fault,' he said. 'Ted's not happy with me being here, that's all'

'Ted's horrible,' I said.

'He's not. I mean, not reelly. By the way, that's not a misprint, is it?'

'No, it isn't. That's the way you talk.'

'I see,' he said. 'You've represented my speech literally, that's good - although it's something of a cliché.'

'Is it?'

'Well, a stereotype maybe,' he told me. 'Being Welsh I suppose I should expect it.'

'Maybe,' I replied. 'But there's nothing more for me to say. It can't be written any other way, I told him. Anyway, it's all been done before: the words I've said have all been said so many times; every story has been told. There's nothing new, I said. It's all cliché to me.'

'It's not, though Sophie. Nobody's told your story. No-one knows what happened to you. Even I don't know. But you do.'

'Do I?'

'Yes, you do. And only you do. No-one else can tell the story. It's all up to you. It's always up to you. This is something that you've got to do, Sophie.'

'That's just what Ted keeps telling me,' I told him.

'True. I know. But you can do it your way. You have to do it your way. You have to write it out to move on, to make sense of it, to make it all worth something. All the things that happen only make some sense if they're your research for the book, you know.'

'I know,' I said.

'So write it then,' he told me.

'I can't,' I said.

'Why not?'

'I'm not intelligent enough to be a novelist. I've read so many books; so many great books. I know that I can never be as good as them. Real writers these days go to Oxford, Cambridge. They're all clever. Where can I say I went? Lowood Lodge – the Adolescent Unit, Cranford Psychiatric Hospital - that's where. They all trained their minds - read books about psychology. What did I do? I had therapy – I had treatment for psychosis.'

'Fuck it!' he responded. 'Jeffrey Archer did it. You can do it, too. Go on. Write something. Get it written. Get it down on paper. Go for it. Go on. Just do it.'

'But I can't,' I pleaded.

'Of course you can. Novelists are nothing special, Sophie. They're just ordinary –like you!'

'Thanks a bunch,' I muttered.

'No, they are. You know what I mean. Look at them: look at what they've written. Ordinary, ordinary, ordinary. They're not famous scientists, astronomers or...or...'

'Nurses?' I suggested.

'Even nurses. They're not famous expert anybodies. They write because they have to write. They write because it's what they write that makes them someone; someone great, maybe. Or maybe just somebody, anybody. That's what you're doing, Sophie. You've got to do it. Write it. Go on. Get on with it now. Get it written.'

He handed me the book that I'd been using, open at a clean page. In the other hand, I took a pen. I took them from him, and I did what he suggested: started writing. I wrote something that began to make me someone. I wrote something that would make things happen. But first of all I wrote what authors call 'backstory': how I came to be here in the first place; what had happened to me; what had brought me to the notice of the medical authorities.

CHAPTER TEN

The prospectus for the residential writing school had stated 'afternoons are largely free for personal creative projects.' That's what Dr Grimshaw had once told me. That was the routine here on the writing course. So after lunch, while the others played or sat and watched TV in the dayroom, I sat with a notebook and invented stories, characters and therapeutic dialogues. For the setting I chose the attic rooms at the top of Lowood House. I wrote a script and put words in the mouths of all the characters I'd created. Everyone took part in the performance. I determined we should all have an appointment; that we'd be alone, the two of us: the patient and the therapist. We, the patients, we would talk to someone one-to-one. It could be anyone. It could be Dr Grimshaw; Jane, sometimes; even Ted. It didn't matter.

Sometimes words flowed; at other times I struggled. Some afternoons I bounded up the stairs like Esther Greenwood on scholarship in Manhattan. The editor of the magazine was waiting. I couldn't wait to start my writing. At other times I was stuck, up on the attic floor like Mrs Rochester. The lights were out; the door was locked. The trees outside the window shrank the afternoon to shadows.

How do you feel? When did it start? What are you thinking? The questions were always the same. I'd heard them all so many times before. Some afternoons I thought I might be on the verge of answering: a word or phrase would suddenly suggest itself; the start of a sentence might appear. Then, just as quickly, it would go. Vanish. Disappear. And then I'd spent the next ten minutes trying to remember what it was I was about to say. And failing.

'Why don't you want talk to me, Sophie?'

'I do. I just can't think of anything to say...'

'You can't think of anything to say. Then don't...'

Silence. Somewhere else, downstairs perhaps, someone shouted for a nurse.

'Don't try to think. Don't think of anything. Just say whatever comes into your head.'

'But nothing does.'

'Nothing does.'

It wasn't a question. But I answered anyway.

'Well.. sometimes... something...'

'Something.'

Statement. Not a question. Don't have doubts about my punctuation.

'Something.... and then it goes again....'

'What is this 'something'?'

'I don't know....' I said.

He sighed, and turned his chair back to the desk and then wrote something in my file. I could tell he was frustrated. I could tell that he was irritated. Impatient. Just beginning to become impatient. But trying not to be impatient. Trying not to show it. And trying not to be it, or to let me see it - that brief flicker of irritation, immediately suppressed; a glimmer of emotion. For a second. Less than a second. Someone else might miss it altogether. But not me. I noticed. That's what authors do, you know. They notice things; they notice everything...

Like I now noticed Lizzie's footsteps on the wooden staircase, echoing along the empty corridor. Any moment now it would be her turn, and so far I had nothing to write down. Damn! My interview today was over. He'd just said so. Soon Lizzie would be sitting in the hot seat here, where I had been. Would it be any better being her? Would she know what to say? I'd never know. As I opened the wooden door and walked out onto the tiny landing, Debbie was there waiting for me.

'Fancy a walk?' she asked.

Of course! I knew now where the plot was going. This was the thing that had been missing. Dialogue. A conversation. That would get the writing flowing.

We went down to our scruffy little bedroom and put our coats on, then went downstairs to sign out in the nurses' office.

'Don't be long now,' Monica called out as we walked along the corridor. 'Back by four or I'll be sending out a search party'.

We walked as quickly as we could to the little wooden hut we called the summer house; the place that we had found one rainy afternoon - the place that was our own. On the way we passed a group of adult patients – men – all bending from the waist and pulling weeds out of the flower beds. Two nurses stood and smoked and watched them as they grazed like cattle. Without straightening up – as we walked past – each of the patients slowly lifted his head and stared.

'I hate it when they do that,' Debbie said.

'Me too,' I told her and we shivered.

We hurried on past the hospital kitchens, past the boiler house with its enormous chimney, through the little patch of ground that no-one seemed to know or care for; nobody, that it, except for us.

When we got there Debbie slumped straight down onto the worn-out arm chair by the door. It was comfy, even if the prickly dusty smelly thing had horse-hair stuffing leaking from the corners. I sat on the floor by Debbie's feet just like a little dog. We were in our own world. If we leaned forward and looked out of the window, we could just see the edges of the hospital towering above us, the chimneys tall and ugly like a factory. But if we didn't – and we didn't – well, we could be anywhere.

'What did you talk about this time?' Debbie asked me.

'Oh, all the usual, you know – what's it like, how does it feel, when did it start; all that crap,' I said. 'How about you?'

'Same thing really,' she replied. 'Except for one thing.'

'What was that?' I asked. But she was looking puzzled.

'Well, he asked me if I'd ever got into a fight at school. If I'd ever lost my temper – hit someone.'

'A *fight*?' I said.

'Yeah, that's right - a fight.'

'And?'

'And what?'

'What did you tell him? Have you? Did you?'

'No,' she said. 'Too scared to, really. I wanted to a few times. I nearly did do once or twice. But I was always scared of what would happen if I did.'

'What would have happened?'

'I dunno. Might have hurt someone, you know – quite badly. Else got hurt meself,' she added. 'Anyway, how 'bout you?'

'What?'

'Well, did you? Were you ever in a fight with anyone?'

'Only with myself,' I said. She laughed.

'No – actually, I did hit someone once,' I added, quietly.

'Why?' she asked. She sat up straight. She seemed surprised, but then she would.

'Well, there was this girl,' I started. 'And this man, this teacher at my school. He caught us, I suppose; he broke it up. He sent me to the headmistress.'

'Wow, Soph. I didn't know you had it in you. What was it about?'

'A boy,' I said. A boy; a man; a man; a boy - what difference does it make? I wasn't lying to her. It was all about him really, what he'd done to me, what he had done with her.

'God - what happened?' Debbie leaned towards me, interested. She tucked her elbows in and stared intently, following my story.

'Come on!' she said, impatient for developments.

But I was thinking. It was coming to me, slowly. It was dawning on me what had really happened, why it had gone wrong back there on that dark Thursday afternoon; why I was in here and why I couldn't find the words - and maybe, why it hurt so much inside.

'I don't....' What? Want to talk about it? That was what I should have said. But Debbie didn't let me finish.

'Come on, Soph. I want to know. What was he like, then? Was he worth it?'

Was he? Was anyone? Was anybody worth it?

'Well, come on Soph. Good looking, was he?'

Oh, *that.* I thought: *that's* what you want to know; that's easy. Not what I am now remembering: how it felt to have confided in him, then how frightened I had been that he might tell someone. Not how unfair it all had seemed.

'He was...' I started. It was somehow difficult to concentrate. 'He was my teacher,' and I left it there. Best not to say too much, I thought, even to her. Best not to say which one or to tell her what his name was. But she didn't want to know.

She simply rolled her eyes and made a whistle.

As we walked back I sketched what authors call back-story. I described what happened next and how I'd ended up in here: I wrote my own biography. Fighting was a serious offence. It was the only thing girls ever got expelled for. But that was not for me, surely? How could it be? I was a good girl, wasn't I? I'd worked hard. I had behaved

90

myself. I did my homework every evening, unlike many of my classmates. And if I was occasionally distracted he was always there to protect me, to stand up for me, defend me. Wasn't he?

As I sat there in the corridor, waiting to be called into the headmistress's office I could hear the sound of voices on the playing field: first-years playing in the sunshine; little girls enjoying school; enjoying life. The window opposite the door was open; white semi-transparent curtains floated like a bridal veil on a gentle autumn breeze.

Behind that wooden, panelled door they were discussing me and making up their story. What was it they were writing? What was she telling him? What was he telling her? Not what I had told him, surely. That was said in confidence. He couldn't say that it was my fault, either. Could he? That I was to blame? But what? What could he say? I didn't know. And yet I wanted to. I should be in there. It was so unfair. I was the protagonist. It was me the minor characters were discussing. It was my story that was being written.

The door suddenly opened, and Mr A stepped out into the corridor. He looked down, briefly; raised his eyebrows almost imperceptibly, then turned and walked away. Miss Nicolson stood behind him like a shadow in the doorway, waiting.

'You may come in now Miss Western,' the headmistress said.

I stood in front of her as she sat back behind her desk, sitting up so straight her back seemed barely to touch the chair behind her. Her wrists rested - just so - on the table; she was balancing a pen between her fingers and her thumbs. I could see the page in front of her was printed. Everything was written down.

Miss Nicolson was a small woman, old and thin. Sitting in her study in a leather chair behind a huge oak desk she seemed to be retreating, shrinking smaller as I looked at her. But posture had always been her speciality – 'Sit up straight, girls; backs as straight as rulers'. *Posture and deportment*, she would say *are fine accomplishments.* She sometimes made girls walk the corridor with text-books balanced on their heads. But now, although her back was straight she seemed almost to be shedding the black gown that she always wore like dead skin: she had grown too small for it. Her hair was tied up tightly, with a few grey strands escaping. She seemed bored, or tired, or both. The interrogation was perfunctory.

'You are aware that fighting is a *most* serious offence, aren't you Sophie?'

Sophie? Sophie? Yes it must be me. I had forgotten for a moment who I had become. I nodded.

'I have spoken to your form-tutor. He informs me that there has been a marked decline in the standard of your homework lately.'

Whose word was that – marked? Was that his or hers?

'Mr Jones – who has been helping you so diligently after school; this man who has nothing but your interests at heart; this man - your own form-tutor – who intervened between the two of you merely to prevent injury! And how do you repay him? You lash out. AT YOUR OWN TEACHER!'

I stood there, waiting for the punch line. But it never came.

'What,' she whispered 'have you got to say to that, young lady?'

What could I tell her? What could I say? What words would make a difference? Would she listen if I said them? I suppose I could talk; I could tell her everything – start from the beginning. Or I could simply stand there listening to what she was saying, waiting for her to draw her own conclusions.

'You have always, in the past, behaved quite reasonably. That is what Mr Jones tells me, anyway. You generally work hard. In many ways you have been something of a model pupil.'

I looked down at the floor.

'And your relationship with Louise Anderson...'

I looked up, suddenly. I felt my face flush hot and pricks of perspiration breaking on my brow.

'...has always been quite cordial - as far as I'm aware,' she went on. I had to smile at that. I had to smirk. That word – the word she chose: *cordial*. Cordial! She knew nothing. This old bag was barking.

'Do you find something amusing?' she was asking. How could I begin to answer her? Just wait until you read the book I'm writing, I was thinking. Just wait until you see yourself in print! Just wait until you find out what was really going on. You're in for a shock. They all are. Everyone. And especially her.

Outside the open window girls were coming from PE, laughing. It was the end of the school day.

'You leave me with no option then,' she carried on. She got up, pushing hard against the desk as if she needed extra help to struggle to her feet.

'Miss Hasnip, would you be so kind as to contact Sophie's mother for me?'

'She'll be at work,' I told her.

'But of course,' she said, a feint tone of disdain.

'Then take a letter, please Miss Hasnip. Sophie will be leaving with it presently.'

She turned to me.

'You will deliver this to your mother, Sophie. Then - when you have served the term of your exclusion - I shall speak with Mrs Western to discuss the terms on which your readmission may take place.'

'It's Miss, Miss.'

'I beg your pardon?'

'My mum's Miss Western.'

'Please LISTEN! You may come back to school when I am satisfied that you have learned your lesson, but understand that there will be conditions. That will have to be agreed. Now – lift up your skirt.'

The pain was nothing. But I knew then, right there and then, that I wasn't going back. My mother wasn't going to see that letter. I could fool her. She'd be far too drunk to notice till the morning. Then I'd get up. I'd get dressed and leave the house. I'd wander into town – go to the library, perhaps. I'd fool them, too: the old, grey-haired librarians. They would never know, not with my outdoor coat on. I had things to do, a place to go. I had research to undertake, although I didn't really know it then. The only thing I knew was it was over – school, him – everything. I wasn't sorry, either. Or I didn't think I was. It hadn't been as bad as all that. Even Louise Anderson, her flaunting, teasing – and my fantasising. What was it, really? Nothing. Not now. Not now that I was never ever going back.

CHAPTER ELEVEN

As I left Miss Nicolson's office I knew that was going to be my last day at the school. If being suspended was supposed to give me a second chance, to prevent me leaving school with no job prospects, it had not succeeded. It was never going to work. I was never, ever going to come to school again. I knew that I would never, ever return. She had failed. She didn't understand. And as for him. Well, I had been betrayed, hadn't I?. What had he told her about me? What if I had told her all about it? What would I have said? That I'd had a schoolgirl crush? I'd fancied someone? That I dreamt at night about the two of us, together? That was all it was. No more. I could see that now. It could never have come to anything.

    'But weren't you worried?' Debbie asked me.

    Worried? No. It was over very quickly. I was angry. Inside me was a raging, burning, throbbing pulsing pain of hot blood beating to the surface of my skin, a fire igniting both my cheeks, making my face flush like a furnace. That was feeling; that was real feeling. Raw emotion. I could have reached across the wooden desk and dug my nails into her cheek. I could have yelled at her: YOU COW! YOU BITCH! YOU STUPID WOMAN, YOU JUST CAN'T SEE, CAN YOU? YOU JUST DON'T CARE, DO YOU? I could have pushed my face so close that she could feel the flecks of spittle as I spoke. I didn't, though. I turned and smoothed my skirt down and marched out, without bothering to close the door behind me.

'What's wrong?' said somebody, as I started walking down the corridor.

'Nothing,' I replied. I couldn't stop and talk. I had to concentrate on making each foot take another step. I hauled my legs along like enormous sides of ham.

I struggled to the cloakroom, each step one step nearer to disintegration. I collected my coat from the peg and walked out of the door. By now my legs were shaking uncontrollably. I climbed over the wall at the back of the school which led to the park, and walked home as quickly as my legs would let me. Don't cry, don't cry, don't cry, don't cry.

Back home I unlocked the front-door, threw my coat over the banister and walked upstairs. I didn't run. I was calm now, I moved slowly. I knew what I was doing. I was opening my door and I was lying on my bed and I was pulling up my knees and then and only then was I going to let the tears roll down my cheeks and let the hurt out and pain and the humiliation and unfairness of it all. But I was going to do it when I chose. When I was in control. I chose not to do it in her office or at school, or in the corridor or on my way to pick up my belongings for the final time. I chose do it now. On my terms. On my own and in my own time and with no-one else around.

Except I didn't. Couldn't. When I tried to cry the tears just wouldn't come. Instead they fed the burning pain inside. The frustration at not being able to let go overwhelmed me. I picked up the nearest thing to hand: it was a table lamp. I wrenched it from the wall and flung it hard across the room.

'Oh God. Poor you!' said Debbie.

The walk to the adolescent unit was now slow. It had to be to allow me to get through the remainder of the story.

As we turned into the drive that led the enormous door we slowed down almost to a standstill.

'I'd have gone back,' she said. 'I'd have finished the bastard after what he'd done to you' said Debbie.

'Perhaps you would,' I said. 'But you're not me. You don't know. To be honest I wasn't sorry to be out of school.'

'Why not?'

Why not? I hadn't really considered that. The more I thought about it, the more it seemed to be inevitable. In fact knowing that I'd never, ever go back was a relief. Now the days were shorter in November and the weather colder; the air was damp it was getting harder and harder to wash my school uniform and get it dried in time to wear again the next day.

'But why did you have to wash it every day?'

'I don't know. I just had to. All my clothes just seemed to get so dirty. All the time there would be some contamination. Sitting on the chairs that they had all been sitting on; touching textbooks they had touched and buried in their bags with all the other things they carried with them: gym kit, tampons, trainers, everything with bits of them stuck on. And then when I touched what they'd touched the bits would stick to me: bits of them, their lives. I felt polluted. And I had to wash. I had to keep myself as clean as possible. It was impossible, but I had to do it. The physical contact of the girls: not just the pain that they inflicted, but their physical proximity, their touch, their presence. Even the air they breathed, the air they breathed out and that I might breathe in. Their skin was everywhere, floating in the air and settling on desks and chairs and windowsills as dust. And greasy marks where their fingers might have turned the pages of a book, greasy smears on handles and on window catches. And the toilets: drips of wee-wee on the toilet seats; toilet-paper that they hadn't flushed away. Bloodied towels left floating in the water. The boxes where the sanitary towels should have gone. The blood inside their knickers. And then on the chairs. It wasn't everyone I was afraid of, it was them. Turning into them. Them becoming part of me. Catching them and turning into one of them, becoming someone that I didn't want to be but feared I might already have become.'

'God, Soph – you had it badly, didn't you?'

'I've not told anybody that before,' I said.

'Not even Will?'

'No.'

'Why?'

'How could I? He would never understand. It's impossible to understand. It was mad behaviour; just like putting all this down on paper. I used to scrub my skin like parchment; I wanted it to be a kind of palimpsest.'

'A what?' she asked me.

'You know, a parchment that you can write over; erase what's happened; start again. Eventually, you won't remember.'

'What?'

'Whatever you don't want to remember. Whatever it is that you're forgetting. You lose it by writing over it.'

'A bit like taping over something on a tape recorder'

'Yes – that kind of thing.'

'And that's what this is,' she asked, nodding to the note book I was carrying.

'Yes,' I said. 'But there's a problem.'

'What?'

'I can't remember some things that I need. They've gone. They're not there any more.'

'But I thought you wanted that,' she said.

'I did. I do. But now I don't know. Memory is such a funny thing.' I said to her. 'Why is it I remember that, but not the other things – things I wanted to remember?'

But she didn't answer. We were almost at the door. We walked the remainder of the journey in silence. Our feet had kicked a light dust from the gravel drive. I remember the thin film of white that covered our shoes like lace. I remember the clean smell of the air: the fresh feel of the breeze on my face and in my hair. I can remember every word of our conversation that April afternoon. I can still recall the words we used, the sentences, the rhythms, their inflections. I can see the words in front of me. They are the things that I remember most - most clearly. But the faces are a little hazy. Sometimes I can't even quite remember what she looked like. I try – I close my eyes; I can see something. But it isn't her. And if I strain hard I can see someone else. Not him. No. Her. Yes! Louise Anderson, sitting in the car outside his house and turning, offering her cheek to him to kiss. She's there. She's underneath my skin; inside my head. A memory I didn't ask for, but one I've got to keep. Why? Why is it there? Is it important? Does it matter? Why can't I remember her? What's happened to my memory of Debbie?

'Everything we are is just a memory,' Will was saying. He was reading what I'd written for him.

'Everything that we remember makes us who we are. We are other people's memories of us, and our memories of ourselves. That's all. Sometimes you think that you're remembering, but really you're creating - re-creating, making something happen that didn't really happen or at least which didn't happen in the way that you remember. How do you make sure that it's accurate? You can't. And yet it's so important.'

'Why is it important?'

'Because you are what you remember. If your memory was suddenly wiped clean but you survived, you wouldn't be yourself, not any more. You'd not be you: you would be someone new.'

'But how can that be true?'

'Well think about it, Sophie. What makes you who you are? It's got to be your memory. If you wake up in the morning it's because you wake up and remember who you were the night before. You have to. If you don't, the person that you were the night before does not survive. You died. Your eyes might open, but behind each one it's empty: there is no one home or there's another occupant.'

'I *do* remember things,' I said to him, 'of course I do. But how do I know what's memory and what's fiction? And anyway, memory is such a fickle thing. Why do you remember certain things so clearly; odd shards of memory? I get her smell, for instance. I remembered her skin's clean odour like the smell of clean towels in a drawer. I could breathe it in like air and close my eyes and think of her. I often do it now when I fold away the washing. But there are so many other things I can't remember. Like my father. Photos look like pictures of a character in a story, rather than a person. He could be anybody. And my mother...

'Let's try an experiment,' Will suddenly suggested. 'I'll talk. You close your eyes and listen. Don't think of anything. Just watch what's happening on the inside of your mind as if it were a TV screen.'

'Imagine that you're five again...' he said.

I closed my eyes.

'Remember what it feels like to be five.... what do you see... what are you doing... what did it feel like, then...?'

I listened to him speaking. Nothing happened. Then slowly, like a long-forgotten landscape gradually appearing through the mist, a memory appeared. As it cleared, outlines began to slowly join together, making shapes, creating images. The shape of my bedroom window back at home; the 'T' shaped division of the glass, with the tiny open window at the top; the deep white windowsill, extending over the front door. I was there. I could see it from the inside, through my eyes. The memory was living, in my head.

'Fix the image in your mind...' he was telling me. But now I wasn't listening. Not consciously, anyway. I was imagining myself in my small bed, looking at the window and the deep blue sky. It was summer. It was early. I was lying in my bed and looking at the morning. The image was so vivid. I must have laid there looking out a dozen times before. But there was something about this morning – what was it? No-one else in the house was awake. It was warm in bed. The window at the very top was open. For some reason I got up out of bed and climbed up on the windowsill. I couldn't have been as old as five. It was certainly before I'd started school. When I started school I got a new bed, and the room was rearranged. This was my first bed. In the place my cot had once been. A straight swap. Same view.

I was desperate to feel the cool breeze on my face. And I was curious, too. I wanted to see what the morning looked like. The deserted street. The trees. The early-morning clouds. A milk-float groaned. I got up, curious to find out what was going on. I wanted to put my mouth to the window and to taste the empty morning air. I stood on tip-toes and put my face up to the tiny gap. There was nobody about. At the end of the street, just out of sight, the town stopped. Countryside began. I sometimes walked up the road to where the buses terminated and just stood and looked at all the fields and hedges. I knew what was there. And now I had to see it in the morning light. I stood on tip-toes, and put my head as far into the gap as it would go. I could just see the fields. The corn was just starting to turn yellow. The morning air washed fresh and clean onto my face. There was no sound.

And then, in the distance, almost out of earshot, a call began to echo down the street. A bird. Birdsong. A cuckoo. Yes. I didn't know it was a cuckoo. But I knew the sound. Not a 'Cuckoo' with a 'c' and 'k' but softer, with an aitch perhaps, but the distinctive falling minor third between the notes: 'Hup –oo; Hup –oo Hup –oo Hup –oo'. And then, as the cuckoo sang, further in the distance out of town, a church bell started ringing. And then, there, at that moment, something happened, something stirred deep inside, some new feeling, some emotion, something that I didn't understand but something that has changed my life forever.

'Really?'

'Oh yes,' I said. 'That's not too fanciful, is it?'

'I suppose not, no,' he said.

101

And as I looked, I saw him leaving: silent footsteps on the path; the front-gate swinging. 'Dad? I called out through the window. 'Dad?' He turned and looked at me and smiled, then walked off down the road.

From then on there was always something, somewhere else that was better than where I was. There was somewhere that I longed to be, and it wasn't here and never could be. Why? Because I was here. And the far off place was always out of reach. The whole thing was an irritant; a grit. That thought, or rather feeling, started on that sunny summer morning. The feeling that there was a better, happier place to be. The land my childhood should have been, but wasn't. From that moment, I was different. I was never there. Not in my heart. Not really. I pretended that I was. I pretended that where I was was where I wanted to be. But it wasn't. Perhaps people can tell. Perhaps that's why I never had that many friends. Perhaps that's why when he had climbed into my little bed I was able to pretend it wasn't happening. Perhaps that's why, when mum woke up and found the note and when she started howling, I knew I would never ever tell her.

It happened, and I didn't want it to have happened. So I just forgot about it, as you can. And then it hadn't happened. But there was a stain, and that's what turned this ache inside so sour, turned a vague longing for something sunny, green and filled with church bells, birds and flowers into something dark and damp and dangerous: depression.

'I can see that it's not working,' he was saying to me somewhere in the silence. But he was wrong: it was working. Somehow it was working better than he might have realised.

CHAPTER TWELVE

So here it is, then – Chapter Twelve: at least it's not unlucky thirteen yet - unlucky for some; but unlucky for me? We'll see. At least I've got a chapter left to do some research for the story. Every writer needs to do research. Even if the narrative is based on things that really happened, and that happened to you personally - things that you have personal experience of - you still need to research it from another point of view. Your perspective might be biased or mistaken. Your memory can play funny tricks on you, especially if you've had some volts of electricity passed through your skull.

Some research is easy: if you're interested in something, you read up about it. Nowadays you surf the internet. You couldn't do that then, of course. That was the great thing about my truancy, though: the things that I could read when I should have been at school. It would have taken years for me to gather all that information. I could have done it differently, of course – empirically. I could have walked the streets: done drugs, had sex, and maybe even had a baby. I could have done it all – I did, a few times and I could have done it more. But I didn't have the time. Books were far more interesting... Research; discovery. Finding out about the things I'd later write about. That was the most enjoyable research: it was invaluable.

But sometimes it has been hard work, too. Think of all the things I've had to do, the medical procedures that I've had to undergo. I've had to: no-one wants to read a book that isn't accurate. No-one would believe it if it wasn't well researched. I've done my homework, and I've got the scars to prove it. I have done it. That's why I can write about it. Of course, I've talked about it, too, to people who might know. Research can take a wide variety of forms. But I still think that the best research an author can do is to live the things that he or she is telling: do them, feel them, smell them, taste them, get a feel for everything about them. That's what I've done here, for you: to make it all authentic and to make your reading vivid.

Interviewing is another typical research strategy. My methodology was easy. I had to find somebody who knew the answers. I had to ask them questions; probe them and uncover facts and then I had to sort them into order. I decided Will would be useful for that purpose. I would use him. The interview took place in the little bedroom while everybody else was still at school. There had been an argument. And then a little speech. Will Caxton, visiting student nurse, sat down beside me. He is young – just twenty-one – and handsome. His appearance has been described by some as 'scruffy' (Ted) and 'dishy' (Jane, but not while Ted was listening). He has a short dark beard, and the stubble makes it look as if he hasn't shaved. In the weeks he has been here he hasn't worn a tie. He behaves in an odd way, too – like helping us with washing up (which we're supposed to do) or sitting on the floor instead of making one of us give up our chair (which Ted would always make us do). I figured he would be a good subject for an interview.

SH: So, Will: you're a student psychiatric nurse; you recently expressed some reservations – in the community meeting - about the use of ECT on me. What does it stand for again?

WC: Electro-convulsive therapy

SW: Thank you. Can you begin by explaining what ECT is, and how it works?

WC: That's difficult, Sophie.

SW: Why?

WC: Well, there are many different theories, for a start. Basically no-one knows for sure how ECT works. Some people don't believe it works at all.

SW: But you do, don't you?

WC: No!

This was not the answer that I had been looking for. At this stage, temporarily, the interview broke down or at least, the interviewer did. Once she had recovered her composure, the questioning continued.

SW: You were saying there are different theories explaining ECT and how it works. Can you explain them to me?

WC: Well, some people claim that it works like the drugs that you're taking for depression, Sophie. It changes the way the brain works, altering the way the brain receptors receive certain mood-related chemicals. That's called the neurotransmitter theory. Other people have suggested that it might actually do some minor damage to the brain, and that this is what relieves the symptoms of depression.

SW: How does it do that?

WC: Well there's a risk that the electric current produces memory loss and disorientation. Maybe this creates an illusion that the problem has gone. I must stress that no-one knows for certain how or why or if this treatment works.

SW: But it does work, doesn't it? Ted said it did and Dr Grimshaw didn't argue. He has to administer it.

WC: Some studies suggest that it does lead to a small improvement in about two thirds of cases. But the benefits then start to wear off over time.

SW: So how long could I expect to feel better?

WC: You'll probably feel better straight away. You'll feel a bit confused and drowsy for about an hour, but after that – and if it's worked – you'll notice an immediate improvement.

SW: And that's got to be worth it, hasn't it?

WC: If it lasts, Sophie, yes. But that single treatment won't be the end of it. You'll need to go back two or three times, maybe more, to make sure.

SW: Ok, then. Let's move on. What can I expect from the treatment?

WC: Well, you've had your medical already, haven't you?

Of course! That was why I'd had to go to Dr Moir. It suddenly became clear. But there was something wrong about the timing, surely? That was before the decision had been taken?

SW: Yes, I have – why?

WC: Because you need to be in good health for a course of ECT. Something very dramatic and invasive is about to happen. The hospital needs to be satisfied that your body's up to it. You must be in sound general health before anyone will consider it.

SW: Ok. I've had my medical. What happens next?

WC: You'll go over to the hospital, that's what. And one of us will probably go with you.

SW: Who?

WC: Someone you trust; someone you like; someone that you feel comfortable with.

SW: Not Ted, then.

WC: Not if you don't want him, no. It'll probably be Jane, or Monica. It involves undressing!

SW: Why?

WC: Oh, just to... I don't know. It's like a surgical operation. You have to wear a gown.

SW: Ok - what happens when I've got it on?

WC: You'll be given a small injection. Then, once you're asleep, you'll be given another drug - a muscle relaxant.

SW: What for?

106

WC: Because when the electric current is turned on, your arms and legs will flail about quite violently, and you could sustain a serious injury. In the early days when people were given ECT without an anaesthetic there were all sorts of injuries – broken bones, pulled muscles, serious abrasions. People suffered badly when the therapy was in its infancy.

SW: How long has ECT been around, then?

WC: Well it was first developed in the 1930s by an Italian neurologist called Ugo Cerletti. He had seen a small electric current being given to pigs in order to render them unconscious. He decided that the same thing could be done for his most severely disturbed patients.

SW: What? To render them unconscious?

WC: Yes – some of his patients could be very uncooperative.

SW: And so he treated them the same way as he'd seen someone treating pigs, originally?

WC: Yes, Sophie. That's right - pigs.

For a while the interview was halted. Both interviewer and interviewee fell silent. There was something in Will's tone of voice I didn't like. He was amused, but hostile too. He didn't think that ECT was any good. But what did he know? He was just a student nurse. He wasn't fully trained or qualified. So I decided to cut short the interview.

Next morning I was taken to the hospital. The day dawned bright and clear. The red bricks seemed to be burning in the golden early morning sunlight. Midges danced in the mild spring air like sparks. I was apprehensive about what was going to happen to me, but I was excited too. As we walked along the little road that led over to the hospital, Jane squeezed my hand.

'No need to worry,' she smiled. Jane had enormous kind brown eyes, the kind of eyes that look as if they're smiling even when she isn't. She made the best of what she'd got: her hair was long and gently wavy like the Boticelli Venus. No wonder Will began to fancy her. She was pretty: interesting instead of beautiful – not classically beautiful, anyway. When someone says 'she set her chin at it' it was Jane they must have had in mind. Determined: confident, but friendly, too; and ready in a flash to smile. A big smile, pulled down by the chin. I'm not describing her here very well. But she was always calm and confident. The kind of person that you might do anything for. Even have electrodes fastened to your head.

We climbed the steps up to the large main entrance. Inside, the reception area was empty – as usual there was nobody waiting at the desk. We turned and walked along an unlit corridor. Here and there the grey expanse of wall was interrupted with bright squares of colour: paintings, done by patients as a form of therapy.

There were other pictures in the tiny waiting room – prints of mountain scenes, of trees and valleys; faded watercolours.

'These are good,' I said to Jane. She smiled, and then went on flicking through the magazine that she was reading. We were the only ones here, although there were a lot of empty chairs. I didn't feel like sitting down. You don't do on the morning of an execution. There was a faint smell of burning rubber in the air. Suddenly there was a familiar voice behind me.

'Ok now Sophie - would ye like to come through now?' I was suddenly gripped by panic. Jane stood up and smiled and moved towards the second door. I followed, then – when we had reached it – she stepped back to let me go through first. But I stopped, too and looked at her.

'I don't want to.' I stepped back, but she was standing in my way now, mouth closed – jaw set.

'Don't worry, Sophie – it's going to be ok.'

'No!'

And as she took a step towards me I lashed out at her. A moment later someone had me firmly underneath my arms. I couldn't move.

'That wasnae very nice young lady,' he was saying, as my legs were pedalling the air. Although he was old, Dr Moir was tall and strong – my feet were nowhere near the floor.

'Calm down!' he ordered as he carried me into the room and dropped me on the bed.

'That's not a very good start, is it? Nurse... could you?' he moved aside and drew a curtain. Jane helped me get undressed.

'I'm sorry, Jane.'

'Don't be.'

'But I am...'

'Come on – put this on quickly, then.'

As I struggled into the pale green gown that they'd provided, metal buckles jingled on each corner of the bed like keys. Leather straps hung loose, just like the lolling tongues of dogs.

'You'll feel a wee scratch...' Dr Moir was saying, as a needle was inserted into the back of my hand. Through the corner of my eye I thought I caught a glimpse of Dr Grimshaw holding up the crown. And then I fell asleep. I knew I had been strapped down by the bruises and the chafing on my wrists and ankles. I knew that the electrodes were attached above both temples. The charge, they told me, lasted for less than a second. And when I woke up I was in another room, lying on a different bed. My body hurt as if I had the 'flu. My fingers and my toes were numb; my eyes were red with blood. My body ached in a new and strange way; in my head there was a buzzing sound, like the noise of a small electric fan. After half-an-hour I got up and got dressed and went back to the unit and went straight to bed.

***

Next day at the Community Meeting, Ted enquired how I'd got on.

'Do you want to talk about it, Sophie?'

There were small brown stains like sunburn just above my temples. If I touched the skin there it felt dry and sore. My eyes were bloodshot. My head felt different, too, as if something somewhere had disappeared, gone missing. I was struggling to find the words to describe what I was thinking. The sensation was like trying to recall something - a distant memory, something that you know you should remember easily but which somehow stays just beyond your reach.

'It's there,' I told them 'but I can't describe it.'

'I think that Sophie's hiding something,' someone said.

'No I'm not,' I shot back quickly. 'But I don't know what to say'.

Ted just laughed, and shook his head. I looked across at Jane, pleadingly.

'Maybe there simply isn't anything to say,' Will interrupted. Ted glared across at him.

'Maybe I can help,' said Jane. 'I was with her, after all?'

Ted smiled. This was the encouragement she needed. She described to everyone exactly what had happened. She told them all about the leather straps, and as she did so I could feel them tighten round my wrists and ankles. She described the sedative that I'd been given. She said how quickly and how peacefully I'd gone to sleep and how – once the anaesthetist had established I was under – they had speedily administered the muscle relaxant, attached electrodes to my temples and begun.

'It was over very quickly,' Jane added. 'Then we took Sophie into the recovery room and waited for the sedative to wear off.'

But there was more to it than that. There was the great blue flash inside my head, as if a lightening strike was earthing on the inside of my skull; there was the fact the muscles of my legs and arms had turned to iron. There were so many things to tell them; although it only took a second, whole universes seemed to be colliding in the darkness. What I couldn't quite believe was how much space there was inside my head. My mum had often said that I had nothing in between my ears. How did she know she was right? But not just my head, every head: there were entire galaxies in there; every time an idea occurred to anyone another pyrotechnic presentation was exploding. I saw the blood cells in my eyes, like small transparent discs with slight depressions in the centre. There were branches, trees and forests taking blood from one place to another. Memories floated in the darkness like sea-horses. And there were strange cells, too, like creatures: some of which were good and some of which were bad. There was a battle going on. That's it. There was a battle being fought inside my head. And in my head the bad cells had been winning. But this white flash, like a nuclear explosion, had stalled them. Not quite stopped them; but it held them back like ants forced underground by chemical attack. The creatures were re-grouping, I knew that. They were still there, lurking in the spaces in-between ideas. They were waiting. But at least now they were hidden.

CHAPTER THIRTEEN

Once the plot gets going, then all sorts of things can start to happen. An author can begin to be a little more creative; experiment a little; try out new ideas and fresh approaches. Once you've assembled all your characters you can move them around in the story just like chess-men on a chess board: try out different moves and combinations, use more daring tactics. It's like a game. And once depression lifts you start to pay attention. You start noticing again, and asking questions. What if Lizzie wasn't anorexic anymore? What if Ted and Will had had a major disagreement? What if red-haired Monica was unhappy? What if she and Jane were both applying for the same promotion?

Once the questions start you're there; you're up and running. Things begin to move off in a new direction. Before long the story will have gained its own momentum. Life emerges from the soil like a flower. You plant the seeds, you water. But you can never know quite how they'll grow. Once characters are created they take on a life of their own. They can start to do all sorts of things that you wouldn't have predicted and behave in ways you couldn't have dictated.

Like Will, for example. How could someone so important suddenly appear and then almost take the story over? Could he personally change the focus of the narrative? Could such a thing occur? Was such a plot twist plausible?

No author could have planned it, that was for sure. Without the hidden factors it would be impossible. And anyway, it didn't happen overnight. Something else was going on, something even I was unaware of. No-one ever knows what's happening in someone else's head. How could we? Nobody knows everything. You can't even know everything that's happening in your own head. No one can. It can't be done. Limited omniscience is the best that an author can ever hope for.

'So, how have you been getting on?' Will was asking. I was sitting on the bed and scribbling. 'Anything that I can read?'

I passed him the chapter I'd just written. He was reading it when Jane came into the room to check on me – again.

'It's time for bed,' she said. I groaned.

'Hey - have you seen what Sophie's doing?' Will asked, and she smiled at him and then at me.

'No don't,' I said as he leant forward, passing her the book.

'Why not?'

'I don't want anyone to know,' I told him.

'But why?' he asked.

'I don't, that's all. They wouldn't understand.'

'I do,' he said.

'You're different.'

'Thanks!'

'I don't mean like that...' I told him. 'You know what I mean.'

'I do?'

'You know you do. But other people...' Jane looked down at the floor. 'I don't mean you' I said. 'The others, though - they wouldn't understand; they'd think that I was being funny.'

'Funny?'

'They'd think that I was trying to be above them; that I thought that I could do this thing my own way, that I thought my story was worth telling.'

'But you do. It is. That's what you do think,' Will said.

'I don't want them to think that, though.'

'No? Why not?'

'I don't know. I just don't, that's all. Don't tell them, will you?'

'Not if you don't want me to.'

'I don't.'

'We won't then,' they replied.

Will handed back the pale blue exercise book.

'Pity though,' he said to Jane. 'There's some good stuff in it.'

'What is it about?' she asked.

'What isn't it about?' he said to her. 'There's a bit of everything – inspiration, writing, memory – you name it: fantasy, reality.'

'Sounds interesting,' said Jane sitting on the bed beside him.

'What I really want to know,' he said 'is where does all this come from?' He pointed to my book. 'Where do these ideas grow?'

'In your subconscious,' Jane replied. 'That's what Freud thought, anyway.'

'I suppose so.' Will stood up to go.

'But what's that?'

'Part of your brain,' she said. 'Your mind.'

'Which one?' I asked. 'What is your mind? Is it just your brain?'

'Your mind is what you are,' said Will. 'It's you.'

'Me?'

'You,' he said. 'That's what you are. Your mind, your brain. Everything we are is in there, in those cells and in that blood; it's really only so much fat, but it makes us what we are.'

'Oh Will, you put it all so delicately.'

'But it's true,' he said, a little hurt.

'You don't believe that!'

'Yes I do,' he said.

'But we're so much more than that,' I said. 'We must be.'

'Why?'

'There must be more to us than chemistry!'

Jane was smiling now, indulgently.

'Ok, our brain is more than that,' he said. 'It's an impressive lump of fat, for sure. It's us; it's who we are, our secret weapon; it's what makes us different – it's what separates us from every other living creature. It's our brain, one hundred billion brain cells – neurons – firing chemicals across microscopic gaps called synapses, making one hundred thousand different links between the cells. That's what you are; that's why you're here. There's something going wrong with all that electrical activity. That's true of everyone. That's why this is the most important hospital in the world. That's why I want to work here. This is the new church. This is where we understand and mend ourselves, and get to know our place in the world. This is where we find the answers to the questions we don't even know we're asking.'

She was laughing at him now, her mouth wide open.

'Really?' she was gasping, though she knew the answer.

'Oh yes, really,' he replied and turned to go.

'Will, wait...' she called as she went after him, their voices growing fainter as they went downstairs.

In the dark that night I thought. I think. I think so. Think. So. I. Think. Think. Is what I do. It's more than what I do. It's what I am. It's me. I am thinking. And I am the things I think. I am thought. That's what I am. I fell asleep.

I needed sleep more during ECT. In all I must have had about four or five such treatments. Sometimes I had to queue up with the other patients; sometimes I was on my own. Each Wednesday I would feel a little scratch before my arms and legs were strapped. Each Thursday morning I would feel the chafing round my wrists and ankles. But I would also feel a little altered. There was something missing, as if a clock had quietly stopped ticking or as if something had been stolen without anybody noticing. My head felt different. Weird. Good. It was nothing that I could define; still less, explain. There was a change happening. To change you need to know where you begin. I didn't know anything but pain. Changing into something different didn't really matter: being someone else might be much better. And I never used the knife again. Not once. Not on myself. No writer is the same, just because we all put things on paper. I'm not Ernest Hemingway, for example.

'I'm cured!' I shouted out next morning, as the lights went on. 'Debbie, I don't ache any more inside. It's over!' and I lay in bed and started laughing.

Debbie stirred and started smiling, sleepily. I went over to her bed and hugged her, tightly, soaking up the liquid sunlight of her body, slowly filling up the emptiness in mine with all her goodness. In that small moment was a future. My future: there was something here to live instead of die for. There was a sense that everything was going to be all right. I leapt up off the bed and danced towards the windows. I stood for a moment before the heavy purple curtains, taking one in each hand ready to dramatically reveal the new day. I imagined golden rays would flood the room and birds would sing in every tree. But when I threw the curtains back the sky was grey; the only birds that I saw were angry rooks and they weren't singing, they were retching and their nests were spreading in the empty elms like tumours. I wasn't even struck by lightening.

How can you go so quickly from elation to despair? One moment everything is flowing easily, the next the words have disappeared like swallows. The flow has dried; if words appear at all they come in one's and two's and do so painfully and slowly. Maybe I'll abandon it, I tell myself.

Maybe I'll just give up. Maybe this is something that I just can't do anymore. Maybe pain is what you need to write, and maybe now, without it, I have written everything I've got to say.

But then I remember the times when words flowed from the pen, when writing seemed to go so well; when words simply appeared on the page before my eyes as if they'd nothing much to do with me; when ideas came out of nowhere and the words got written effortlessly: those are the days you should remember. Days when you read through what you've written and it all makes perfect sense – as if it's always been there in the background and just faded into view. Those days seem so necessary. I go to bed on days like that so happily. I think about the next few pages in my sleep. Sometimes I begin to write as soon as I wake up. Instead of lying there and waiting for the ache to start, I write. I have a pen and paper by my bed. Debbie doesn't mind. The light goes on 'Good morning girls,' a voice calls and before I'm even wide awake, before I wake up and remember who I am, I'm writing some idea or other from the night.

The fluorescent strip-lights clatter into life, and hum. And I lie back in bed and think about the words I have just written

'Morning, Sophie – sleep well?' Monica asks.

But I don't answer. Debbie turns and yawns, then groans.

'Time to get up, Debbie – you're on breakfast duty!' Monica tells her.

Debbie groans again, but I don't hear her. I'm already writing.

'Ok then girls, I'll see you two downstairs in fifteen minutes. Don't be late.'

'Mmmm,' I say my tongue between my lips. I'm concentrating. It doesn't last for long. But when it's done, it's good. It's written. And then I can get out of bed.

'Come on Debbs,' I shake her bed. Her breathing's deep: she has gone straight back to sleep again. I sit down and bend towards her ear.

'If you want sex Debbs it's got to be right now – I've got some writing to get done.'

'You what?' she mumbles sleepily and turns towards me.

'Come on,' I tell her. 'Let's get the bathroom used before the boys get up.'

She moans again, and rolls out of the bed on to the floor.

'Ok,' she says, her eyes still closed. She collects her towel and pads out of the bedroom, eyes still almost shut.

We cross the open landing to the bathroom, looking out over the staircase at the world outside the window. One door say 'engaged' but Debbie – half-asleep – still opens it and walks inside. Steam billows out around us, making it impossible to see who, if anyone, is in. I step inside and draw the shower curtain.

'Hey!' a boy's voice shouts from somewhere in the steam.

'Sorry,' we both mumble, giggling, and we hurry out to try the next door: empty. I follow Debbie in and wind the rope cord of my dressing gown around the handle and then knot it on the rail.

Once the door is fastened, Debbie squats down on the loo and shivers like a hamster. She leans forward with her elbows tucked in underneath her. I take a look, then take my nightdress off and step inside the shower. Water trickles down from the enormous metal shower rose. Steam begins to billow out into the bathroom like a fire.

Suddenly she is there beside me, naked. We take turns to wash each other. I go first; I lather up the soap then take each limb in turn and rub them in my hands until the wet and shiny skin is covered. She stands there with her eyes closed and her head up as I rub her chest. Her breasts are small, like little buds, barely protruding from the sharp-ribbed smoothness of her boyish chest. She turns, so that I can do her back. Her shoulder blades protrude like two small trowels. Her spine runs down the middle of her back like beads, before it disappears between her tiny adolescent buttocks. Her legs are long and thin and sleek; in-between there is a small tuft, softer in the water than the hair there ought to be. I want her just the way she is now, and I want her like she is forever.

How does it feel?

It feels wonderful.

It does, too. I stand up and help her rinse the soap from her pale body, damming water with my hands and then suddenly releasing it and running down her shoulders and her arms, her back, her bottom and her legs until the suds have disappeared. It is so warm here, so warm and steamy in the shower. It is warm and we are close. The white-tiled cubicle is small. We stand so that our bare feet touch as we manoeuvre round the shower tray together. This is a strange dance. Warm water trickles down my neck as I move my head beneath the flow. I lower myself a little, just a little, and I bend my knees because I'm taller than her: then I'm there. I'm level with her open face. Her eyes are closed; her lips are pursed, her mouth just open. Drops of water drip down off her chin before I shield her with my head like an umbrella, move my face to hers and place my lips on hers so gently that a sudden shiver runs up through my body. I feel her tongue alive inside my mouth and open wider as it searches deeper. Both our mouths are now competing, each one trying to engulf the other. Her lips are taken into mine, then mine into hers. Finally I stand back and I hold her hands and look at her. Her eyes are wide, her mouth still open. What is that expression?

I decide I know and kneel down on the hard white wet tiled floor. The tiles are cold against my legs. With water dripping off my nose I push my face between her thighs and let my tongue explore. Her eyes close and she leans back to get the jet of water full into her burning face. My tongue goes deeper and she starts to shake. As her knees bend I hook an arm round each leg to brace her as she crumples back against the wall.

I kneel there for a moment, watching her. I let her get her breath back with the water pouring down on top of us like warm rain.

'Oh God!' she might say. Then again she might not. Words are so inadequate. Nothing she can say can tell you how she feels; only I can try to do that. I'm the author. I know. This is what I do. But what can I say? How can I describe to you what she is feeling? Do I really know? And if I do, what words are there that could come close to telling you? The drugs they give us can't do this. The talking can't. Only we can do this for each other. Only I can do this to her; and I feel it too. Her. Us. Together, in the shower. And I love her, too. At least I think I do. How do you know? I can't be certain. But it feels like love which means it feels like what I think that love should be. But I don't know for sure. How does anybody know? How can you tell? I'm sixteen, and I've never felt like this before. I never thought I would. I never thought I could. Would. Should. And with her, too.

I suppose I must feel guilty, too. I'm not supposed to be happy. I'm supposed to ache: I do. But now the ache is in a different place, and it is warming, too. And she is happy, too. Just look at her. Her face is flushed all morning. When I catch her eye she looks away and smiles. She knows exactly what I'm thinking when that happens. I do, too. We're both remembering this morning. We are thinking one another's thoughts. We know what happens when we're with each other, and we know that it's our secret. And that is what love is – a secret. No-one knows about it. No-one knows that it exists. It doesn't – not for them. For us. Our secret. Something only we know. Something only we do. We are special. Me and you. I love you. Yes I do. I know you might think that's impossible. I know that you might say girls can't love girls, but I love you. I only have to think of you to know and I must know that I love you 'cos I think of you so often and you're lovely. That's poetry, really. When you think about it, that is poetry.

I love you Debbie,
You might think that's strange
You might say to me 'girls can't love girls'
But I love you: it must be true.
I only have to think of you to know.
Inside things suddenly go sunny
As if deep inside my body
Somebody is giving me a secret,
Telling me of all there is or ever was.
And that is you.
And you are everything to me.
All I need and all I do –
I love you.

CHAPTER FOURTEEN

Will had created quite a stir with all his new ideas. He wanted to experiment – with us, on us, I don't know. It didn't matter. He stood up to Ted, however - who now referred to Will sarcastically as 'student nurse' the whole time. But Will didn't seem to mind; he wasn't bothered. He might have only been a student nurse but he still seemed to have a lot of confidence. He was in awe of nobody: he broke the rules deliberately, living dangerously - came into our bedroom when we lying in our beds to say goodnight to us; he talked with calm authority to Dr Grimshaw about our drugs and even got our dosages reduced. That helped. I started feeling more alert. I noticed things around me more than I had done; whether that was him or what had happened to my brain or changes to my drugs I didn't know. I didn't really care. I felt that something deep inside was slowly thawing; things were starting up again. It was like waking after a long and dreamless sleep. It was like learning once again what life was like and who you were. It was a rebirth, I suppose. For the first time I became more interested in everything around me: with a clear head breakfast was a meal that I enjoyed again; I began contributing to the community meeting; lessons in the schoolroom started to become fascinating.

Afternoons, though, had always been a problem. Walks – if they occurred at all for me since my escapade – were always closely supervised. The teacher, Mrs Turner, left once lunch was over. The boys might kick a ball around; some would sit and watch TV. I might start to do some writing. But all that came later. First, we had a painting class to go to.

'I've invited Mrs Lotinga from Rehab,' Will announced one morning. 'I hope nobody minds'. He looked at Ted. 'She'll set up in the classroom after lunch. She's bringing all the equipment that we'll need.'

'Well,' Ted said. 'Who wants to paint, eh? You don't have to go. It's not compulsory. It's a nice day – I might go out for a walk if anyone wants to join me. Or perhaps you'd like to paint – who wants to do that then? Let's do this democratically. Let's have a show of hands.'

A few of us slowly lifted up our arms. Then more.

'Well I think that it's a *great* idea,' said Jane emphatically. 'I'll certainly be there!' and her hand went up as well.

But in the end she wasn't. Ted decided that they had to meet together in the little nurses' office. Monica came to watch us paint instead.

'You need to work in daylight,' Mrs Lotinga was saying as we arrived. She was opening the windows and turning off the yellow artificial lights.

I didn't really want to paint. I couldn't see the point. But at least it was a break from all the other things that we would normally be doing. It was something different. And we didn't have to go. Ted had made that clear. But most of us had wanted to, if only just to try out something new. We were interested, for once. Even Lizzie came – it was a change from being stared at for an hour after lunch.

'Welcome along everyone,' Mrs Lotinga was saying, glancing as she did so at a clipboard to remind herself what we were called.

'This is Mrs Lotinga,' said Will once we'd all assembled. 'She's very kindly come to help us do some painting for the afternoon'.

'Thank you nurse,' the woman said. 'Ok, ok – thank you everyone!' she clapped her hands.

The girls smiled. Lizzie stalked off towards an easel in the corner, muttering something about needing to be near the lavatory. But Mrs Lotinga was wise to that.

At school, I'd been quite good at art. I'd always enjoyed drawing. I was moderately good at it. I liked the freedom of the art class, too; I liked the individual attention. We'd had Art every Wednesday afternoon. We sketched and painted things that Mrs Cash had brought in: pictures, vases, tangled heaps of metal.

This was different. This was unlike any art class I'd ever attended. Mrs Lotinga had no props. But then, this wasn't art. This was therapy. I'd forgotten. We weren't painting to improve ourselves as artists; we were painting to explore our problems and emotions.

'Think of the page as a window...' she was saying. 'Let the light flood in; look through and see what lies beyond. What do you see? What do you want to see? Fix it in your minds and capture it, transform the paper into what you see.' As she waved her arms the bangles jangled on her wrists.

'Adolescence is a wonderful time for painting,' she was saying. 'It's when you're all constantly drawing and re-drawing pictures of the world around you.'

I glanced around the room to see what the others were doing. There were huge amounts of thick paint, blacks and reds and oranges, on most easels. The boys were simply daubing colour on the paper, laughing at the rude shapes they were making. I was staring at my sheet of paper, waiting.

'Paint whatever comes into your head,' she said to me. 'I want you to capture your ideas – to fix your inspiration. Paint,' she said. 'Just paint. Paint anything.'

Will suddenly appeared at my shoulder.

'Not working, then?'

'Not really,' and I showed him what I'd done – precisely nothing.

'You'd rather paint with words, eh?'

'Yes I would.'

'Don't worry – she's not used to it, that's all.' He nodded to the corner of the room where Mrs Lotinga was scrutinising Lizzie's painting of a plate piled high with food.

'At Rehab,' Will went on 'they just paint whatever they want to – most of the patients there just like the colours.'

I thought of the pictures in the long grey corridor.

'I just need an idea,' I told Will as I stood there staring at the large white sheet of paper clipped to the easel. It was creased and there were other pages underneath. There had been others on the top. It was a large pad with the pages curled up at the corners. The random lines traced patterns up and down the paper. It looked a little like a map. As I looked closely I could make out roads and trees; field boundaries. And up there, in the corner, almost hidden by the trees I hadn't painted was a small house.

I picked up a paintbrush and I started filling in the lines and patterns of the landscape. The boundaries of fields; the trees; the blue stream running down one side of the estate - the stream where I would swim, naked, on a summer's afternoon, turning over like a dolphin in the cool, clear water, and the house in the corner where I lived, alone. There weren't very many facilities: no 'mod-cons'. I wouldn't be able to afford much as a struggling writer. But it didn't matter. I would wash in the river and rise in the early morning with the sun. If I needed light after sunset I'd use candles. Life would be as simple as it could be. I marked out fields where I would grow my own food and would keep my horses. Suddenly, everything was all so clear and well-defined. I'd only really used three colours: black for the boundaries and outlines, the borders of my world, the moat, protection; green for the fields and trees - by the time I'd finished, most of the paper was green; and blue for the stream. And then I put a little dot of yellow on the top. That was my self-portrait. That was me. I was there, with just my sun-bleached yellow hair above the water.

It wasn't a particularly good painting. It didn't matter. It was different to the others, I could see. But everything was clear and bright. The colours were vivid. I didn't have to think about a thing. It painted itself. I was possessed. I was amazed when Mrs Lotinga called out to tell us that the class was over.

'Put your brushes down now,' she was saying. 'Stay where you are, and I'll just have a look at what you've done.'

She was standing at my shoulder, looking at my painting. She was leaning forward and the chain around her neck was hanging like a pendulum outside her tie-dyed blouse. I held my breath. I knew that if she peered any closer I would have to hit her. I felt the anger boiling up inside. If I touched her the experiment was over. Another good idea ruined. Something else I'd spoil for the rest of the community. I didn't want to hit her but she was intruding. She was too near. She was too close; too near to me; too near to what I'd done; too near to everything that I'd created.

'What's that?' she asked and stepped back, pointing to the yellow dot. I felt my shoulders drop.

'That's me,' I answered as I sighed. 'Swimming.'

'Do you do a lot of swimming, Sophie?'

No, I thought, but didn't answer. Instead I carefully unhooked my picture and I rolled it up. That was enough analysis. I'd painted what I'd wanted and it worked for me. Talking would do nothing for it. Why did everybody always want to talk about it anyway? Words would simply spoil the atmosphere.

***

126

A few days later I went back to finish off my picture. I'd been thinking about it ever since the afternoon I'd painted it. I'd seen it in my mind; I'd thought of different things I could include and ways I could improve it. The stream would bend, for instance, and would run across the bottom corner of my land. The trees would fringe the boundaries on all sides, so that I'd be screened off from the outside world. And in the middle there would be an open space. The sun would shine and things would grow: vegetables, flowers; ideas. I'd keep some chickens, too. There would be some outbuildings built on to the farmhouse. I – we - could use them for our storage and for stabling the horses.

By the time I'd finished I'd created an idyllic landscape of trees and gentle hills, big hedges and small flower-scattered meadows fields. The overwhelming impression was of greenness: lush fertility. It was much more than a single picture. I'd painted the same scene now on several occasions: sometimes as a plan with details; sometimes as an overall impression. They were much more than merely pictures. What I'd painted was a future.

We would both live by the things we grew. We would live here in the house alone. We had no need of company. We wanted no-one but each other. All we wanted was to be alone and live our lives without the interference of other people. That meant boys. We would survive entirely by our own efforts. Every time I painted the bucolic fantasy the impact was the same: calm, safe, green. Sometimes I'd allow myself to glimpse the house at the end of a long drive, shielded by the tall trees. Sometimes I would paint myself or Debbie in the picture: somewhere in the distance, me with long fair hair and her complete with tiny bunches like a young deer's budding antlers. But mostly all the views were simply scenes of fields I longed to own and meadows I would walk through, land where no-one else would ever go, fields where I could wander naked if I wanted to and feel the constant sunshine washing on my bare, bronzed skin. I'd wander round like her, proud of my body. And now she would be watching, hidden in the trees.

I enjoyed the painting classes. At least I did at first. Painting pictures made me feel there was a future for me: something better, somewhere I could travel to as soon as therapy was over. It was an addictive high. Like a junkie, I kept returning to my new drug. I wanted this new feeling that the painting classes gave me, even though I knew it wouldn't last. Like everything I did my mind would start to build a natural resistance. Sometime soon the pleasure would wear off. That time came sooner than I had anticipated.

Three weeks after starting Mrs Lotinga decided that we should hold an exhibition of our paintings.

'You've all done so well that I think we should show the people at the hospital what we've been doing. We'll take your work with us to Rehab.'

Rehab – the Rehabilitation Unit - was a big, modern building at the opposite corner of the hospital site, as far from the main Victorian asylum and as close to the outside world as it could be. Deliberately? I don't know. But I did know that from Rehab you could see the world beyond the ring of trees: the world outside; the world of normal people, looking normal, doing normal things instead of in here doing occupational therapy.

The town lay in a valley several miles away. In the distance, framed by the surrounding trees, the spires and roofs and chimneys of my home stood out clear against the sky. Normality. So near, and yet so out of reach. If I stared for long enough I could just make out my school. I could work out where my house was. I could see the clock above the entrance to the library. It all looked small and safe from up here. On Sunday you could even hear the church bells ringing in the tower, clanging out their nursery-rhyme refrain. It was all like something from a story, so clearly contained and well-defined. It was difficult to imagine all the things that were still happening: my mum at work and drinking herself stupid in the evening; the girls at school all learning lessons in the classroom. Everyone just carrying on with life while we were here. It made me want to be there, with them: to be anywhere but here. But it was safe up here. The outside world was tidy, in its little box. And when we turned around and went inside it was as if someone had simply put the lid back on.

In Rehab patients almost looked like us; they didn't look mad like the other patients did. These people would recover. They had lives to live. They would get better. Here, they were being trained - in pottery, in typing, cooking, anything that might be useful; anything that would also keep them busy. That was Rehab's duty – to keep everybody occupied.

Sometimes the mask would slip, though. We had overheard strange stories. Like the man who once ate all the goldfish. Or the woman in the typing classes who pretended she was running it; the man in pottery. But most of them would leave here one day. So would we. One day we would walk out of here and take our places in the world beyond: re-born; renewed; repaired. Rehabilitated.

'Welcome to Rehab everybody,.' A woman in a long blue kaftan was looking at a clipboard as we walked in.

'Lizzie, it's down the corridor on the left,' Mrs Lotinga was saying. Lizzie stalked off in the opposite direction, muttering to herself.

'No – left,' the woman shouted after her as Lizzie turned the wrong way.

'Oh well,' the woman sighed. 'I suppose she'll find her way eventually.'

We set our paintings up around the art room walls. The boys were keen to show off what they'd painted. Debbie's landscapes drew admiring glances. Jason had drawn highly detailed pictures of an imaginary world he had invented. As I unrolled my own attempts an overwhelming wave of disappointment washed over me. The drawing was so poor. The depth and light were non-existent. There was no perspective. In my head, it had been different. In my head

I'd seen it all. There had been symmetry between the paper and the picture. One was the cause of the other, and – however crude – the picture on the paper would always re-create the picture inside my mind. That way, everything I drew was good. Until I looked at other peoples' efforts now.

'I've invited everyone to come along,' our tutor was calling out to us. 'Ted and Monica are both coming; Jane too. And Will is here already, isn't he?'

Will was helping pin up all the pictures.

'And Mr Garland too: you know, the Senior Nursing Officer – I've invited him along as well.'

'Why all the fuss?' asked Lizzie quietly as she crept back quietly from the lavatory.

'Beats me,' I told her.

'Ok now – are we all ready?'

The room was large and light, specifically selected – or maybe it had been designed – for painting. There were windows on three sides like a conservatory, making it difficult to identify any of the silhouetted figures who were walking round inspecting all our paintings. I sat behind an easel in the corner, next to my pictures. That was the idea. We were to be there to talk about our work if anyone should ask us any questions. What else? After all, that's what we were here for. I looked at all my efforts, deciding what to say. They were almost identical; like studies for one, big final painting. Only there would be no final painting. There would be no more paintings from today. And the paintings I had done would be destroyed.

'What's that?' asked Jane.

'That's me,' I told her.

'Oh – and that?' She pointed to a house.

'A house,' I told her.

That's really nice, she'd say, and 'You've got quite a talent'. But I hadn't. The words were simply said to make me feel a little better. I knew that. And the questions she was asking weren't genuine expressions of interest in the paintings. They were gentle interrogations of my inspiration.

130

Anything I said would be reported back. And another small piece of the jigsaw they were assembling, the one called 'Sophie Western, school-refuser, suicide-risk, depressed' would be neatly put in place. As a result, I intended to say nothing. I was pleased by the kind words. But then I felt stupid for allowing myself to feel pleased. I knew what they were doing. But I had to tell them something. I said that this was where I was going to live when I left school. And they all smiled and said how beautiful it looked.

All the time, over my shoulder, I was scanning the room to see where Ted was, hoping he wouldn't find me in this corner. I needn't have worried about that, however. Ted was far more interested in the boys' efforts.

'What on earth is that?' he snorted, wagging a finger at one of Patrick Randle's pictures.

'That's a woman Ted,' he sniggered.

'I can see that, Patrick. But...' he rumbled 'do you really thing that that's appropriate - here?' He scanned the room, anxiously looking-out for the Senior Nursing Officer.

All of Patrick's pictures were unusual. They looked more like prehistoric cave art than like proper drawings. They were covered in religious symbols. There were people, too. And the people were all naked. Things were happening; things you couldn't quite make out but which you knew were naughty. Patrick was a naughty boy.

'Hey – get off that!' he was shouting.

'We are NOT having these up here when Mr Garland arrives!' Ted was muttering as he tore them down. 'And you are going straight back to the unit, Patrick Randle – Will?'

Will walked across to Patrick's easel. Ted was shaking.

'Take this boy back to the unit will you, Student Nurse? And...' he spluttered 'put these disgusting objects in the bin'. He dumped a pile of screwed up sheets on Will's arms.

Somewhere, in the corner, Mrs Lotinga was crying.

CHAPTER FIFTEEN

'I don't suppose that was a great success?' Will said later when we got back from the exhibition.

'Oh I don't know,' Lizzie said. 'I thought it was great. Mr Garland loved my paintings – said they were so realistic that they made him feel hungry.'

'Yeah and Ted was really interested in Jason's mini-universes' Debbie added, 'asking him loads of questions and telling Mr Garland all about them...'

'No he wasn't,' Jason murmured.

'Yes he was,' she said. 'He really liked them and he said so too to Mrs Lotinga and everything.'

'Oh well then – maybe it wasn't as bad as I had feared,' Will added.

Patrick, though, was sitting in a corner, sulking.

'Can we do more painting, Will?' asked Lizzie.

'I don't think that's a very good idea at present,' Will said. 'Anyway, this afternoon I thought that we'd try something different. We're going to do some drama. I've invited the local theatre director over. He'll be here in about an hour. Help me move the furniture in the day room, will you?'

We pushed the chairs and tables up against the wall to make a large space in the centre. This would be our studio. As we did so, Will explained what we would do.

Role-play was what he called it; no script – we would all invent it as we went along - take a situation, live it, act it, be someone that we weren't and think their thoughts and speak their words.

'That's a bit like writing, isn't it?' I said.

'I suppose it is,' he told me. 'But it's like real life too. We're all so many different people when we have to be or want to be – we've all of us got different facets to our personalities.'

'Really?'

'Yes, of course Sophie. We all put on an act.'

'We don't.'

'We do,' he told me. 'How would you describe someone like me, for instance, if you had to? How would you describe my character – my personality?'

'I don't know,' I replied. What I meant was that I didn't know where to start. Will was so sure of everything; so confident; so certain that he was correct in anything he said and did. I'd like to be like that, I thought: to be so sure of everything you're doing; to be certain - even if you're wrong; to have the confidence to make it seem that you were right. Or arrogance.

'You're confident,' I told him.

'There you are,' he said. 'You think I'm like that, and I want you to – but that's not who I really am, not always anyway. Sometimes I am insecure: as insecure as you. I'm not confident; not really; not inside.'

'But you're older – you know more than we do; understand more.'

'But you don't suddenly get more confident because you're older. You just learnt to act as if you are. And sometimes, maybe most of the time, the act appears to work.'

'Well you always seem as though you're totally sure of yourself – even with Ted!' I told him.

'That shows that it must be true. The acting works. You have to look as though you are. You have to act as if you are. You have to play the part. That's the only thing that starts to get a little easier over time as you get older.'

'We can explore this concept further,' said the theatre director when he arrived a little later.

'What I want you all to do it to act the part of somebody you know: someone that you know well, someone close but somebody who isn't you. I want you to be that person in a situation that you've been in. I want you to see it happening from the other person's point of view; I want you to see what's happening through their eyes, to see yourself, preferably, from inside the mind of someone else.'

We stood around and looked at one another.

'Think of somebody,' he started. 'Someone close to you. Now close your eyes. Imagine them.' And I imagined mum.

'Think of something that defines them. You are going to act it out in front of someone, and then they will tell you what you've shown. Ok? Now, choose a partner.'

Debbie acted out her brother, sitting in a chair and watching television. I was my mother, coming home from work on Friday night and drinking.

'Right. So. Ok, then, everyone?' I could tell that he was struggling.

'This time, I want you to work together on a piece of drama. One of you is the character, and your partner...'

Yes?

'...your partner, he or she plays you.'

Me?

'You!'

Oh.

'We need to see some interaction, too. Invent some dialogue this time. Invent a scene. Conflict is always useful. Make up something that brings your character into conflict with your partner – who is you. Or remember something, if you don't want to invent it.'

Will looked a little anxious. Everybody else just looked confused.

Find a corner and then act it out,' the director told us. 'And remember... you've got to be the person that you're playing. Get inside them: see the world through their eyes – see yourself as they see you.'

We messed around a bit; there was a lot of noise. The man was moving round the room offering advice and watching what each group had done. When he reached our corner we were talking.

'Ok: what scene are you rehearsing?'

We looked at each other; then we laughed.

'I'm my mum,' I said. 'And Debbie's me.'

'Ok – what's happening?' he asked.

'Nothing,' we both mumbled.

'Never mind. I'll help you. What I want is this,' he said. 'You – Sophie – be your mum, and...'

'Debbie,' I reminded him

'Ok then – Debbie,' and he turned towards her, 'you be Sophie. Go on.'

'What?' asked Debbie.

There was a pause.

'Act it out...' he said.

'Act what out?'

'Act out the situation that you've thought of... what was it that you said? You've been allowed home for the weekend...'

I thought I'd better help him out.

'Yes. Two weeks ago. I went home and my mum found out what I'd been writing.'

'Great... ok then... off you go.'

She sat down smiling, imagining herself pleased to be back home after months in hospital, even for the weekend. I closed my eyes and thought about the Saturday afternoon mum had read what I had written about her. As I walked home from the library I could see her waiting in the street, unable to contain her anger for a moment longer.

I marched over to where Debbie stood, and grabbed her roughly by the arm. She winced and screwed her eyes up as she pulled away.

'What,' I hissed at her 'is *this*?' jabbing my finger at the imaginary book. She knew, of course, exactly what it was. But I was not expecting her to answer and she didn't; couldn't; wouldn't; didn't want to, I don't know. She knew exactly what was happening. Something in her expression seemed to be asking me a question. Do you want to do this, she was saying? Do you really want to do this? Is this really what you want? Do you want them all to know?

'Why not?' I thought, and I looked into her eyes. What is there to lose? Let's just get on with it.

So Debbie froze, in character again. I knew what she was thinking: how the fucking hell has mum found that? It was so well hidden. She must have ransacked half my bedroom looking for it. But how did she know that there was anything to look for? Why look in the first place? And why there? I'd hidden them so carefully behind the photo of my father on the bedside table.

'You're sixteen!' I said as mum, as if that made a difference. Then I repeated it more quietly, just like she had done – '*Sixteen*, my girl. Right – inside: NOW!'

At this point Debbie's mind was racing. She said nothing. There was nothing that she could say. She couldn't tell the truth. She couldn't tell her mum that she was wrong, because her mother – me - was never ever wrong about anything. What could she say? *You see, it's like this mum – you know that there's this student nurse called Will who's helping me get better? Well, he's helped me with a bit more than my therapy. He's getting me to write a book. A work of literature. I'm going to be an author once I'm better!'*

'YOU – AN AUTHOR? YOU? Don't make me laugh.'

'But I am, mum. I am already writing.'

'Oh I see – so everyone can read about us, can they? Everyone can find out all our business - know that you're mad, for example.'

'I'm not mad!' I said. 'Dr Grimshaw told me that there's no such thing as madness.'

'Dr Grimshaw....DR GRIMSHAW. He's responsible for all this, he is. It's his fault. I should never have let him take you there. That's where all this... all this... WRITING nonsense comes from.'

Writing. The way she said it sounded so sarcastic, like it wasn't, which is what she wanted. It was all part of the show: the act, the pantomime. But I could never act my part. I never told her she was wrong. I never had the courage to stand up to her. No. And she was close enough to me now, close enough to slap her face? Why not? I wanted to; I mean I wanted her to: Debbie to as me, as I had never been. I wanted her to scream and shout and let it all out but she wouldn't, couldn't, didn't, all because I hadn't.

'This is disgusting,' she went on. 'You know what you are – you're a pervert! That's what you are.'

'But it's only something from a story,' she was telling me.

'A STORY? Don't you story me, my girl. I've had about enough of all your stories.'

'But it's fiction,' she was saying. 'It's just a piece of fiction.'

'FICTION? FICTION?'

'Yes,' she said. 'I made it up; it's for the book I'm writing.'

And then I started reading...

...shouldn't that be with him? Shouldn't that be 'make love with him'? Or even 'Did he make love to you'? And why is it called 'make love' anyway? What's that supposed to mean? Why do people say that? Why didn't he just ask me if we'd had sex; fucked, shagged, screwed, right there in the kitchen, on the kitchen floor with all my schoolbooks open?

'Here's a good bit!' and she pointed at it with her finger.

Why didn't he ask me how we made love, or how we came to make love? How I'd got closer and got closer, inch by inch, shuffling my chair across the carpet until our bodies almost came so near they touched; how I'd slowly felt his warm breath brush against my cheek; or how his arm had rested loosely on the chair back and then curled around my back so that suddenly, but naturally, his arm was round me, resting on my shoulders. He was holding me now; his face was close so that I could feel his breathing start to quicken.

'Mum!' I said, or rather Debbie did, as me.

...I'd like to fix your lips on mine and stroke your skin...

'Mum!'

...I'd like to taste your body with my tongue...

'I could go on,' I said as mum. 'I SAID I COULD GO ON!'

And I was yelling at her now; screaming in my own face, firing question after question, not waiting for an answer, never listening to her, never pausing, never stopping for a moment, filling all the gaps so that she couldn't get a word in because if Debbie started speaking she might say something I couldn't bear to hear. So she just stood there, saying nothing, just like I had done, just like I always did. I listened as she bawled obscenities at me, and never said a word. I never did with mum. It did no good.

'I suppose you think that sex is grown up, do you?'

With a grown up – yes, I do.

'Who is he, anyway?'

She didn't really want to know.

'He must be desperate. Who'd look at you unless they were, eh? Look at you.'

I looked, by way of answer.

'Dirty little whore. That's what you are.'

'If your father ever got to hear of this he'd...'

What, exactly? What would daddy do?

'It's a good job he's not here, that's all – a bloody good job for you.'

I know. That's true. And now I'm here as you, you're telling this to me and all the time you knew – you really knew, you knew what was happening. You know all about it, didn't you?

'Of course I knew,' I said.

'Then why, mummy? Why didn't you say something to me – or to him?'

'How do you know that I didn't?' she said. 'Why do you think he left, eh?'

End of show.

***

'That was fascinating,' somebody was saying. 'You're very angry, Sophie' someone added. And I was surprised to find the others had all finished. Everyone was watching our play. We were back now in the day-room where we had started. Debbie – look at her – she looks a little startled.

'You were really getting into that,' he told me.

That was true.

'Ok, then everyone. Sophie's shown us what to do. I want some passion, now – some real emotion. Most of you are just play acting – feel it this time. Go on. Have another go,' he said to all the others.

'You two can take five,' he said to us. 'Sit down for a moment. Get your breath back.'

We did as we were told.

'What happened next?' she asked as we sat quietly in the corner. All around us there was shouting – anger. Everyone was making loads of noise.

'Nothing much,' I said. 'She took away what I had written.'

'And did you ever... you know?'

'No!'

'Why not?'

'He wasn't interested in me, that's why not. He wanted me to be a different girl. But it doesn't matter anymore.'

'It doesn't?'

'No, because I've got a plan.'

'A plan?'

'A plan for him. I'm going to get him, just you wait and see. He'll be back one day, and he'll be back for me.'

'But how, Soph?' I could tell that Debbie was concerned. She didn't want to see me hurt a second time.

'Don't worry,' I said. 'I've got everything worked out this time. Just read on…'

CHAPTER SIXTEEN

I'm being interviewed about it all today. I've written down so much now that they want some answers – they want explanations and elucidations; they demand conclusions. That's something that you have to be prepared for when you're a writer. People always want to ask you things, like where you get all your ideas from. Even if it's fiction that you're writing; even if it's feigning, even if it's only fingering, *fingere*; even if you've made it up like I did, people always want to ask you questions. People want to know what real events the story might be based on. What they really want to know, of course, is how much of it might be true. People always want to know: they're know-sy. They were nosy about me and Debbie: wondering where we went together, and what we both got up to. There had been gossip in the unit; then one day we had been followed. Finally, someone had found out our secret; somebody who must have then told all the others. Who? Not Debbie, surely. She would not betray me, would she? Then who? Patrick Randle, maybe? If so, how? And who could possibly believe him after what had happened at the painting exhibition? We knew he knew but we made sure he couldn't tell – we wrote it differently. Didn't we?

    'I think you've both let yourself become...well - too close,' Ted began. 'Don't you?'

I didn't want to talk about it – not to him at any rate. The spoken word would spoil it. It was better in my head or on the paper. Then it didn't matter. Saying it, and seeing words go into his ears and then imagining the pictures that they were creating in his head was wrong. He couldn't understand.

'How did you...?'

'Let's just say that someone saw you.'

What did they expect? You're not allowed to go out on your own; you're not allowed to use the bathroom on your own; you're not allowed to sleep alone.

'Who?' I asked.

'It doesn't matter: let's just say he...'

PATRICK RANDLE! Fucking Patrick Randle, that was who! Sometimes ideas do actually light up inside your head, and this one burned. This was burning brightly. Fucking Patrick Randle on another perverted power trip. I hated him. I hated him. What he had done was getting in the way of everything. And now I hated him more than I ever thought it possible to hate anyone.

'So it was a "he",' I said.

'Maybe,' Ted replied, but it was too late for that now. I knew; I knew everything. We'd been betrayed. I had to act, and act fast.

***

'You ought to let the readers in on it you know,' Will told me, later.

'Why should I?' I was more angry than upset. 'What's it got to do with them?'

'Well, nothing I suppose. But they're going to find out anyway. You might as well tell them yourself, the way you want to.'

'But I don't want that in the narrative. I only wrote it to get rid of him. He wouldn't go away.'

'I know. Sometimes that happens, though. The story takes you in a new direction: one you hadn't really wanted.'

142

'But this was supposed to be our secret. I was never going to use it. He promised me. He said provided that I wrote it for him he would keep it secret. He said he wouldn't let anybody read it.'

'But it hasn't worked,' Will said. 'It's all out in the open now. We need to hear what happened from your point of view. We need to hear your version of the story. When did it take place?' he asked.

'Oh, ages ago.' I told him. That was true. Back when we had still been allowed to go out for a walk – that long, just after I had started writing.

'But before you found the knife?'

'Before I found the knife, yes. Otherwise I might have used it on him there and then.'

He'd followed us, you see. He'd gone out for a walk with Jason just as normal, but then as soon as they were out of sight of Monica he ran off, leaving Jason crying on his own. We weren't too far ahead of him. He followed us without us knowing. Had he planned what he was doing? Had he fantasized about it? Drawn it, even?

It was a sunny afternoon in early spring, the kind of day when you first begin to notice that the sun is warm again. Then you see the earth is drying, and green shoots are growing. Then you notice that the leaves are budding on the hedges, that the trees are covered in a light green haze.

'Isn't it beautiful?' said Debbie. She was happy. I was happy too. I mean, we weren't. We were depressed. I had my ache; Debbie cut her inner thighs. But we were feeling something else as well. Perhaps it was the drugs that we were taking? Or the weather? Whatever, things were starting to get better.

Then we noticed him. As he drew nearer to us we both ran. We didn't think about it. We just ran and ran and ran as far as we could. We ran into a dense clump of trees in the far corner of the grounds, behind the nurses' residence, behind the big elms near the wall. And there, in the corner, almost hidden by the trees we reached the summer house.

143

'God – do you think he saw us?' Debbie panted as she shut the door.

'I don't think so,' I replied, and looked out through the window. There was no sign of anyone. We were alone again. I sat down in the chair and she sat on my knee. The warmth of her body next to mine was everything I wanted it to be. Her freckled face so close that I could feel her warm, sweet breath. Her button nose so small, just like a child's nose – not yet hardened into bone. Her cheeks were soft and flushed from running.

'You're so beautiful,' I said to her, and swept the hair back from her face.

'I know,' she said, and laughed. 'It'll work so well, Soph, won't it?'

Soon there was no-one else at all, not in the whole wide world. We were there together and our bodies gradually grew closer. Then our lips were touching softly and her voice was like a feather in my ear. Our hands explored each other's bodies, first on clothes and then on skin. Then we were lying on the rough floor without knowing how we got there. And when I looked up he was standing at the window, watching.

'Oh GOD!'

'What is it?' Debbie jumped up quickly. And then suddenly there he was, inside.

'I know what you're up to,' Patrick smirked.

We could see what he was up to, too.

'I'll tell,' he said; he would have done, as well. 'I will. I'll tell. I'm telling Ted. I'm going to tell them all tomorrow.'

I looked at Debbie. I didn't know what to do or say. There was a chance that she would. She seemed to know much better than me what to say and do. She always knew exactly what to do with me.

'Sophie needs me, Murphy... It's difficult to explain. It's all part of a plan.'

I did. It was. But didn't she? Didn't she need me, as well? I thought we both needed each other. I thought that we were both in this together. Didn't she enjoy what we were doing here? Was she doing it for me? Was it just a duty? Was it something she was doing just because I'd asked her? Had it grown out of that evening weeks ago when we'd talked for so long that we'd almost been locked out of the adolescent unit and they'd almost sent the nurses from the men's ward out to look for us?

She seemed suddenly exhausted. Just saying what she'd uttered seemed somehow to have tired her, and she sank slowly into the wicker chair as if part of her was melting. This was Debbie he was speaking to. Debbie who could think of an answer for almost everything; the one I talked to about things I couldn't talk about to anyone. And she didn't know what else to say.

She looked at me. I didn't know what to say. I didn't say anything. I just sat there opposite her, looking at her, waiting for her. I wanted to say something that would make her feel all right. I wanted to say something that would make her stay there with me, something that would make him go away. Then I remembered one of Patrick's paintings. The one he'd done of her.

'I'm sorry Murphy,' I said at last. I knew it wasn't good enough even as I said it. I knew I'd ruined everything. He looked at me. His glasses were too large for his face. He was young. But in his eyes there was an odd, old look.

Words were slowly coming back inside my head. He moved over to the door. He didn't say a thing but as he reached out for the handle, he looked back. He was tall and thin. His face was bony. He had grown up, quickly. Too quickly almost for his body to catch up with him and fill out. I hadn't noticed. And his head hadn't grown up at the same rate as his body.

All I could see was the back of his head. The short hair. And the stubble on his neck. The back of his big ears. I'd never really seen him from the back before. He was about to push the handle of he door. He was about to leave. He was about to go back to the unit and to tell them everything and...

'STOP!' I shouted. It was my voice that said it. But I didn't mean to say it. It just spilled out of my mouth.

'Wait...' I said to him. Come on, I thought. Come on, come on. Think of something. Come oooonnnnn. And then I thought of something. Wait. That's what I thought: just wait. Not much, but at least I thought of something. Now I had to think of what to say to stop him going. He would have gone, just then. The door would close behind him and then next morning he would bring it up in front of everyone: in the Community Meeting. Everyone would know what we were doing.

What were we up to? Now my mind was racing. What should I say? What should I do? How could I stop him? As I thought, the ache returned. The glow inside that Debbie had provided disappeared. It all turned cold again. A big cloud covered up the sun.

'I'll write you something. Yes – I'll write you something - anything you want!' I volunteered. 'Tell me what you'd like to happen, and I guarantee I'll put it in the story.'

What could he want? What could I write? I thought about the cave, his drawings. Was there anything that I could do to stop him telling? Patrick Randle. Fucking Patrick Randle. Damn him.

'Well I can't do it,' Debbie whispered.

'Why not?' I asked.

She looked at me. 'You know why. I'm still...' and then she mouthed the word so Patrick couldn't hear.

'Well at least I'm not a lesbian like you two,' he was shouting. 'So what if I am? Ain't going to be for too much longer, am I?'

'Aren't you?'

'No I'm not. And you're gonna write about it for me.'

146

'Write about it?'

'Yeah, or else I'll tell.'

'You've got to do it Sophie,' Debbie was telling me. 'You've got to.'

'But I don't want to, Debbie; I don't want him in the story.'

'I don't think you've got much choice.'

I looked at him. He was standing there, looking back at me.

'Patrick?'

'What, exactly, Sophie?' He was cocky, now. He knew that we were trapped. He knew he had us, both exactly as he wanted. But he was unsure how to press home his advantage. And it might be what we wanted too.

'Patrick,' Debbie started. 'Soph and I...you know. We just need to sort a few things out. Will you let us have a minute to ourselves, please?'

She didn't wait for him to answer. At the same time as she finished, she was opening the wooden door for him. He stepped outside.

'Just for a minute mind,' he said, as Debbie closed the door behind him.

'What the hell do you think you're doing Sophie?'

'Me?'

'Yes. Telling him you'll write him into the story – our story. Telling him you'll put down what he wants.'

'I don't know.'

'And then telling him you can't write down what he's suggested.'

'But I can't! I can't write that down. It'll ruin it!'

'You managed well enough in Chapter Fourteen.'

'That was different!'

'How was it different?'

'You *know*...'

'No, I don't know Soph – explain it to me.'

'Debbs,' I said, 'you know...you do. Don't do this to me. You heard what he said. It's you he wants, not me.'

147

'He wants us both; he wants us both to do it.'

'Well I don't want people reading that.'

'But...'

'What?'

'What option have we got?'

'I don't know Debbie. But it's horrible...'

'It's not,' she said. 'It's just like snogging someone you don't fancy, really – a bit of heavy petting.'

'But...'

'There's nothing to it!'

'Have you ever done it?' Have you?'

And she smiled a little smile of satisfaction.

'Have you done it with him?'

'Might have done...'

'How could you Debbie?' God, I don't believe it... I thought...'

'Look, Soph. It doesn't matter; doesn't count.'

'You what?'

'It's nothing. What harm can it do?'

She just looked at me. She knew I had to carry on. I closed my eyes, imagining the scene. And when I opened them again I started writing...

CHAPTER SEVENTEEN

'It's hard for you to talk about it Sophie, isn't it?'

'Yes it is. But I can write about it.'

'Good. Because we need to know what you are thinking...'

'What?'

'We need to know what's going on inside your head.'

'Oh I see, *you* think that really happened.'

'It's ok,' Will said. 'It doesn't matter.'

'But it does. It bloody does. It matters quite a lot.'

'Why?'

'You might get the wrong impression.'

'Wrong impression?'

'You might confuse what's fact and fiction.'

'Fact and fiction?'

'No-one knows for sure what's going on when I am writing. Nobody can tell what's really happening.'

'Yes we can – your reader can.'

'Not necessarily.'

'What do you mean?'

'I mean that no-one knows what's really real now, do they? No-one knows which bits are fact and which are fiction any more. No-one knows what I'm reporting or inventing.'

'No?'

'And that's the way I want it. Secret. Nobody can see inside my head and find out what I'm *really* thinking. Nobody can do that. No one can ever know what's going on in someone else's head. Do they know about the plot? Do they know about the twists? Do they know about the inspiration? No, they don't. And no-one does - sometimes not even me. No-one knows what I am thinking. Nobody can see inside my head. No-one's listening in to my thoughts. My thoughts are mine. I can think anything I want and nobody can stop me. Nobody can tell. I could be thinking anything right now: anything at all. You'd never know, unless I told you. Unless I chose to tell you what was going on, you would have no idea of it at all. You would never know; could never know. And even if I told you, you would never know if I was telling you the truth. So you'd still not know what I was thinking: *really* thinking, in my head, on my own; my own ideas; the things that only I was thinking. No. Because they're mine - my thoughts. And they belong to me. I make them. I think them. I'm the one that has them. They are mine. Only I can make them happen. Most of the time. Sometimes they come from somewhere else. Sometimes thoughts come into my head from nowhere. Well, from somewhere, but I don't know where. They just appear. And they're the ones to fear. They're the ones that worry me. They're the ones that might either be the most exciting and original ideas I've ever had or else the most frightening, destructive and derivative. Does anyone know where these thoughts come from? The thoughts I'm having right now, for example. What's causing them? What's putting them inside my head? Is it me? Am I doing it? I'm not aware I'm doing it. But I must be doing it. I might be doing it a split second, fraction of a second before they come to me. But am I? How would I know if I was? Where could they come from, what could they be if I wasn't? How can he know what I am thinking? How can he possibly know anything unless I tell him? He doesn't know; he's lying. I'm the only one that knows what happening in here, I tell him.

'You might be,' Will says softly, 'but I know you're hiding something.'

'Do you?' I say. Then we sit in silence for a bit. Outside the window, trees begin to sway. The wind is gathering strength now. Rain has just begun to fall. That night I would be writing up a storm. The wind would soon be roaring in the tree-tops like the sea. On wild nights like this the hospital was a huge ship and the trees were crashing waves. We were miles from the safety of the shore and we were sinking. Who would send the lifeboat? We looked from our bedroom window for the flare, as lights flashed on and off and rain sprayed noisily against the dark wet glass. We fell asleep to the sound of wind whipping branches of the trees against each other; water thrown against the windows like angry fists of gravel, setting up a soundtrack for a nightmare night of strange dreams. I remember everything about those nights in the hospital. Wet leaves slapping on the wet glass like a hand across the face. Us sitting up in bed and listening, frightened but excited too. The things we said; the tone of voice and every word that passed between us in the darkness. I remember everything so clearly – well, almost everything. There are other things I can't remember quite as well. Other senses are more difficult to recall. I can't remember textures, for example, and I can't remember smell or...

'Taste?'

'Oh God!'

'What?'

'That's it!'

'What?'

'That. What I just said. What I just typed. That there.'

'What?'

'That – the taste. That stuff. It happened. I was terrified.'

'Terrified of what?' he asked.

151

'Terrified of what was going to happen; terrified of the effects, of what would happen if I didn't, what would happen if I did. I thought he loved me; thought he cared. But he didn't tell me what it tasted like, or what I had to do with it.'

'What did you do?'

'I swallowed it,' I said. 'Every bloody word of it. I swallowed the whole damn thing - hook, line and sinker.'

'You really had it bad for him,' he said.

'I did. I had it bad.'

'And now?' he asked. 'Now what do you feel for him?'

'I want to kill him. Yes, that's what I want to do – I want to introduce a murder, add another chapter to the mystery,' I told him.

'That's a bit extreme,' he muttered.

'Yes I know,' I said. 'Although it's just a character; authors are allowed to kill their own creations, I believe.'

'Maybe,' he said. 'But there are consequences that you must consider.'

'Like?'

'Like the police; the courts; a trial.'

'I know,' I said. 'I've got that drafted.'

'Have you? Show me.'

So I did. I sat and watched him as he read...

'Mi lud, the defendant was provoked by an outrageous offence against her committed by the deceased whilst she was only seventeen years of age.'

'And how old was the deceased?'

'Er... twenty-six, I believe mi lud.'

'Twenty-six when the alleged offence that you refer to was committed, or was that his age when the crime your client is now standing trial for was perpetrated?'

'He was.... I think; it happened quite some time ago, mi lud'

'And yet you tell me it was because of this outrageous offence committed all that time ago that the accused reacted in the way it is alleged?'

'Mi lud?'

'Tell me, Mr Parkville - what exactly was the nature of this so-called offence?'

'Mi lud - the deceased had said to the accused he loved her.'

'Loved her.'

'Yes.'

'He told her that he loved her, did he?'

'Er, I believe so, yes mi lud.'

'He used the words – I love you – spoke them to the accused, so that she could be in no doubt of his feelings?'

'I believe so, yes mi lud.'

'And then?'

And Mr Parkville looked down at his notes.

'And then, mi lud, the deceased performed a 'sex act' with my client.'

'With her?'

'With her, yes mi lud. But without her consent.'

'I see. What sort of sex-act Mr Parkville?'

'Er... she.... the deceased placed his penis in my client's mouth, mi lud.'

'He placed his penis in your client's mouth?'

'He did, mi lud.'

'What for?'

'For... I... I venture to suggest it was solely for his own sexual gratification, mi lud.'

'Mr Parkville, you will have to help me here.'

'Mi lud?'

'If you say your client took the deceased's penis in her mouth, how could she not have done so without giving her consent?'

'Mi lud?'

'Surely she could simply keep her mouth shut?' said the Judge.

***

'I'm not sure that this works you know,' he told me, and he put the book down on the bedside table.

'No?'

'I'm not sure that it's plausible. It doesn't strike me as a very satisfactory explanation.'

'Why?'

'Well, you're suggesting that she murders him because of something that he's done.'

'I am.'

'And then it goes to trial...'

'Yes.'

'And then what?'

'She gets off, of course... and everyone lives happily ever after.'

'But you can't do that' he said.

'Why not? I have to have a happy ending.'

'And you can. But write a truthful one as well.'

'But how?' I said. 'It's fiction.'

'Yes I know. But even so it still needs to be true - true to the characters and plot; true to the circumstances and the personalities involved. True to yourself, as well.'

'I'm not sure that I follow.'

And he took a deep breath. I could tell there was a lesson coming.

'Just think about it for a moment. Think about this thing called "truth". What makes something true?' he asked.

I thought about it for a moment.

'Well a thing's true if it can be proved, for one thing. Like in a court of law when they decide if something really happened.'

'Ok. So can you prove what you are feeling?'

'Well... no.'

'And does that mean that what you're feeling isn't true?'

'No.'

'No. And is the Bible true?'

'How should I know?'

'Do you believe there really was an Adam and an Eve?'

'No.'

'So it's not true?'

'Well, not exactly.'

'But it *is* true, Sophie. Even if it didn't happen, it's still true; it still describes the loss of innocence, the fall from grace, the pain of self-awareness perfectly.'

'You make it sound like adolescence,' I replied. He smiled.

'There's something else,' he told me.

'What?'

'There's something else about the story.'

'Well?'

'It's Debbie,' he went on. 'I'm not convinced about her motivation.'

'What?'

'Why does she want to help you in this way?'

'To keep him quiet, of course. To shut him up forever. And, of course, to keep what happened to her – what I wrote - a secret.'

'But we know about that *now*,' he told me.

'Yes, I know' I said. 'And?'

'Well, things have moved on haven't they?'

'What do you mean?'

'Well, Debbie doesn't hate him any more,' he said to me.

'She doesn't?'

'Hasn't she told you?'

'Told me what?' I suddenly felt sick. I hadn't thought of that. I'd not planned that new twist. After all that we had done together, all that we had shared; after all that we'd agreed.

'She's... they're – well, an item now,' he said.

I felt the room go cold and start to spin.

'I can't go on with this,' I told him, and I stood up. 'It's all too personal; I'm getting too emotional.'

'But you've got to go on, Sophie.'

'No I haven't. I don't like what's happening.'

'Ok so change it then,' he told me calmly. 'All you've got to do from now on is to write it differently. If you don't like what's been written so far, make a change. Write yourself a different plot. It's easy. Adjust the style; try a new perspective; change the narrative. That's what happens when you're the author of a story – anything, in other words. You're in control. It's up to you.'

'But things are happening; things I don't like; things that I'm not planning.'

'And...?'

'And I'm supposed to be the author.'

'Yes, you are.'

'But I'm no longer in control.'

'You are.'

'I'm not. It doesn't feel like that. This feels like someone else's book. It's just like all the others that I've read. And I wanted to write something different.'

'So change it then,' he said again.

'I can't. The book I want to write just isn't happening. There's no point going on.'

'Look, Sophie - when a book gets written there's a reason: something missing in the other books, perhaps – I don't know - something new, some new discovery or a new idea or just a different way of saying something that's been said before. And because it's new it breaks the rules. New things can happen. Anything can happen. Things that haven't happened, things you didn't want to happen, things no-one would think were going to happen, happen. And they happen just because you've written them. And once you've written them they have to happen, they were always going to happen. Things have to happen because you've made them happen. Make them happen, Sophie. Do it. Write it. I'll be here to help you. Now – get on with it.'

'I'll try,' I said. 'I'll think about it....'

'No, don't think about it – do it: write it. Go on - now. Get on with it' he ordered.

'What, right now?' I pleaded.

'Why not?' he responded. 'What's wrong with right now? Do it now. Get on with it.'

'I will... I promise, but...'

'Then do it. Do it. Do it now, this minute. Write down what we're saying.' But she wasn't listening. She was smiling now; not looking at me: looking instead at some distant image, some idea – the whole idea of writing something not because it happened, but because she wanted it to happen. She wanted that to be the reason. And I wanted her to think that was the reason. What other reason was there? She wanted me to read the words. She wanted what she wrote to be a possibility. But there was another motivation. She wanted to discover my reaction. She needed me to stay calm, for my face to stay calm; what she needed was a non-reaction. What she needed was for me to act as if the whole thing had been a perfectly normal arrangement, something all girls did, a common day-by-day transaction. But she'd gone silent now. She was embarrassed by the things she'd written.

'It doesn't matter, Sophie. You can say all sorts of things in books and no-one minds. You can say all sorts of things you don't believe, and you can say things that you do believe but don't want anyone to know; things you wouldn't really want to own up to – nobody will ever find out. Nobody can tell the difference. It's just your characters speaking – not you. No-one knows what you think. So you can say anything. Make them say it, that's all. Make them be your mouthpiece. You can even pre-empt the reaction that you think it might provoke in other people. You can have fun with this. It's wonderful.'

'It's not,' she said. 'It's horrible. I hate it, and I've lost the plot. You carry on with it if you think that it's worth doing. I'm fed up of it.'

'I can't do that,' I said.

'Why not?'

'It's not my book,' I told her 'or my story. This is all about you.'

'Yes, I know.'

'And you have to be the one that writes it.'

'But it's about you too,' she said to me. 'You started it. I wouldn't have done anything without you.'

'Maybe, Sophie.'

'No – it's true. You're more than just a character – you're my editor, my tutor; you're my facilitator.'

'Ok, then. If I am, I'm telling you you have to carry on,' I said. 'You have to keep it going.'

So I gave in, she wrote, *and started writing. I didn't bother replying. I just did as I was told, which was vanilla - boring. Instead, for the story, for my character maybe, I should have made a stand and argued with him: perhaps provoked a violent reaction - throw things at him, maybe rip the pages I had written into little shreds and stuffed them down his shirt. And maybe he would grab my wrists and hold my arms to stop me causing further damage. It was something he'd been taught in training: physical intervention can sometimes be necessary. Then, when he released me I would slap him hard across the face, as he deserved. I'd watch him as his hand went up to rub his cheek, and tell him I had gone too far. We were alone in the room, after all. And I would have him where I wanted him. And as I stalked out of the room he would be wondering – where's she going? Who's she telling? If I didn't tell, of course, he'd still be wondering if and when I would. He would be waiting. All the time he would be thinking, is she going to do it? Is she? When? What is she going to say it? And to whom? Well, I suppose he wouldn't think 'to whom': too posh. He wasn't posh. He used big words, but only used the words in simple sentences. He didn't make a bed for them to lie on, or arrange them on the sheets seductively.*

No. He just threw them down like dirty linen, left them lying in a heap upon the floor.

And where did all that come from? Nowhere. No idea. It just happened as I sat here, looking at the trees. It just appeared.

Inspired?

No. Not inspired. It's not inspired. It just appeared, that's all. Appeared. Six-hundred words, or thereabouts. Six-hundred bits of language put together. Ideas put down on paper. Your ideas. Or my ideas? Somebody's ideas. From somewhere. Now they're here. Mine. Finished. Job done. End. Or the beginning? Wax or wane, or ebb or flow? Up or down? Half empty? Or half full? Who cares? It's here. It's down. It's happened. It has happened. Here. This afternoon. Right now.

'That's good,' I said to her. But she was having none of it.

'You think so?' she responded flatly. 'Is it really? I'm not sure. It doesn't work for me. I'll never be an author. I'm a failure.'

CHAPTER EIGHTEEN
(Will)

Within days of the beginning of my placement I had gained a useful first impression of each of the adolescent unit patients. Debbie, for example, showed all the classic symptoms of a long-term anorexic. Her refusal to maintain a normal body weight had weakened her to the point where she was dangerously thin and bony. She'd stopped menstruating, and her breasts had shrunk to nothing as if denying the inevitability of growing up. Lizzie, though, was one of the more obvious successes of the regime. She was close to being discharged when I arrived, having finally attained a healthy body weight and established normal patterns of eating. She had clearly regained a healthy attitude to food after suffering from bulimia. When I first saw her there were few external signs remaining, apart from a continued need for eating greedily and hurriedly.

Patrick Randle – 'Murphy' as they called him, rather unimaginatively – was more worrying. He was the only patient with what I'd been informed was a potentially 'criminal' history. I never quite found out all the details, but I suspected it involved some form of sexual encounter, underage; he had been charged – but not convicted – (like his namesake, maybe?) but the case had not proceeded to a trial. There were other similarities between him and his

160

fictional alter ego, like a resistance to authority. But in other ways he couldn't have been more different. He was not a leader, certainly. He was led – dick led. He found it impossible to control his basic instincts; he drew pictures of the girls, when he wasn't drawing pictures of himself. Even his routine behaviour violated almost every social right and norm. Ironically, the one thing that he probably needed most was beyond us to prescribe: a normal sexual relationship with somebody his own age, someone with their own agenda – a feisty, Becky Sharpe-type character: somebody like Debbie, maybe. But she had problems of her own, not least chronic self-harm. That was rather common in the adolescent unit. As a result all knives and scissors, razor-blades and even mirrors were routinely confiscated on admission. Cutlery was counted back into the padlocked kitchen drawers after every meal.

And what of Sophie? She was quiet, but not withdrawn. At least, I didn't think so. Nevertheless, she had remained a closed book for the majority of her stay here. There was a hint of mystery about her: secrets – things she kept from other people, maybe from herself. I liked her, though. And I saw her as a challenge. She became my student project, I suppose.

In the arrogance or confidence of youth I concluded that there was a chronic over-reliance on psychopharmacological interventions at the unit. Mind you, that was the classic psychiatric orthodoxy in the nineteen seventies. Drugs, the medical establishment seemed to be suggesting, would be the solution to every possible mental problem. But hypnotics also dampen down the flames of adolescent sexual adventuring. And my initial training had confirmed the contradiction that libido could present a useful indication of recovery. That is why - although what had happened recently wasn't something anyone could condone, still less encourage – knowing it had happened had revealed some interesting information. Things were improving, both for Debbie and for Sophie. Maybe writing therapy was working. Ted, for one, would find that difficult to swallow.

'Why don't we simply let it run its course?' I suggested in a staff meeting one morning, while the patients were in lessons. They were pretty much the first words that I'd spoken in that meeting since arriving.

'We can't,' said Ted. 'That's irresponsible,' he added. 'What if something happens?'

'Like what?' asked Jane.

Ted looked somewhat embarrassed and he tried to laugh. But frankly he looked better with a frown.

'I know, but Jane...'

'What are you saying, Ted?'

'They're kids – well, she is anyway. Debbie. It could lead to problems.'

He was right, of course. It could. But it was fascinating, too – like watching flowers grow, not knowing quite what might be growing.

'We'll have to bring it up at tomorrow morning's meeting,' he continued. 'And let's be clear about this, everyone – we've got to be united. We've got to make it clear there'll have to be an end to such relationships.'

He stared across at me menacingly.

'Remember, Will – you're only here as an observer.'

'That's unfair!' said Jane, suddenly. 'He's a member of our community. He should be able to express his views just like the rest of us.'

The effect her interruption had on Ted was interesting. Anyone else would have been instantly shot down. His head turned sharply, and he couldn't quite disguise the glare which flashed across his face like lightening. But then he smiled. At least, his mouth did.

'Perhaps you're right Jane,' he began. I didn't know him very well by then, but his reaction was surprising.

'All right, Will – you can say something if you want to.'

'It's fine Ted,' I said. 'I'm happy listening.'

162

The Adolescent Unit was what's known in psychiatric circles as a therapeutic community. The day was highly structured, and that was all part of the treatment – establishing normal patterns of behaviour in sometimes woefully chaotic teenage lives. Wake-up was at seven-thirty, breakfast was at eight o'clock and then the community meeting was at nine. As most of the patients were of school age, lessons (until one p.m.) took up the remainder of the morning. Lunch came over from the hospital canteen in three enormous heated metal trolleys. The idea was that everyone helped to serve it out and then to clear away, although I noticed Ted seemed not to want to soil his hands with such a menial task. Afternoons were usually more flexible. There was individual therapy with Dr Grimshaw, the psychiatrist. I liked him. He was young. This was his first real post since qualifying. He had some good ideas. But what he lacked compared to Ted was practical experience. He hadn't yet attained the magic title of consultant. Ted could always gainsay his suggestions by referring back to thirty years experience of adolescent psychiatric medicine. That was what he did to me when I suggested things like painting therapy, or the drama idea.

'There's no point. We know what we're doing. Leave it be.' he'd say.

But there was also Jane to consider. She was young – not beautiful, but pretty in a 'Head Girl' sort of way. And there was clearly something going on between the two of them. I'd seen the way he looked at her. And she played up to him, no doubt about it. I felt a little guilty trying to exploit it but how else was anything new going to get done here? Before I dared say anything about the painting, for example, I had talked to Jane and made sure of her support. She was keen. I knew she would speak up for the idea.

That way I had been indulged with a couple of experiments. They were easier to agree with, anyway. They had been one-offs. But writing is a more sustained therapeutic intervention. Ted wasn't going to let a student undertake such a radical innovation without discussion.

Writing it down like that makes me sound so *arrogant*. It makes it seem as if I – a mere student nurse - knew best. But it wasn't like that in reality. In fact, the opposite was true. My training cohort had been told of plans to close the old asylums. I never really thought that it would happen. No-one did, back then. But I was keen to try out new ideas; to put into practice some alternative therapies. Who wouldn't? I was enthusiastic, and I was emotionally involved (as you are before you learn professional indifference). But it's strange how sometimes, one completely unrelated incident takes on such huge importance. You could argue that the whole plot hinged on it. What was it? A game of Rounders, that's what. It's ironic, isn't it? If it hadn't been for a silly game this book might never have been written. That's what finally persuaded Ted to let it happen (or at least ensured that he was too ashamed to hold out against it any longer). Now it's up to me to tell a story...

'Final item,' Ted said at the morning nurses meeting. It was approaching half-past twelve. The trolleys full of food would already have arrived. There was no time left for a discussion. 'We've been asked to play a Rounders match against the Rehab patients'.

'That's interesting,' said Jane.

'Yes,' said Ted, changing his expression. 'That's just what I was thinking. Why are you smiling, Will?'

'Oh... I agree with Jane – sounds interesting,' I said.

'Ok, then – if the kids agree at tomorrow's meeting, then it's scheduled for Thursday afternoon, weather permitting'.

The 'kids' of course, were always likely to agree.

'I declare this meeting open,' Randle lisped next morning.

The day room was a big space on the ground-floor of the house with comfy chairs around the edge. The nearest thing that it resembled was a school common room, complete with moody dark paint on the walls and posters covering the cracks. The carpet was so badly stained it was impossible to tell what colour it might once have been. The air smelt permanently of stale cigarette smoke. Patients sat all over: on the floor, on chair-arms, on each others' knees. Staff, too, seemed unconcerned about the seating plan, and crouched or sat wherever there was space. Except for Ted, that is. He always had the same, big chair. Sophie sat in one of the big soft armchairs; her long legs at full stretch to the floor. Debbie lay beside her, with one leg bent at the knee and folded underneath her body. As I looked at them, I felt a twinge of sympathy. I knew what was about to happen.

'Next item,' Ted announced, and looked down at his notes.

'There have been some... what shall I call them – secret conversations here in recent weeks. We've been told that two of the people in this room have been taking too much interest in other, to the exclusion of the rest of us.'

I looked at Jane. She caught my eye and looked down at the floor. Ted carried on.

'Sophie? Debbie? Is there anything you want to tell us?' he said, smiling.

They looked at on another. Debbie looked bewildered. Sophie blushed.

There was a long pause. Then gentle sobs began to well up through Sophie's body.

'We're listening,' Ted continued. 'Aren't we, everyone?'

He glanced left and right, theatrically.

People nodded. But it didn't matter. He wasn't looking at them. Others murmured their agreement. But he wasn't listening. He was looking at Sophie as she sat there in the arm-chair, with her head down and her long hair covering her face.

Eventually she looked up.

'I...' she started.

'Do you want a tissue, dear?' asked Monica, leaning forward.

And she wiped her eyes.

'I... I'm... I think I might... I mean...'

'Go on...' Ted growled, like a big brown dog about to bark.

'I think... I might.... I might... I mean I might be...'

'What is it, dear? You can tell us, can't she everyone?'

More nods and murmurs of agreement from around the room. Everybody appeared to be supportive; interested. We were. That was how we did things here, in Ted's words.

The clock on the wall sprang forward by another minute. In a quarter of an hour, the meeting would be over. Somebody would ask if there was any other business. Nobody would speak. And so they would announce: 'then I declare this meeting closed,' and all the kids would troop off down the corridor to the classroom for the morning's lessons. Time was running out for Sophie.

Then she spoke.

'I think...' she started.

'Take your time,' said Jane.

'I can't,' she said. 'You tell them. Go on, tell them Debbie,' Sophie shouted.

We listened, shocked, to what she had to say. Patrick, as the chairman, said nothing. But as I looked at him I saw the smug expression on his face. And then...

'She were a virgin!' he was laughing.

'Order!' shouted Ted. 'This isn't what we're supposed to be discussing.'

'I thought we had it all planned?' Sophie spluttered.

Debbie bowed her head. 'I know,' she said. 'We do, but...'

'What?'

'Well - things move on, that's all. Me and Murphy, we're...'

'...at item!' Patrick shouted, grinning.

'Murphy – SHUT UP!'

Patrick pulled his head down quickly, like a tortoise. And then Ted and Monica smiled a tiny, barely-noticed little smile of satisfaction at each another.

And before I knew what was happening someone was inviting me to speak.

'Yeah let's have a new perspective,' somebody called out.

I suddenly found myself the centre of attention, struggling to know what to say. I looked around the room. Everyone was looking at me, waiting for an answer. I struggled for a moment; I mumbled something about not really seeing what was wrong provided everybody behaved and hoped that it would be enough. I didn't want to be specific. And I didn't want to tell them what I knew.

'Well,' said Ted, with a sigh. 'Let me explain. We have a rule here that was decided by this meeting; ooh... about six months ago. The rule is this – no secrets from this meeting. Everything we do is open for discussion. Everything.'

There was a pause. He looked at Sophie, then at Debbie.

'But that's unfair,' said Debbie. Her voice was different. She had a slight, west-country accent. 'We're all in here together. We're with each other every minute of the day. We know what's going on; we talk, we do. We talk when you're not listening.'

'It's not that we disapprove of secrets, Debbie.' Jane had joined in now. 'You mustn't think we disapprove. But excluding others like you do makes so many members of our community unhappy – look at Sophie.'

'...and we're all here because we want to help you,' Jane continued. 'If you only talk to one another, then we can't give you the support you both need.'

'Dr Grimshaw?' Ted said.

'Well,' he began. 'Sophie's still very reluctant to communicate; she resists all my entreaties. I'm not much nearer getting her co-operation than I was when she first came here. Besides, what you and Debbie have got up to is almost common-knowledge.'

'I see,' said Sophie. 'So it's fine as long as no-one knows about it is it?'

'No.' The doctor shook his head 'It's just that you'd invested such a lot in such a close liaison; it was inevitable that it wouldn't square with other things that happened. And then, the other night you....'

'Yes, I know' she said, and held her wrist as if on cue.

'I think we need to try some radical new therapy in Sophie's case,' he went on. 'I propose to recommend Sophie for a course of ECT.' he said. Ted put the motion to the meeting. There was voting. But of course the whole thing had already been decided.

No-one else spoke. I was too shocked. The next voice was that of Jane.

'I think we'll leave this one for now. Has anyone got anything else they need to say? Ok, then' she decided. 'Subject closed. Ted – is it time to tell them all about the Rounders match?' she asked.

CHAPTER NINETEEN
(Will)

I quite liked Sophie. She was thoughtful girl, and she intrigued me. Of all the patients she was the one towards whom I felt the greatest professional curiosity. To get her to open up would be a real challenge, the kind an arrogant young trainee is bound to rise to. The other patients all had problems that were defined and being treated: Lizzie with her anorexia; Jason with his autism; Debbie was a classic self-harmer, and Patrick I suppose was almost pathological in his behaviour. But Sophie was depressed, apparently. No, not apparently: I don't mean to imply I doubted Dr Grimshaw's diagnosis. It's just that there seemed so much more to her - something hidden; something not spoken. It was me that suggested writing to her, with the painting and the drama over. I encouraged her to put her thoughts down onto paper. It's a common enough strategy. It was discovered accidentally when people noticed that the pulse rate and blood pressure of criminals was lowered once they had confessed. They had relaxed. But I knew Sophie would resist it if it were presented to her as a form of therapy. I had to plan it as a new activity for her.

'Just let me try,' I pleaded. Dr Grimshaw smiled at me and nodded. Only Ted objected. But I'd talked to Jane about it first. So, at the case-conference two weeks later, she leant her support. She was wearing a rather pretty low cut top, I noticed. Now the air was warmer she had put away the baggy jumpers for the summer. For the first time I began to think how interesting she was – not beautiful, perhaps, but certainly attractive. She always made the best of what she'd got – clean hair, nice clothes; accessories. Her eyes seemed larger than they were: her gaze seemed to widen as she looked at you. The eyes were so brown that they didn't seem to be defined by anything as physical as an iris. Instead there was a space into her mind; it made her face expressive. Her chin protruded slightly when she smiled. She smiled a lot.

'Well I think that it's a great idea,' she said emphatically. Ted looked at her.

'I'm not... I don't know.'

'Oh, what harm can it do?' she said, and laughed.

'She resists strongly all conventional forms of therapy.' added Dr Grimshaw.

'*Does* she?' Ted asked mockingly. 'She seemed to do well enough with ECT the other day.'

'I know,' he said 'but that won't last forever. We've got to find a way to reach her. This might be the key.'

Ted wrote something in the file. 'Ok,' he sighed; we'll give it three weeks. But I want to see what's being written.'

'Why?' I asked him.

'No, Ted – it'll ruin it,' said Jane.

'I think he's right – she'll never do it if she thinks that we're all reading what she's written,' Dr Grimshaw chipped in.

Ted turned to Monica. She said nothing. He looked down at the file and mumbled something. 'They're all reading everything she's written now though, I suppose,' he sighed.

'Will – perhaps you'd like to explain some of the background to your new idea,' invited Dr Grimshaw, coming to my rescue.

'Not mine,' I added, and he nodded.

'Go on.'

'Well,' I started. 'Writing therapy is actually an empirically based collection of therapeutic interventions. I did a meta-analysis of it as a final year project.'

'A *what?*' asked Ted.

'A meta...look, it doesn't matter. What I mean to say is that it's nothing new. You could argue that there are any number of examples from literature.' I paused, but nobody responded. I took that as an indication that I should keep talking.

'It's one of a number of new attempts to deal with psychiatric illnesses. Early work grew out of more orthodox reflective practices. Writing – anything – isn't far removed from standard Cognitive Behavioural Therapy. But it can help when people are reluctant talkers, just like Sophie. And it can help fill in the gaps between appointments. Patients can start to feel they're in control of their emotions. They start to take control of what is happening to them.'

That, of course, was always going to be a problem. So was the fact that most of the initial research into the practice was American.

'They do things differently there,' said Ted. 'We're not like them.'

I laughed. But there wasn't any hint of irony in what he was saying.

'We need to make sure that what happens in the Community Meeting is what matters' he went on. 'That's where the patients start to take control – when they realise that they're not alone, that they're part of something bigger and they've got responsibilities to everybody else in the community. If we're not careful there'll be no need soon for places like this. They're already moving people out of the main hospital. I suppose you want a job when you qualify, do you *Student* Nurse?'

'Yes...of course I do. But there are other ways that we can try. This might just work,' I said, although I knew that I was struggling. 'There's so much time spare - after lunch, for instance. We could do it then.'

'Oh, so now you're suggesting that we fill up every waking moment, are you?'

'No, but...'

'What, then? That we get everybody writing in the afternoon as well as in the morning? Do you not think they'll have done enough of that in lessons?'

I looked down. There was a lot more I could say. But instead, I waited – kept my powder dry, as it were.

'Come on,' Ted said. 'It's nearly twelve o'clock. Lunch will have arrived. We need to get it early so that we can be in time for the Rounders match this afternoon.'

And that, I thought as we left his office, was the end of that. After lunch we walked around the hospital to the Rehabilitation block. Teams of adult patients bent low over flower beds and vegetable plots. A few looked up like cattle as we passed. As we approached rehab, though, the vista opened. The hospital sports field overlooked the town. The curtain of surrounding trees was parted, framing the spires and roof-tops like a nineteenth century landscape painting. In the fields beyond, the first few crops of rape were beginning to flower. Elsewhere, there was lush green waiting to be ripened into golden corn.

'Who's your captain?' somebody was saying.

'I am,' Ted replied.

'Ok, then – heads or tails?'

Ted lost. We fielded first. Or rather, most of us just stood around and waited for the ball to come in our direction. Fielding implies a certain dynamism which was sadly lacking in our team's contributions in the field. Lizzie, for a start, kept running in the wrong direction. There have been studies since the nineteen-seventies suggesting anorexics might have a problem with basic navigation. Back then though, it was just another source of irritation.

'Lizzie – watch the ball!' Ted shouted as she missed another catch.

The rehab team were good. They enjoyed Ted's bowling, hitting him so far that sometimes they were able to complete a double rounder, or whatever the exact description of the score might be.

'Thirty-nine to win then,' Mrs Lotinga was trilling as we lined up for our turn at batting.

Ted went first, and scored a couple before holing out to someone in the deep. The rehab team could catch. I went in next. I thought I did ok. I scored a few more – so did everybody: even Lizzie. But gradually we began to fall away, either run out, caught or – in the case of Debbie - missing the ball completely.

Jane was last man in. Three more Rounders needed, and some tricky bowling. She hit the ball and started running. Ted was screaming at her, but she wasn't awfully athletic. A fielder in the deep returned the ball just as she set off home from the penultimate post. With a flourish the man at fourth base demolished the post, and she was out.

'Oh bad luck Jane,' Sophie shouted. 'Yeah, well tried!' we echoed.

All that is, except for Ted. He said nothing. But you could see that he was fuming. And the frustration at being unable to vent his anger must have been overwhelming. He stormed off the field and marched back to the unit, missing out on the post-match party. It was quite amusing, really. And, once he'd gone, we started talking about him. Someone said how childish his behaviour was. We all joined in, including Jane. All that is, except for Monica. She was listening.

'So was that it?' Sophie was asking once she'd read what I had written.

'What?' I said.

'That incident? The thing that started all this writing?'

'Yes.'

She sounded disappointed.

'What's the matter, Sophie?'

'I don't know. I thought there might have been more *story*, I suppose - some drama, hidden meaning: something tying all the loose ends up together. Some ending, some concluding incident or happening. Anything.'

'That's all there is,' I said.

'I know.'

'Sometimes it's just the simplest things,' I told her.

'So there's no great overarching narrative?'

'There isn't.'

'And no big denouement?'

'No big denouement, no.'

'Oh.'

'That's it then.'

'Yes.'

'The end.'

'The end.'

Or maybe the beginning! Ted simply gave up any opposition to my plan. 'Do what you fuckin' want,' he told me when I next brought up the writing therapy. He was still annoyed, and probably embarrassed, about the Rounders incident. He'd made an exhibition of himself. He'd lost a little bit of his authority. He knew he had become an object of ridicule.

'But why should that have made him more amenable?' Sophie asked. 'Why wouldn't he want to argue with you to re-establish his authority?'

'I don't know, Sophie. Interesting, isn't it? You're learning some psychology this morning. I think Ted was probably re-grouping. He thought he'd give me something, then step back and watch me fail. That way he could regain his superior position.'

'That's Machiavellian!' Sophie said to me.

'That's right,' I told her. 'But we're not going to let him, are we?'

'No.'

'That's right,' I repeated. 'This is going to work.'

'Yes,' she answered. 'How do we start?'

'Well, there are a number of things that you can do,' I told her, even though I wasn't sure where to begin. Some research suggests that patients write a journal: not a daily diary record of mundane events, but a reflective log of feelings developing into an analysis of motivation.

'Perhaps we should start by writing a type of diary?' I said. But Sophie shook her head. I didn't like that, either. I'd heard of therapists describe a 'mind-dump' where people write for a short period of time without stopping, without editing and without worrying about style or grammar.

'How about we take a piece of paper,' I suggested 'and you write for five minutes without stopping. You put down everything, without thinking about what you're writing.'

'Could do,' she replied. At least I'd got her interested.

'Try it then,' I said, and with a sigh she sat down with a pencil and a piece of paper. I sat down a few rows back. The old-fashioned wooden lift-top desks in the schoolroom were scored with decades of graffiti, so much that I concluded that they must have been discarded by a local comprehensive. There must be generations of graffiti etched into the surface. I ran my fingers over some of the letters, like brail. Most were names, scored deep into the wood. Others were hearts with arrows and initials. One drew my attention: 'SH' and 'DA' together with a ball-point arrow. I suddenly felt very sorry for a girl so obviously lost in her emotions. At the same time something of the strength of this attachment suggested a reaction to another incident.

'Will?' she asked.

'What is it, Sophie?'

'I can't do it.'

'Why not?' I asked her.

'I just can't get going. I need to know what I am doing. I mean, what's this for?' she asked. 'What good will it all do?'

'It'll make you feel better for a start' I told her. That was true. That was how the therapy had been discovered, in the USA.

'You know when they do lie-detector tests and such-like in America?'

'Yes?'

'Well, they sometimes do that when a suspect's writing his confession.'

'And?'

'And they've found that their equipment shows that criminals feel better once they've written their confession.'

'Really?'

'Yes. Polygraph operators notice that the heart rate, breathing, even blood pressure of the criminals whose confessions they've been monitoring are all slower once they've finished writing.'

'That's interesting' she said.

'You're right: it is. And the first real English novelist began life writing criminal confessions, too.' I told her.

'Who was that?' she asked.

'Defoe,' I said. 'You've heard of Robinson Crusoe?'

'Yes' she said, and then she thought about it for a bit. 'I'd like to do that one day,' she added.

'Well, you can - why don't you start then?'

'What?'

'Get on with it –get writing.'

'Oh, *that*.'

'So?'

'I didn't mean that,' she said. 'I meant live on my own like Crusoe on an island somewhere.'

'But Crusoe wasn't always on his own.'

'No?'

'No. He had Man Friday.'

'Just two characters, in the entire book?'

'There were others: minor characters. The cannibals, for instance.'

'Oh.'

'But yes, essentially the book was all about one man's experience.'

'But I need to have more characters than that in my book, don't I?'

'I suppose so, yes,' I said.

'All the people here, for instance – you, and Ted and Jane; then there's school - there's Louise and there's my teacher and my mother and...'

'Yes?'

'And another character,' she added softly, staring at me. 'Someone...'

'Who, Sophie?'

'Someone else.' was all she said, and she sat staring into empty space. 'Another author; someone older. Somebody without a face.'

CHAPTER TWENTY
(Sophie/Will)

I suppose there was nothing to lose. I'd quite liked writing stories when I was at school. And poems, too. But it was difficult to get started. At first I couldn't write as myself, for instance. I had to write as other people, and let them take up the narrative. But it was all me, really. All of it was me. I was putting words into the mouths of all my characters. I was making up the things they said and did.

'What is it that you're working on today?' Will asked me as he walked into the classroom. It was hot. Summer had arrived, at last. The wall of glass had turned the school into a greenhouse. As soon as he walked in, Will began loosening his collar.

'A letter,' I replied. 'I'm writing letters, like you told me to.'

'I did? Oh. Who to?'

'I don't know. I'm not writing them. I mean I am, but I'm writing them as someone else. This one is Dr Grimshaw, writing about one of his patients.'

'Which one?' he asked.

'You have to guess,' I told him, smiling.

'No!' he said. 'You're kidding!' His eyes widened suddenly. I could tell that I was already sustaining the reader's interest.

'Do you want to see?' I asked. How could he possibly resist? He had gone red and was perspiring. Now he was almost shaking.

'If you want to show me,' he was saying. He walked towards me and I handed him the paper. He took it from me and just looked at it. And then he started reading.

...Sophie Western was my patient for approximately two years. She was referred to the Child Guidance Clinic initially as a result of school refusal. She was first seen by my colleague, Mr Drewery, a clinical psychologist specialising in child and adolescent mental health. His initial diagnosis was that of a depressive illness, and accordingly she was referred to me. She exhibited – make that 'presented', Will suggested – *she presented with a wide variety of symptoms, including washing* – that's obsessive-compulsive behaviour, he informed me - *sleep disruption and anxiety. There was hostility towards my early attempts to engage her in routine talking therapy. Something was preventing her from facing up to some past event or trauma. Her relationship with her mother was difficult, and as our meetings continued it became apparent that her condition wasn't making the kind of progress I expected.*

My initial objective had merely been to stabilise her condition, which I did by administering a number of tricyclic antidepressants, beginning with dothiepin, imipramine, and amitryptyline, initially at a dose of 5mg daily...

'Yes that's good,' he said. 'They work chemically by blocking the re-uptake of neurotransmitters, thereby increasing levels at the receptors. They can be slow to take effect, though: up to two weeks before they start to work,' he said.

'I know,' I said to him '– read on.'

...and so appointments during this initial period were scheduled for every second day. I needed to see her to gauge the effects of the medication and adjust the strength and dosage. I was fairly confident that they were being taken correctly.

179

'Is that true?' he asked me.

'Yes of course,' I answered. 'I did want to get better.'

'Sorry.'

Thereafter, she saw me at the child guidance clinic twice a week. There was a high degree of hostility to many of my enquiries, and establishing an effective counselling dialogue was difficult. I interviewed the mother, and established certain background details. Mrs Western was – if anything – more hostile to any medical intervention than her daughter. She denied my colleague's diagnosis, and would only consent to continued therapy following the intervention of the Education Welfare Officer. Sophie had been truanting.'

'You haven't told me that before.'

'I haven't told you anything so far,' I said to him.

'Why do you think your mother was so hostile?' he asked.

'I don't know,' I lied. I knew, all right. I'd done my amateur diagnosis. Some books I'd read suggested that as many as one person in every six becomes depressed at some point in their lives. Not all would be diagnosed as 'clinical' depression, though. But she didn't think that such illnesses were real. All she would say is that I had to pull myself together, or snap out of it. She would never have allowed that diagnosis. She didn't think that it was serious. Not even later on.

Sophie was admitted to the adolescent unit of Cranford Psychiatric Hospital as a voluntary patient: that was the term in use prior to the 1983 Mental Health Act. Nowadays such admissions are referred to as 'informal'. Hers was deemed to be necessary due to the lack of progress with her therapy and the fact I was concerned about the apparent lack of response to the drugs; hospital admission would give me the chance both to ensure that they were taken, and taken correctly, and to closely monitor their effects. It is not uncommon for psychiatric patients to resist medication, or indeed resist attempts to make them better. In this respect, Sophie was unusual. She was intelligent and articulate and although she resisted medical intervention in the form of cognitive behaviour therapy, she nevertheless appeared genuinely to seek relief from her symptoms. She was, however, reluctant to discuss their cause.

'See!' I told him. But he went on reading.

At the time of her admission her sleep patterns had been severely disrupted; so, in addition to the anti-depressants I prescribed low-dose hypnotics in an attempt to re-establish Sophie's normal sleeping habit. Until then, she had reported little disruption to her sleep; if anything, she was sleeping more than usual which – of course – added to her fatigue and is not an uncommon symptom of depression.

Interpersonal therapy (IPT) focuses on people's relationships and on problems such as difficulties in communication, or coping with bereavement. There is some evidence that IPT can be as effective as medication or Cognitive Behavioural Therapy but more research is needed. In the case of Sophie Western, traditional forms of therapy broke down to an extent that – in her second month here – she underwent a short course of electroconvulsive therapy.

'No mention of the knife, then?'

'No,' I told him. 'I don't want that fact in my notes for everyone to see.'

She was closely monitored and her voluntary status was rescinded following an incident in early March. She was sectioned on March 27th 1981 and spent a further three months at the adolescent unit. She formed a close relationship with another patient and eventually found someone she could talk to in the person of a student nurse, with whom she seemed to strike up a rapport. Her subsequent recovery from depression and her discharge from the hospital coincided with engaging on a course of writing therapy.

'Wow!' he said when he had finished. 'That was fantastic! Recovery... discharge, everything – it's all there. Wonderful!'

I looked down at the floor. I knew that it had pleased him. I was pleased with it myself. Not that it had been as good when I had started. Don't just write it and forget about it, he had told me. Go back to it; revise it; draft it. Make it better and improve it. And with his help, that's what I was doing. I was learning. This was how to be a writer: use everything, and everyone. Use him. Use what I'd done. Use everything. Write about it all then learn from my experience. I'd drafted and re-drafted it – perfected it. I'd done my homework, too: I'd read about the drugs. I'd even sneaked a quick look at my notes when Ted had left them on the table in the nurses' office.

'You know a lot of books use letters to convey the narrative,' he told me afterwards. 'It's what writers call an epistolary form.'

'A what?' I asked.

'Epistolary - a letter; writing an imaginary letter.'

'Why?' I asked him.

'Well it's something writers sometimes do as an alternative to ordinary narration. Letters can reveal a lot about what people think and do, you know. Just like our conversations.'

I was thinking, now.

'Some great books have been written in that way,' he told me. '*Pamela*, for instance – or *Virtue Regained*.'

'I've never heard of that!' I laughed. 'What was it about?'

'A young girl – in fact, a servant who receives unwanted sexual advances from her master, Mr B.'

'What?'

'I know, I know,' he said. 'But Richardson got there before you. Over two hundred years before, in fact.'

'What happens to her?'

'Oh she marries him eventually. He sees the error of his ways and makes an honest woman of her.'

'Bollocks!' she exclaimed.

'Best-selling bollocks, at the time,' I told her. 'Some people think that was the first proper novel in the English language. It was a sensation, selling millions. And all of it was written as a set of letters.'

She was sucking on her pencil.

'How about another one?' I suggested. 'Write to someone else involved in the story. Ask them something. Somebody important, maybe. Anybody. Doesn't matter.'

'Nah,' she eventually responded. 'I don't want to write another letter. I'm not *Pamela,* or whatever she was called. I'm nothing like her. And I've got other plans for him...'

'Ok, then – try a different strategy. Here's something that I read about a while ago – you write an A to Z of all your favourite words.'

'Like a picture book?'

'Sort of,' I replied. 'Just write the letter down the left-hand side and then for each one write a word. Don't think about it for too long. And if you can't think of any words go to the dictionary, open it and stick your finger in at random: *sortes virgiliane,*' I said to her, although she wasn't listening. Of course she wasn't. In fact, she was already writing. This was wonderfully gratifying. One week after starting, things were really happening. I left her in the classroom for a short while. I thought that it would be ok. She was absorbed in what she was doing, and I could see her through the almost floor-to-ceiling windows on both side of the unit classroom. Back in the main building everything was happening: Pat and Debbie, bickering; Lizzie scowling; Ted and Jane – what were they doing? A short time later I went back to find out how it was going.

'Any good?' I asked her.

'Well, I think so. I've got a list,' she said. 'I've even put a word down that I'm not quite sure exists. I've looked in the dictionary.'

'What is it?'

'H – Homunculus,' I told him.

183

'That rings a bell,' he said. 'That's interesting'

'Why? Is it a real word?'

'Yes, of course it is.'

'What does it mean?' I asked him.

'Well, it's ....it's sperm actually,' he told me.

'What?'

'Sperm. Or more precisely, it's the 'little man' that people once thought was contained in every individual sperm - before they found out any better.'

'What?'

'Before they found that women have a part to play as well, instead of simply growing what a man implants inside them.'

'They thought *that*?' she said.

'Some of them still do,' I whispered.

'Yes I know,' she told me.

'Ok, ok. You've done the word list. Good.' This was moving on quite quickly.

'Now what do I do?' she asked me.

'Play a game,' I told her. 'Move the words around. Choose a few; make sentences of them. I know, choose a word and write the letters down the page.'

'Yes?'

She chose the first word in her alphabet – A – P – P – L – E.

'Now what?' she asked me.

'Now choose words that begin with each of those initial letters. Choose another 'A' word, if you want to – you'll need another 'P' as well.

'Like an acrostic?' Sophie asked me.

'Yes, like an acrostic.'

'Then what?'

'Then you write a sentence using each of the words you've chosen.'

'Is that all?' she asked me.

'Yes, that's all,' I told her. 'That's the exercise.'

'But what's the point?' she asked me. 'What's the reason?'

'There is no point,' he told me. 'And there is no reason. You are writing. You are learning. You are healing. That's not a reason. That is happening. Something is always happening. Even when you don't think anything is happening, slowly something is beginning – you are starting to get better. You are getting better. Slowly. Writing is a way of getting better. Putting words on paper, one after the other. And when you've done it, look at it. Look at all the letters. Look at the words they make. Look at the lines and paragraphs. Look at the patterns that they make on the paper. Count the pages, feel the weight of paper. See the chapters; see the words that stand for what you've done. It will be where you want it: outside, on the page in front of you instead of here,' I slapped my solar-plexus.

'But what if no-one wants to read it?'

'Look – it doesn't matter. It's there to read when someone wants to, or else be shut up in a drawer. Doing it is what's important. Writing is a way of learning. It is a way of something happening; recovering. That is what is happening. Recovering is happening. You are happening, recovering, writing, learning, growing, healing. That is always happening. Always. Happening. Always. Always. All the time. Even when nothing happens, that is happening. That is always happening. You are slowly healing. All the time. Healing. Healing. Healing. Healing.'

She was marking out the paper as I told her.

A Apple
P Plan
P Poison
L Lonely
E Eve

'Now make a sentence up for each one of the words.'
'What?'

'Write a sentence – any sentence – with your word in it. Don't think about it. Do it. Go on. Get it done.'

She took an apple for the teacher
That was what she needed for her plan
Although the fruit was sweet it hid a poison
The lonely hours as I sit writing
Why am I the one who's being punished, and not Eve?

'Now what, Will?' she asked.

And I read what she had done. I didn't really want to be her teacher. But she was good; a model student. She had done exactly what I asked of her. That was frightening. I was making all this up as I went along. I was trying desperately to think of something else for her to do, something to expand on these ideas, to develop them (and hoping that something might come out of them).

'Poetry,' I suddenly announced. 'That's a form of writing therapy. Let's try writing poetry.'

Poetry therapy requires an all-round literary appreciation more than other forms of writing therapy. Anyone who has learnt to write can string some sentences together. But poetry is literature distilled; the ideas and emotions concentrated, focussed, analysed. It takes time, and knowledge.

'Have you written poetry before?' I asked her.

'Yes,' she said.

I knew she must have. It was in her nature. Sophie was a thinker; and a reader. She had read a lot of books. We'd talked about her favourite authors, and the books she'd read whilst truanting from school. Put the two together and you've got an author. She was having none of it, however.

'Try and write a poem using one or more of the phrases you've created.'

'You can't just write a poem!' she protested. 'You have to sit and wait for inspiration.'

186

'No you don't,' I told her. 'Writers don't just sit around and wait – they write; that's what makes them writers.'

'But I'm not a writer,' Sophie said to me.

'You might be, one day. Would you like to be?' I asked her.

'Yes,' she told me.

'Well, start writing then. Start making something. Use the word-game you've completed. That's your inspiration.'

And so she started writing. Not quickly, and not easily. There were lots of crossings out, experiments with different rhyme and metre, drafts and re-drafts. In the end, the following lines took over three days to produce. Then Sophie typed them up on the old, black Remington her grandfather had given her. The result, I thought, was quite remarkable...

Fall

Some girls at school seem not to care who sees
Their bodies wet and naked from the shower.
The others hide behind a towel, like me,
And fret about it all for hours and hours.
One girl, though, just doesn't seem to care:
She seems to love the thought of being bare.

She likes all the attention - no fig leaf for her.
She doesn't care if what she does is wrong.
But she's not sweet or innocent, she's aware
Of what she does, and knows it won't be long
Before he turns from her and goes for me.
And that's her motivation - jealousy.

To set a trap you need to have a plan,
And tempting fruit is such a common feature.
How could she ever hope to trap the man
Without bringing an apple for the teacher?
She offered him her gift and knew he'd bite,
And I was left to watch, consumed with spite.

The ripe fruit was the bait, my sweet temptation.
Once bitten, though, the fruit turned brown and sour.
And now I sit and wait for inspiration,
As the lonely classroom clock ticks down the hour.
How could she eat, like Eve, and still be free?
I ate the apple once: it poisoned me.

CHAPTER TWENTY-ONE
(Will)

Poetry, of course, is never easy. Something about the discipline of line and rhythm helps to shape ideas and to transform them into something that you maybe hadn't first considered. That's true of writing generally, I suppose, but is more acute in poetry. The finished verse is significant enough; but if it's any good as therapy it should be able to withstand interrogation.

'So where did all that come from?' I asked Sophie after I had read it.

'I don't know.'

She sat there, staring at the page. 'I was just thinking, really – thinking on the paper; thinking round the words. The idea came from somewhere, but I don't know where.'

'But you're supposed know,' I told her. 'You're supposed to be the author. If you don't know, then who does?'

'I don't know - the reader?' she suggested.

She was right of course.

'But you must know more about it all than that?' I said.

'I don't though,' she replied. 'Haven't you heard of the unconscious?'

'I think you mean *preconscious*, actually.'

'Same thing,' Sophie told me.

'No, not really.'

'You tell me what it is, then; you're supposed to know.'

'Sophie!'

'Well, anyway - that's the 'somewhere' that ideas like this might come from. That's what Freud said, anyway. You've heard of him I take it?'

'Sophie!'

'Well then,' she replied. 'It's not just in psychiatry you know.'

'I know.'

'It's called creative memory – confabulation, even.'

'Oh!' I said. 'I see you've done some reading.'

'Yes. In fiction, things slowly become true by virtue of the fact that they've been written. Things that didn't happen, happen. Things that did, but don't get written, haven't. That's something that our minds do, but it's not necessarily what's true.'

'What do you mean?' I asked her.

'I mean it hasn't really happened but we think it has,' she said.

'And if we think it has...'

'It shapes the way we act and think and it can change the way that we behave.'

'In other words it shapes the narrative,' I added.

'Well, it would do if there was one.'

'Isn't there?'

'No, and that's the problem. There is no narrative in all this - just events; just one damned thing after another. That's all there is – no story, and no continuity: nothing.'

'That may be true,' I said to her. 'But your job as the author is to make a narrative - you've got to invent one. Narrative can be the easiest way to understand a situation, even if it isn't true. That's what we do. That's what we all are - storytellers. And we tell the story to ourselves. That's your problem, here. You don't tell a story - you know, one with a beginning and a middle and an end. You don't have to start at the beginning: you can start a story in the middle: you can even start if at the end if you want to. But you have to shape events into their parts. Writing a book is like assembling a jigsaw puzzle. Each piece has to fit, and has to be connected to the adjacent pieces. Otherwise the picture won't make any sense.'

'But it doesn't. Life's not like that. My life isn't, anyway.'

'Then you've got to make it like that, Sophie. Make it fit. Impose the sense. You're the author. You're in charge. You can do anything.'

'Anything?'

'That's right, Sophie. Anything.'

'But that's not what is happening. That's not real; I can't make up a fairy story and pretend that it is happening to me.'

'No.'

'Why bother, then?'

'Because you have to; we all have to. It's all part of the game we're playing. That's what we do – we're storytellers. Humans always have been. What we do is make up stories.'

'But why?'

'I don't know - to help us understand; to work things out; to explore our motivations and to find solutions to our problems.'

'You're making it up!' she shouted.

'No – honestly!' I told her. 'Some of the earliest stories ever written were about working out dilemmas: not just writing down what happens but explaining *why* things happen. Books like the Decameron were essentially...'

'The what?'

'*Decameron* - ten people fleeing from the plague in Florence, each one telling a different story to the others.'

'What about?' she asked.

'About the world they live in, life as they lived it; about all sorts of difficulties people faced. The characters are all just working something out.'

'You make it sounds like maths,' she muttered.

'Sorry. But they're doing it through story. That's what we're all doing all the time,' I added. 'Working out what's happening; changing the way we see things; taking in new information. We're all just looking for a way of understanding.'

'And how do stories help us to do that?' she asked.

'Because what we do is we construct a narrative, one with ourselves as the central characters: we interrogate events and find connections; we control the rising action. Then finally, there is some concluding moment when the strands are drawn together and the meaning suddenly becomes clear.'

'Is there?'

'Yes, of course there is.'

'No, I mean *really* – not just in a story: in reality?'

'I don't know about that, Sophie. I'm not sure. Perhaps not.'

'Then why should we pretend there is and write it in a book?'

'Because we have to: that is what we're here to do. We need to. Stories are the only thing we've got.'

'I can't, though. It's not working for me,' Sophie told me. 'There are so many things I still don't understand.'

'That's natural,' I said. 'It's like that in a book. You don't know at the start why certain things have happened. You don't yet understand their place in the story. That comes later. Somewhere there will be some resolution. There will be explanations. Honestly. You've simply got to write them.'

'You mean a denouement?'

'Possibly. Or just some rising action. You'll realise where things go and how they fit in. It'll happen.'

'But what if they don't fit? What if I don't like what's written?'

'They might not; and you won't like everything. You'll find you have to change things - write yourself a different plot, move things around, change details here and there. That happens as we read on. The more we know, the better we can understand the way the story is developing.'

'But what if I don't like my story, once it's written?'

'Write yourself another one. There isn't one defining narrative in our lives, there are many, and the story changes. How we understand things changes over time. We come to see that certain things are more or less important than we thought they were. We re-invent the past and re-create ourselves. We do it all the time.'

'Ok - so if I don't like something, I can simply write it up again, and write in a different way?'

'Of course,' I said.

'And even change the ending?'

'If you want to, yes.'

She thought about it for a moment. 'But I don't know now what I want to happen in the end,' she said.

'That's fine,' I told her. 'It doesn't matter. It'll happen if you let it. The story will take on its own momentum. It'll take you into areas you'd never have considered.'

'Like what?'

'Like this discussion, for example. Who knows where it's leading?'

'That's my difficulty,' Sophie told me. 'If I can't see where I'm going then I cannot see the point in writing.'

'Yes, but there are lots of other reasons we might have for writing.'

'Such as?'

'Such as making sense of things; preserving things; enjoying things.'

'Enjoying things?'

'Yes. Enjoying things. Telling someone what you've done is half the pleasure. If there's nobody to tell, the enjoyment of a thing is halved.'

193

'Just because you haven't told someone?'

'I think so. Imagine if there was nobody to tell; if you were all alone.'

'I'd like that,' she replied.

'For a while, maybe. But think of all the things you'd like about it. Go on. Think about them. And then imagine what you'd want to do when one of them had happened.'

'Tell someone about it?'

'Tell someone. And writing is another way of doing that. A better way. A way of making the enjoyment permanent, because the record of the pleasure will be there forever; you can work on it and get it right, and make sure everybody understands; you can go over it again and again improving it until you have distilled the essence of the thing forever.'

'Sounds serious.'

'It is serious. That's what you're supposed to be doing, here. Not something cheap and nasty and unworthy of the things you're trying to record.'

'But what am I trying to record?'

'I don't know, Sophie. That's for you to tell me. That's for me to find out when I read the things you've written.'

'I'll try,' she said. She looked down, and her hair flopped down and hid her face from me as if a curtain had been drawn around her. Occasionally, she flicked it back and I could see her tongue between her lips. Something was happening. She was concentrating. And the pencil was scratching words out on the paper. I could hear it. I could see the graphite creeping slowly on the white sheet like a frost. I found myself increasingly intrigued by what she might be thinking.

***

I tried hard, but found it difficult to begin. I sat and thought about the things he'd said. And then another voice began. I took hold of the pen and held it like a knife. I cut words onto the paper. I carved out the descriptions of my characters. I sharpened my ideas. I sliced through the confusion. And a story started slowly appearing. Characters were invented. Friendships formed and friendships ended. Problems were confronted. And the book grew. The small blue exercise book was soon filled up with words. There was another. And another. Words flowed like a river. And the book went on and on forever.

CHAPTER TWENTY-TWO
(Sophie)

People always ask me, they say - 'when do you do your writing, Sophie? What is your routine? When are you inspired?' I have to tell them that there is no inspiration, no routine: I'm writing all the time. I'm always writing, every moment. In my head, the words are always forming. And in bed when I'm asleep, and in the morning; in the afternoon and evening, something's always happening.

When do you do the writing, though? When do you put the words down on the paper?

Whenever I can is the answer. Sometimes I have to scribble something down on little bits of paper. Then, once lunch is over, I go back into the classroom and I type them up. I add another page. I put it on the pile. And then I go back and I join in with what everybody else is doing.

Which is?

Watching TV; playing games. There is a pool table in the bay window of the day room. There are some board games, too. And some of us are still allowed to go outside for walks.

Not you, though?

No.

What do you do when all the others go outside?

I write. At least, I try to. Sometimes it is difficult to do.

Is it?

Yes, it is. Have you ever felt it, sitting there, the blank page, bursting with the urge to write but nothing's happening? Nothing's happening at all? No words? Nothing. And you think there's nothing there, but at the same time you can feel the pressure, bulging in your brain, the pressure to say something, anything, to hit the keys and get the words down on the paper, covering the paper with black ink, with characters, with Serif letters making patterns on the white sheets, making words and making sentences and paragraphs until the paper's full of words.

Do you need any special conditions to complete your writing?

No. But I write better without any interruptions. I like to sit and type alone. Writing by hand is too slow now. I need to hear the rattle of the metal. The noise is useful. Sometimes Debbie comes to see me. Sometimes Will checks up on what I'm doing. But mostly it is solitary. And I like it like that. I don't like it when I'm interrupted, but sometimes living in a community interruptions inevitably happen.

'You've got a visitor,' Jane told me.

'And another chapter,' I said *sotto voce*.

'Hello, Sophie. How are you?' And Mr Jones walked in and sat beside me.

'Oh fine,' I told him. 'I'm writing a book, actually. It's called Writing Therapy.'

'A book?' he said. 'That's interesting. What is it about?'

'Me,' I told him.

'Oh!' he said. 'Am I in it?'

'You can be if you want to be,' I told him. I didn't tell him he was already. 'You can write a chapter for me if you want to. I'm asking lots of different people if they'll make a contribution.'

'But I wouldn't know where to start, Sophie.'

197

'You would,' I said. 'Why don't you tell me all about that day, you know...?'

'Your final day in school?'

'That's right,' I told him. 'Tell me what happened from your point of view. There's so much that I want to know.'

'Like?'

'Like what you said to her and whether or not you knew what she would do.'

'No, Sophie... I don't think so.'

'But you've got to,' I insisted. 'The readers need to see it from your perspective.'

He stopped. We were alone. I knew what he was thinking.

'Anything could happen now you know,' I told him.

'Oh.'

'If I scream they'll all come running: you should see what I've already written.'

'Well, ok then - maybe just a word or two.'

'Oh no,' I told him. 'The full story. I want everything.'

'But won't that... you know... disrupt the narrative perspective?'

What did he care about my narrative perspective? He had another.

'It won't,' I said. 'And even if it does, that's my problem isn't it, not yours?'

'Ok. I'll see what I can do.'

I handed him the book. English books at school were always red. This was blue. He flicked his thumb through some of the early pages.

'Can I?'

'No,' I told him. 'Not yet – write your contribution first.'

I got up. He moved into my seat. I imagined the warmth that I'd created spreading through his body. And he started writing...

Sophie; Sophie Western – I remember. How could I forget her? I'd been her teacher long before she reached the sixth-form. I liked her; she was a dedicated student and she used to help me – you know, run small errands, get the register and such-like. She had an attachment to me, I knew that. I was no fool. Well, yes I was. But she was pleasant and polite. I knew her mother wasn't all that keen on her continuing at school. She wanted her to leave and get a job, like she herself had done. But I encouraged Sophie to stay on, to study English. And I told her that she should apply to university, study literature like I had done. I thought that I was helping her. I was. But maybe she was also helping me.

I was at a low ebb at the time, you see. The job was getting to me. I had not intended to spend long in teaching. I'd never really wanted to go back to school: two, three years I thought and then I'd be an author. That had been my strategy. Now, five years later, I was going nowhere. I had published nothing – just a few small lines of poetry. And recently I'd written hardly anything. There was something standing in my way; something large, something I couldn't quite see, a shadow, like a tumour on an x-ray.

Not that life was difficult; not really. Teaching girls was easy, at first anyway. That's what I did. I taught girls how to read books properly; I taught them to dissect a book as if it were a scientific specimen; I taught them how to suck words dry, to wring all meaning from them, to get inside them, wear them, then discard them. That's what I had done, and done successfully. I'd never really given it much thought. It was a natural facility, one that I exploited readily. I'd done well enough at school, I'd gone to university; I'd got a good degree without once considering employment. Teaching seemed the obvious thing to do: teaching a subject I was good at, something that came easily to me.

But there was more to it than that. If I'm honest I had never been that happy at my own school. I'd worked hard and I'd kept out of trouble; been successful academically. But I'd never been happy. No - or popular. Socially, I'd always been on the fringes of the action: observing, commenting, describing rather than participating. I'd missed out on something and the thought of going back to school to teach must have been at least in part to do with a nagging feeling there was unfinished business in my life. I hadn't achieved what my psychiatrist describes as 'closure'. In that sense this chapter should start even earlier, at my own school twenty years before. But then it can take twenty years to 'climb clear' as Philip Larkin says, of this particular wrong beginning.

When I agreed to coach her after school I thought it would be easy: going over set books, finding different things to say about the texts. And I knew what kind of things to say. But she told me she was sick of Chaucer, Shakespeare and the Faerie Queene. It was her idea that we should read Justine. *And I thought, if word got round, that it might do myself a bit of good as well.*

I'd started to have problems at the school, you see. It had been difficult for me recently. Girls can be so cruel. Then Sophie came along and wouldn't let me go. She hung around so much that people in the staffroom had begun to talk. Miss Nicolson cornered me one afternoon. She had waited for me specially, and made sure that there was no one else around.

'How are things going?' she asked. It was her way of being informal, I suppose. Everyone else would have just said 'How are things?' But the extra word, the way she said it and the way she nodded told me that she didn't really want to know. No - she was going to tell me. She was going to let me know how things were going: and that was badly, in her opinion and in the opinion of the other staff, or so she said. She remarked that several people had suggested that she speak to the Governors. But no, she told me, she had said that she would talk to me herself. She had a duty. She was my Headmistress. She had been responsible for my progress as a young, probationary teacher and she'd never really relinquished the responsibility.

'I didn't want to hurt her feelings,' I lied when we spoke later in her study after school. The huge sash window right behind her desk was open, as it often was. The white, almost transparent curtains floated in and out as outdoors, on the field, the gang-mower was pulled back and forth across the grass. 'Yes, I coached her for her Oxbridge interview. She asked me to. She said that she'd arranged it with her mother.'

'Was anybody else present?' Miss Nicolson enquired, in clipped tones. She was so businesslike and so dispassionate. She could never understand what really happened. What was the point of trying to make her?

'No. Her mother would still be at work.'

'Ah yes.'

'But I would only stay an hour or so. Her mother knew.' I knew now that it wasn't true. It couldn't be.

'I've spoken to the mother,' Miss Nicolson interrupted. 'She tells me she knew nothing of the arrangement.'

'Then she's lying.'

Silence. The mower slowly edged a little nearer to the open window, trimming the grass next to the mock-Tudor sports pavilion, all showers and steamy windows. It was a pleasant school, I thought as I stood before the boss's desk considering my future. I had enjoyed it here. Who wouldn't have? I was a man, it was my first job. And I wasn't that much older than the eldest of the students. Not that I'm a paedophile or anything. I didn't watch the small girls in their PE knickers running on the field, although there were a few who might have done. But the older girls – well, they were more young women really. They were mature. And they were sexy. And they flirted with me. And I was never quite sure how I should react. I was never really comfortable with that. I hadn't had the practice, and it showed. They knew. Louise Anderson had known when she was in my form. She made sure everybody knew through her Socratic inquisition.

Honestly: the questions she would ask: always innocent; yet always fully loaded.

'Did you have a nice weekend, sir?'

'Yes thank you, Louise.'

'What did you do, sir?'

'Oh...you know. A bit of this-and-that.'

'Who with, sir – with your girlfriend?'

'No. I haven't got a girlfriend.'

How many times had I told her? Why did she always have to ask? And then the look of mock surprise that spread across her face when I admitted that I hadn't. She didn't need to say any more. Someone else might, but it was never necessary. I could feel my face begin to burn. I would hastily look down and start the register. But by then it was all done. The snide remarks might come. A copy of 'Gay Times' was left anonymously on my desk. What could I do? I mentioned it to someone in the staffroom. There weren't that many men. But Hugh had always seemed ok to me.

'Don't think about it,' he had told me, puffing on his pipe. The first years were attempting to play hockey on the sports field. He was gazing at them through the staffroom window.

'And whatever else, don't ever let them see it's got to you.'

'No,' I said. 'I won't'.

Too late, I thought. I already have. They know.

'The trouble is,' he went on 'people don't really understand what it's like in school. What it's really like, once they've found some little chink in your armour. They don't realise how scared we all are. That's the only reason why we do it: shout and bawl; act tough; go wild. It's fear: we have to make them frightened of us, and do you know why?'

'Why, Hugh?'

'Because we're all running scared of them, that's why. Oh, I've seen what they can do to a young teacher; seen it on teaching practice when I was a student. Completely

202

destroy them, they can. They're like animals - even girls. In fact, especially girls. That's the only reason we're aggressive with them; aggressive talk; aggressive body language. Just talking, asking, issuing instructions in a way you'd never dream of with adults. It's necessary. We need to be. It's needed. No-one would learn anything if it wasn't like that.'

'Not all the girls are like that though,' I said and thought of one who wasn't, and another that I wished was not. 'Sophie never joins in all that banter.'

'No?' said Hugh. But I could tell he didn't know her, or believe me.

She was different from the rest. She'd sit pretending to be getting on with something. She tended to sit at a desk near the front, on her own. Not that she was friendless. Just that she didn't seem to mind being on her own, unlike me. It didn't seem to bother her. She didn't seem to care what people thought of her, or didn't seem to mind. Until that stupid fight, that is. That was when it all unravelled. And I felt responsible, somehow. I should have seen it coming I suppose; I should have stopped it sooner - should have sent Louise Anderson to the head teacher. But, as usual, I wanted to impress her. She took over. She was in control, even as she stood there out-of-breath, dishevelled. That was the first time I'd ever seen her like that - looking anything except composed – cool, you might say now. She wasn't cool that afternoon. She was panting, and she looked a mess.

'Did you see that, sir? Did you see what she did to me?' she gasped. Her hair was wild and her tie was pulled down. The top of her school jumper was hanging off her shoulder.

Sophie didn't say a word. She was lying on the floor. And she was crying.

'You're not going to let her get away with it, are you? She went for me, sir.'

And, in an instant, I began to doubt what I'd walked in on. Louise Anderson was like a bird of prey. And in that fraction of a second, she had pounced on me; she held me

203

fast. And I had nowhere else to go. She was as ruthless as she'd obviously just been with poor Sophie when the two of them were brawling on the floor. And whatever had just happened, whoever had been right or wrong, soon everyone began to understand the accepted version of events. Her version of events.

'Are you all right, Louise?' I asked.

Sophie looked up through her tears. And that was when she lunged at me.

'Whoa! Look, sir. She's mad.' Someone shouted as I grabbed her by the wrists.

'She belongs up in the Cranford, she does.'

'She attacked you sir,' said Louise. 'Send her to Miss Nicolson. We all saw it. We saw what she did. We'll back you up. Go on, sir – send her to the Headmistress.'

So I did. And that was that. Miss Nicolson saw her chance, and took it. And a scandal was avoided. And I'm still there, and she's up here. And now no-one will ever know what really happened. I've got away with it, you see. I'm free to try again, with someone else. And this time, well... that's another story, isn't it?

'By the way I've brought you this,' he said and reached inside his briefcase.

He handed me the package. I could tell inside there was a book. I took it out and held it out at arms length and squinted at the title: Sons and Lovers.

'It's about... well, you can see what it's about,' he said. 'I thought you might... you know, our lessons and all that? Didn't Lawrence say the novel was the one great book of life?'

I smiled at him. At least I think I did. He sat there, on one of the small chairs looking awkward and embarrassed.

'So?'

'So what?'

'Is what I've written any good?' he asked me.

'It's ok,' I told him, and he looked a little disappointed. 'No, I mean it is good – really. Thank you. It explains a lot. I'll make sure it gets included.'

'Thank you.'

And with that, he rose to leave. But at the classroom door, he paused.

'I'll come again,' he said.

'No, don't,' I told him and as he made to turn I stood on tip-toes and I kissed him on the cheek. And felt nothing.

CHAPTER TWENTY-THREE

This thing is taking over everything I do now: everything is geared to doing this. I don't want to do anything but this: I don't want to go anywhere or read anything or even talk to anyone. All I want to do is sit here, writing this and putting words down on these sheets of paper, one word after another, then another, then a sentence: full-stop. Capital letter and another line begins. Another thought. Is this the best way to express it? Is this word or phrase the clearest? Should I try another? Experiment with different possibilities? No. Just do it. Write it. Get it down on paper. Check it later. Tap, tap, tap-ping on the typewriter. That's what I enjoy. Tap, tap, tap-ping; typing: writing. Getting what I'm thinking out of my head and out there in the world, in front of me. Writing is the only thing that's real, now; writing makes things real. If things aren't written then they're not real anymore. What a bore I must be. That's what Debbie tells me. But I cannot help it. I have to do it. Tap, tap, tap and if it's not tap, scratch out with a pencil on a scrap of paper, put an idea down before it disappears forever.

'But why?' she asks me.

'I don't know,' I say to her. 'I have to.'

'But it's all you ever do,' she says.

'It's all right for you,' I tell her. 'You've just got to sit there while I write about you. I've got to turn what we do into words. You don't have to; you can just get on with it but I've always got to think of what to do to get it down on paper.'

'Why?' she asks again.

'To make sure that other people understand what happens.'

'What for?'

'So that they know.'

'So who'll know?'

'Everyone.'

'But why does everybody need to know?'

'I don't know – they just have to, that's all.'

'I don't think they do,' she told me. 'Anyway they can't - you won't let anybody read it.'

'Not yet, no,' I said. 'But one day – maybe.'

'Why would anybody want to read it, though? Just because you might have put the words down on the paper doesn't mean that others want to read them. What is there in your book worth reading?'

'I don't know,' I told her, and stopped writing. The question was a physical interrogation. Suddenly, in my stomach, there it was: what makes anything we write worthwhile? Why add to all the books that have been written? Are we saying anything that hasn't been said already? She sensed that she had hurt me.

'Tell me what it's about?' she asked me, sympathetically.

'Debs,' I started. 'It's not about anything.'

'It has to be,' she responded gently. 'It has to be about something.'

'No it doesn't,' I replied. 'A book just *is* something; it isn't *about* something as well.'

'Ok then,' she went on. 'Tell me what it's like,' she said. 'Describe it to me.'

'That's not easy either, Debbie.' I replied. 'It's like... it's atmospheric really; episodic – there are episodes: finding the knife, discovery, the painting, writing – and they all take

207

place before a backdrop of therapy and thinking – musing, quietly reflecting, including all sorts of things like passages on what is real and other passages about stuff that I haven't written. This is a book about writing a book. This is a book with the back off: this is a book whose bones you can see. This is my way of confessing. This is my way of telling, and of understanding. This is the way that I'm learning to face up to what has happened and to who I am.'

'But is it any good?' she asked.

'The truth is I'm not sure; I don't know if it's any good or whether anyone will want to read it when I've finished. But I've got to do it. That's the truth. The truth is if I didn't do it then I wouldn't be doing what I want to and need to do. I'd be doing something else. And that wouldn't be the truth. The truth is doing what I'm doing, whether anybody likes the things I do or not. The truth is that I've got to do what I am doing; if I don't then I'm not doing what I feel is true - I'm lying. The truth is that I'm not a writer; I'm a girl who's sitting at a typewriter. I'm someone staring at an empty sheet of paper. There's no noise from the keys; there's nothing happening. I've reached the end, now. It's all over. No more words are coming.'

'So I'm in there then, am I?'

''Course you are,' I told her.

'Why?'

'Because you're such an important character. You've helped me get the story written. And you're important for the action; I need you for what will happen later,' I told her.

She smiled. I think that, secretly, she liked the thought of being in the story. I was glad that I had pleased her. It was like before. The sun was shining. Then her face changed, and the clouds came over.

'But what if people recognize me? What if my dad finds out and reads what I've been doing?'

'He won't know that it's you,' I reassured her. 'I've changed all the names.'

'But...' She suddenly looked worried.

208

'What have you written about me? Tell me?'

'It's ok,' I told her. 'I've not written anything that's nasty, or untrue.'

'But what?' she suddenly demanded. 'What have you been writing?'

'Everything,' I said to her.

'Everything?' she shouted. 'Like him, for instance? Is he there?'

'Yes, he is - like him.'

'Is that there, then? The summer house?'

'Yes.'

'And what he did to me?'

'To you?'

'To me, yes – while you stood back and watched. Yes, that.'

What could I say to her?

'Debbie... no! It's not like that. You know...'

'I don't see why,' she said. 'Oh God! What if someone recognises us?'

'Look,' I said, 'they won't. This is a story written in disguise - a *roman a clef*?'

'A what?' she asked.

'*Roman à clef* – a real story written up as fiction. Will explained it to me. Everything happened as I've written but just not to you or me or not with me here as a character; at least not in the same order.'

'That's confusing,' she told me.

'Very,' I replied.

Or did she?

Did I? Or is it all just in my head?

'But who am I disguised as then?' she asked. 'And who is Patrick Randle?'

'Well, you're called Frances,' I replied.

'Who?'

'Frances Nolan.'

'Why?'

'Because you... you just have to be, that's all.'

209

'Oh, thanks. And him?'

'Oh he's just nobody,' I told her. 'I've not mentioned him by name. He could be anybody.'

'Sophie, we both know that's not true.'

'Yes, but...'

'No. You're going to have to let me read it,' she demanded. 'I want to read what you've written about me. I demand to. I have a right to see it.'

Reluctantly, I handed her the notebook.

Of course, I knew from the very first time that he came round that 'it' would happen. It was always going to happen. It was inevitable. It was our destiny. Him, and me. And me and him. I knew he'd want me, even though I knew I wasn't pretty, not like she was. But I was clever; he knew that. Why else would he bother? Why else would he give up all his time to tutor me? I knew deep down he must have felt the same way that I felt about him – love, in other words. And love makes everything all right.

'Frances? Oh, Frances!' he would whisper. 'If only you were older.'

And I would sit there hardly breathing, knowing what was about to start happening. The covers of the books were all turned back. His warm breath started pawing at my shoulder. Then his hand started inching, inching up along the inside of my thigh, beneath my skirt. Then my arm was round his shoulder, guiding him, his lips to mine. And then his fingers. I could feel them searching me, between my legs. With his other hand he took my wrist and moved my hand until it rested on the pulsing shaft he was to put inside my body. Him, in me; me, with him inside me: one. The two of us, as one.

And then things started happening so quickly. Unbuttoning his shirt. Unbuckling his trousers. My blouse up above my head. My school skirt like a puddle on the floor. His boxer shorts; my knickers. Socks.

'Take your bra off for me.'

Me fingering the clasp nervously and looking down. My breasts spilling out in front of him. His hand on them. His lips. His kisses on my tummy. And his tongue's soft flicking on my fanny.

  'Are you sure?' he says.

  'I love you.'

  'I love you too.'

  'Yes,' I whisper, and he stands in front of me. I touch him, softly: stroke his chest and run my fingers down his belly.

  He even asks if I'm a virgin.

  'Yes,' I tell him.

  'Me too,' he replies, and takes me in his arms.

***

  'Oh God!' Debbie shouted, sticking out her tongue mock retching.

  'What?' I asked her, jumping up. 'What it is? What's the matter?'

  'This is garbage,' she was saying, crossing out what she'd been reading. 'This is bloody Mills and Boon stuff, this is. I could do much better.'

  'Debbie...'

  'Don't you 'Debbie' me. This is dreadful. And from now on I'm not part of this, ok?'

  'Debbie... no. You've got to let me write about you. Please - I've got to. Don't forget about the plot. You know what we've been planning for him. And it's coming, soon. I'm getting to it. Honest!'

  'And in the meantime I just lie there while he shags me?'

  'In the story...'

  'In the story and...'

  'What?'

  'In reality,' she murmured.

  'I...'

'Try writing that!' she told me.

'But...'

'But NOTHING Sophie. NOTHING.'

'But he's...'

'WHAT?' she shouted. 'WHAT IS HE? A CHARACTER? A WORK OF FICTION? SOMEBODY FROM YOUR IMAGINATION? WELL, I'VE GOT NEWS FOR YOU, SOPHIE. THAT'S EVERYONE: WE ALL ARE; EVERY ONE OF US.' She paused for breath. 'And so are you.'

'But... Debbie, please?'

'No, Sophie. You know nothing. Nothing. You might write this garbage but it's us that has to live it.'

'Debbie, please... don't do this. You write it then. Go on. You write it how you want it.'

She paused and looked straight at me. And I knew then, at that moment, it was true. The whole thing. Everything. And so she started writing...

I knew that this was going to happen, ever since the extra lessons were arranged. And I was curious. I knew he was. I knew he wanted me, even if perhaps he didn't fancy me. I knew it would be like this, that he would try it one day after school and I would let him, I would want him to. I knew there'd be this moment, in this room, with no-one else around. I knew I wouldn't stop him. I knew everything. I am the omniscient narrator. And I also knew that I'd have wanted so much more. It would be warm but there would be a breath of cool air from the open window. His dark form standing by the bed would be like a ghost. I would not be able to see as he climbed in beside me. I wouldn't see what he was doing, what he looked like, what was happening in his eyes or see how big and stiff he had become.

I'd seen a diagram at school. I knew where babies came from and how they were made. What I didn't know, not really know, was what he'd do. I suppose I could have guessed that he would push inside me like he did. I should have guessed that it would hurt. I didn't know he'd push and push, and then pull out and then push in again. I didn't know that I would bleed.

I couldn't scream. I could have done. I could have screamed the walls to rubble. Deep inside my head the noise was almost unbearable. He had said he loved me; told me he respected me. So how come he was hurting me?

For an ordeal, it was over very quickly. No sooner was he in than he had finished. His body had been rigid as he lay on top of me; I could feel his bones and the flesh stretched hard across them like a door. Then, all of a sudden, he went soft; his body flopped on top of me as if he was a big balloon deflating. Just at that moment, and only for a moment, I imagined that he was someone other than my teacher; I imagined that he really was my lover; somebody or other. It didn't really matter. I could imagine slowly winding my arms around his back and holding him; I felt what it would feel like; in my mind, and it felt fine. We'd kiss. He'd stay with me instead of going back to his house and we'd be together in the darkness for the remainder of the night. We would wake up together in the morning. But he rolled off me, left without a word. He climbed out of the bed and vanished.

And next morning it was as if the whole thing hadn't happened. There was no smile in the corridor, no hint of recognition. He ignored me. And I had to talk to him; I had to. And that was when she walked in.

CHAPTER TWENTY-FOUR

'So how's it going?' Will asked, next day in the schoolroom.

'It's not,' I told him. 'Not any more - it's finished.'

'Finished?'

'Not like that: I mean I'm finished. I'm not writing any more. I can't'

'Why not?'

'I don't know,' I said. 'It's no good. No-one will ever want to read it, so it's pointless. Debbie told me...'

'Oh, come on Sophie.'

'But she's right. I'm never going to be an author. Writing's stupid anyway,' I shouted. 'You must be mad to want to be a writer. And anyway, it's rubbish – look at it.' I tossed the book across the desk.

He picked it up and started thumbing through the pages.

'It's so much better in my head than on the page,' I went on. 'In my head it can be perfect. It can be the best piece of writing in the world. But once it's written it's so shallow. There are mistakes. Errors. Things I don't like. Things I want to change. All the time. Words I wish I hadn't used. Others that I wish I had. I read it and I don't see what I meant to write; I see what actually got written.'

'That's always going to happen, Sophie. Nothing's perfect. There will always be something that you wish you hadn't written; there'll be something that you wish you'd written in a different way. There will be words you want to change and passages you want to re-write but be careful - you could revise a piece of work forever.'

'Perhaps I'd better...'

'But then the writing would never be over. The process would be endless. And you'd still be in the middle of the story.'

'Now this is confusing me.'

'You need to finish – properly. You can't simply abandon it.'

'I can,' I said. 'I want to.'

'No you don't,' he told me. 'You're just frightened.'

'No I'm not,' I said.

'You are.'

'What of?'

'The ending,' he replied.

'I didn't want to do this anyway!' I cried. 'But now I'm stuck with it, and if I do go on, and if I do get to the end, then what? What's it going to be like when I've finished? What will I do when I get to the final chapter? When I've written the final word; when there's no more writing to be done, when the last thing gets put down on the paper – what then? It's fine if you're a real author. You have other books to write; more words, and more ideas. I'm not, though: this is not a real book, as you know. So what am I to do when it's all over? Writing this is what I have become? If I finish, what will I be then? Something? Or nothing? If there is no writing, is there anything else at all?'

'Of course there is,' he told me, and he pointed to the book.

Of course there is! There was. And this is it. I have to finish. He was right. If I don't finish then I'll never be a writer and I'll not recover. I have to keep on going till the end: 'keep taking the tablets' as they say. 'Continue taking the prescribed medication and ensure that you complete the course'. It means the same thing. I just want to write it. And

I want to finish it and see it printed, hold it in my hands and see my name along the spine. I want it all to be between the covers, trapped on paper where other people, if they want, can read it. I don't want it to do well or sell or anything; it doesn't have to be the next blockbuster. But I want to see it published, finished, managed. End-of-story: over. Only then can I begin another chapter.

My head was teeming with ideas now: with words, with things I had to hammer down on paper quickly, fingers rattling the heavy metal typewriter my grandfather had given me. I had to do it swiftly too before they flew out of my head forever; things I had to put in black and white and trap like insect specimens before they could escape. I stretched my fingers, stiff for typing. I pushed against the heavy keys: there was resistance, but my thrusting always made them yield. The keys were tense and hard, resisting like a virgin; the mechanism unyielding through lack of use. Only once I'd started did the rhythm of the typing begin flowing. My words gathered their own momentum, tap – tap, tap- tap – tap, tap – tap –tap –tap – tap TAP, until I felt I'd reached a natural conclusion. Then I'd pause for breath and read what I had written.

Slowly other people started to find out what I was doing. The noise alerted them to the things that I was writing. I didn't want that, though. This was supposed to be a secret. I didn't want anyone to know, especially him.

'Still writing that book, are yer Sophie?' he was asking, placing his hand on the back of my chair. I leaned forward, slightly, shielding what I'd written.

'You know, we could still, *you know*...'

I turned. He was taller than I remembered; I could see right up his nose. He mouth was smiling, sort of; the effect, though, wasn't comforting. He was trying, but not succeeding. I turned the platten round to hide what I'd been writing.

'More about me is it?'

'No,' I lied.

'I bet it is!' he said. He bent forward and his breath was hot and sudden in my ear.

'I still fancy you, you know,' he whispered.

I said nothing.

'I could...you, know. I want to. And I've got a massive willy.'

'Yes I know' I said. 'Put it away, Murphy.'

'No'.

'Yes'.

'Won't'.

It was my turn now to try and smile. Where was Debbie when I needed her? Where was the murder weapon? Somehow, in the smallest void between my chair and his stiff body, I managed to push myself back and then to turn a little. He straightened suddenly. I looked up at him.

'I want you.'

'No you don't...' I shouted. 'You want her and she's not here.'

His mood changed, suddenly.

'Yeah, you're right' he said, and turned his head away. 'But you are. You'll do.'

'No I won't,' I said. 'You don't even fancy me. You know you don't. You told me. You don't find me sexy.'

'Don't I?'

'No you don't.'

'Then why have I come back?'

'You tell me?' I said. 'Go on – explain! And if it's any good... well – I might just think about including it.'

'Look, I never said you wasn't sexy,' he was writing. You are sexy – to me you are. I like the ones that no-one else will have. I like them girls whose bodies don't get seen. I want to be the first. I want to watch them get undressed, all shy and glancing up to check I'm looking, taking off their clothes in front of me. I want to be the first to touch them and to see them shiver with excitement, maybe fear. I want to be the one who makes them feel things that they've never felt

217

before – I want to explore their heads at the same time as my hands explore their bodies.

I want them to be thinking, 'what's he up to?' as I'm doing it to them, instead of just feeling what I'm doing. I want them to be thinking 'what's happening to me?' as they're taking what I'm giving, feeling it inside them without shrieking. I want to be inside their heads, you see, as well as in their knickers.

I want to hear the sharp breath that they take as I push hard right inside them, and then while I'm working on them I want them to be wondering – what is he doing? Is this normal? Should I be enjoying what is happening? Should this be what is happening? Is this what always happens? Everywhere? To everyone? And am I one of them now? Am I in? Have I arrived? Am I a member? Is that it, now? What happens next? A celebration? Am I in the club now? Am I a member?

***

I looked down at the latest page and suddenly felt sick. This wasn't the story I had planned on writing. I could feel my head go heavy on my neck and roll as if it might fall off and bounce onto the floor. This was no good. It had to stop. The talking therapy was over. Now was the time for action. The time had come now to fast-forward to the ending. And if Debbie wouldn't be the bait for me then *I* would have to do it. Not this minute, maybe; and not necessarily right here. But somewhere not too far away, not too much later. That's what authors are allowed to do with characters, you see. I knew the plot. I would recover. Yes – and Debbie and I would live together in the country. I could hear the birds sing in the trees and I could feel the warm breeze through the open window. As long as we could be together everything would be all right.

But *he* would find us; he'd come back one day and I would come back home from work and find him sitting at the kitchen table, both hands round a mug of tea. It would be so easy.

'Mr Jones,' I'd say. 'Hi! How are you? I haven't seen you here for a while.'

And he'd say nothing. He would hear, of course, but he'd ignore me. He'd be sitting at the kitchen table holding hands with Debbie. I was under no illusions now. I knew all about him and his tastes. And she was just his sort, just like Louise. So he would come for weekends, maybe. She was just part of the deal: his weekend shag. She was his to use.

But I would have a job by then. I'd get an office job, and I'd be good. Not every eighteen-year-old former psychiatric patient would be able to type as fast and I could, and not just fast – but accurate as well. And I'd have money, too. I would support her. That was fine. It would just be for a little while: just long enough for me to get my own back. Yes, that's it. I'd have a life and I'd be well again and he would come back like a cancer. That's what happened. Just like this. One day I got back home from work and he was there again. Debbie had made *him* a mug of tea. And he was sitting on a chair, leaning back, his long legs stretched out so you had to pick your way around them, making no effort to move out of the way, to let me pass.

'Hiya, Sophie!'

Debbie was sitting up close, leaning forward over the table, holding her mug in both hands, looking at him, listening to him talk, and hanging onto every word he said. Paying him attention.

'Tom's staying over,' she would say, still looking at him.

I would freeze.

'Haven't you got anything to say to him?'

I was standing at the sink, filling the kettle. My hand would tighten round the handle.

'Oh!' I'd say. 'Why's that?' and try to make it sound a friendly, innocent enquiry. I'd try to make it sound as if I cared. I'd try to write it so it was convincing, so they heard a simple, innocent and airy enquiry. I would make it sound so normal. But it wasn't. It wouldn't be convincing to the readers who had stuck with me. They would know it sounded just like me.

'Sophie's working at the council now Tom, aren't you Sophie?' She went on, ignoring my question. Why should she bother answering? She could do what she wanted; have round whomsoever she chose; say what she wanted to them; listen to them and nobody else: listen only to what she chose to hear. She didn't need an answer from me anymore, that was certain.

'Yeah, Tom. Filing. Moving bits of paper; putting 'em in folders.'

I could feel a slight lump swelling at the back of my throat. Don't cry. Don't CRY! Not here. Not now. Not in front of him.

'Tom's still at the High School you know, Sophie. And he's been promoted!' Debbie said.

I closed my eyes.

'Not mad then anymore?' he asked me.

She laughed. I didn't. I said nothing. Inside, my stomach churned and my body raged. As I plugged the kettle in I noticed that my hand was shaking. I could throw it at them both. I could rip it from the wall and hurl it at them. No. Maybe not. Best to boil it first, I thought.

'I'm… I'm just going upstairs to get changed' I said.

'Well don't be long. Tea'll be ready in ten minutes. You still like sausages Tom, don't you?'

I went to my room and sat down on the bed. It couldn't happen. I couldn't let it. But what could I do? Things were going so well at last. My job, my new life, and my boyfriend. Yes, I had a boyfriend then.

So I decided that I had to act. If he was sleeping over then I would seduce him. Easily. I wouldn't need to, anyway. He'd want me, just as he had said when he'd come talking to me in the classroom. Not because he fancied me. He'd made that clear. But he would come into my room because he could, because he wanted to get inside my head, as well as in my bed. He'd stand and stare down at me as I lay sleeping. Then he'd wake me.

'Shift over,' he would say.

And I'd make room for him. Then would come, his clammy hands against my thighs, beginning just above the knees. He wouldn't kiss me. No. He would just mount me like an animal. And here he was on top of me again, his grunting face stuffed in my pillow. He would never even look at me. As far as he was concerned, I was just an object; I existed solely for his pleasure. Nothing I could do to him provoked any kind of reaction. I tried. I sometimes squeezed my pelvic floor hard just to see what he would do. I held him close to me while he was there on top to see what it might feel like. He did nothing, ever; never spoke to me or held me; never told me that he loved me. He did nothing. Until now, that is. Until the knife I found was sliding in-between his ribs and going deeper into him, through layers of skin and then through muscle and right into tissue. God knows what he felt then. Something. At last, he was feeling something for me. I had to make him feel it; I had to teach this man a lesson.

He stopped moving in and out and made a kind of hissing noise, as if he was deflating, as if I'd punctured him and he was just a big balloon and once the air was let out of his lungs he would just stop working like an empty blow-up toy.

'But where did you hide the knife?' the readers would be asking.

Weren't you concentrating? Weren't you listening? I gave you all the clues! I stretched my arm as high as I could manage, and then I brought it down hard into his back. At the same time he seemed briefly to rise up, pushing hard against the mattress as he strained hard to abuse me. And this allowed the knife to slide inside his body, in-between his ribs, like it was sliding into butter. It was so much easier than I'd anticipated; so easy that at first I thought I must have missed. Then, suddenly, he collapsed on top of me. There was a low groan from somewhere deep inside him; it didn't sound like his voice, or like any voice. It was just a sound, as if he were deflating. I felt the warm and sticky blood spread around the knife and in-between my fingers. And I screamed, loud: screamed for the first time, screamed for all the times and everyone, and for the first time I had ever seen it written down. Rousseau said one page of *Justine* and a girl was lost forever. He taught me the whole book.

CHAPTER TWENTY-FIVE

Setting is important in a piece of writing. Get the back-drop right. It sets the mood, and it determines action. It's like another character. And so far in this book that character has been the hospital: the psychiatric hospital, dark and brooding, hidden in the forest like a fairy-story dungeon. We all lived our lives as patients in its shadow: we were on the edge, but it was always there. Through my eyes it was alive. It made a noise you couldn't hear. It spoke. The windows were all eyes. It was watching. It was a monster. It controlled us all. We'd never leave, it said. We were here forever just like everyone else. No-one will recover; no-one ever gets away. But it was wrong.

'I think we should escape somewhere,' said Will one morning in the community meeting. Spring was slowly giving way to early summer; birds were singing and the evenings were light and fragrant with tree pollen. Flowers opened in the beds tended slowly by the patients while their nurses stood around and smoked and made sure nobody escaped.

'How can we afford a week away?' Ted asked, scornfully.

'We don't need to,' Will replied. 'I know someone; there's a cottage in the Dales. We can use it for a week in June. We can have it rent-free.'

'What does everybody else think?' Patrick asked quickly, before Ted could think of anything else to say.

'Great idea,' said Lizzie. There was a murmur of agreement from around the room, excitement even.

'Well... I propose that we look into it,' said Ted.

'Done that already,' interrupted Will. 'If we want to go it's ours.'

'I mean from the hospital perspective,' Ted went on. 'We'll need to check with them that it's ok. That is, if no-one here as any objections?'

He looked around the room, hopefully.

No-one spoke. Dr Grimshaw sat and smiled benevolently, as he always did on everything that went on in the community meetings. And Jane seemed as interested in Will's idea as we were.

'It's a chance to get away from our day to day routine here, I suppose. It could be interesting. We can see what everybody's like in a different place' she said.

'Change the setting?' I suggested.

'Yes, I suppose so; change the setting,' she repeated.

Ted was silent now, no doubt planning some petty act of revenge on Jane.

'I like it here,' said Debbie suddenly.

'What?' The whole room looked at her.

'I said I like it here.'

'I know... but.'

The dull wallpaper on the wall above her head had started peeling. Little holes appeared where people sat and scratched the white cocoons and released the little larvae wood-chips from the paint and paper.

'I don't want to go away.'

'Aw, Debbie. Come with me. Please. We can't go there without you.'

She was silent. She was going to go. We all knew that. When community decisions had been taken, everyone abided by them. It was all part of the therapy. Democracy;

responsibility; community. Decisions were always made by the whole community. But the nurses still set the agenda.

'But there'll still be a cost,' said Ted, sulking.

'Of course – but we can do things to raise some money,' Will countered.

'I know...' said somebody. 'Let's organise a disco!'

'Jason...' someone shouted out sarcastically.

'No Sophie,' Will held his hand up in the air. 'I think that's quite a good idea.' I turned my head away.

'We can invite our friends... and family,' continued Jason seriously.

I suddenly had a vivid image of my mother, standing in the corner in her hat and coat while coloured lights flashed on and off and music thumped out from loudspeakers. 'What's the point of this?' I could imagine her complaining 'you can't even hear the words.' And I was smiling.

'See. Even Sophie thinks it's gonna be a fun thing,' Jason said, triumphantly.

Memory is a strange thing; you think that you're remembering, but really you're creating - re-creating, making something happen that didn't really happen or at least which didn't happen in the way that you remember. How do you make sure that it's accurate? You can't. And yet it's so important. Everything we are is memory. Everything that we remember makes us who we are. And there are things we'd rather not remember; other things we can't recall.

So how come I remember everything? Even all the small things people said. The words they used, the sentences, the rhythms of their speech? The words are the things that I remember most - most clearly. Naturally. It's only when we learn to speak that we even start remembering and understanding; knowing. Before words there is nothing: no memory, no thinking. Think about it. When you think, you think with words. Without words therefore, there can be no thought. Just feeling. Even faces can sometimes be a little hazy sometimes in my memory. Sometimes I can't even quite remember what Debbie looked like; what she really looked like - little details like her ears, the way her hair was gently wavy. But I know exactly what I was feeling on the night of the disco: I remember perfectly. How could I forget that night? How could I possibly forget what happened?

One week after it had all been democratically decided, preparations for the disco were in progress. At the far end of the day room, bits of kit were being put together. Plywood boxes painted black were being clipped around enormous sets of loudspeakers. Somehow coloured lights had been embedded in the structure, and behind the barricade two record turntables were being tested.

'Hey Sophie, this is great!' Debbie shouted in my ear. The music hadn't even started playing yet, but somebody was booming 'one, two,' into a microphone.

I walked back out again and went into the breakfast room. Ted and Jane were standing talking in the corner. Well, Jane was standing in the corner; Ted was leaning over her with one arm on the wall.

Then the music suddenly exploded. A raucously catarrhal shout of 'BABY BABY BAB-EEE' followed by a three solemnly plucked notes on the guitar indicated that the disco had begun. Then the drum and bass joined in like someone stamping up the stairs. Lights flashed. Noise vibrated deep inside my ribcage. I fled into the kitchen.

Ted's wife was standing by the cooker, on her own. She was small and thin with tight black curls sitting on a tiny head like an enormous hat. She was holding a glass of wine and smiling, but at no-one in particular. Nobody was talking to her. Nobody was even looking at her, except for me. But she was smiling anyway.

'Hello.'

'Oh, hi love. Hi!' she said, and smiled again, then looked away.

I stood there, trying to think of something I could say. But everything I thought of had to do with Jane and Ted. And when I looked again she wasn't smiling anymore.

I picked some food up, put it on a paper plate and I walked out. Debbie was there in the hallway, looking at me, desperate to tell me something.

'What's going on?' I asked her.

'It's him,' she said. 'He fancies her.'

'Who?' I asked.

'Ted of course,' she hissed.

I put my finger to my lips, but nobody could hear above the noise.

'Who does he fancy?'

'Jane,' she said.

'He doesn't.'

'Yes he does. Haven't you noticed how much time they spend together?'

'Well, yes I have...but..'

'And the way he looks at her?'

'He's married!' I protested.

'Call yourself a writer!' This is the biggest story ever. His wife's here, she'll see them together and there'll be a huge row. Make sure you get that put down on paper.'

'But...'

'No buts,' she went on. 'You just look at 'em. Look at them in there, now: they're dancing. Look at them together. Look at the way they're looking at each other.'

I peered through the door. They were dancing, just as Debbie said, and in the middle of the room. Ted's arms were round her waist and hers were up around his neck and they were swaying from one side to the other. He was smiling down at her.

'She doesn't fancy him though,' I protested. 'Surely?'

'Why not?'

'Well he's old,' I said. He's...arrogant...he's...he's...'

'...in charge,' Debbie continued. 'Some girls like that, don't they Sophie?' and she winked at me. 'They like it when the boss pays them attention.'

'But he's bald!' I shouted.

'Makes no odds,' she said.

227

'I don't believe it.'

'Don't want to, more like.'

'No... I can't.'

'It's obvious...'

'It might be but I still can't quite believe it's true. I never thought that Rochester deserved her.'

'But she's not Jane Eyre; she's more like Becky Sharpe.'

'I know. But I still don't know what she sees in him,' I said.

Then suddenly, from nowhere, he was looming up behind her. I tried to stop her going any further, tried to tell her with my eyes that he was there behind her. Suddenly she stopped, but it was too late.

The way her eyes switched from excitement to panic in an instant, as if somebody had flicked a switch, is what I remember most about her. The sudden wave of panic that seemed to ripple through her body. Ted could be quite frightening. He was large and liked to use his size to reinforce his status. When he spoke he came so close that you could feel the moist warmth of his breath, and smell his awful *Tabac* aftershave. Only when he had fixed you with his eyes and when he came so close to you you couldn't move, only then did he feel totally in control and almost sexually excited. He didn't need to be that close. But he liked being that close, because he liked being boss. He liked Jane because he was her boss. She did the things he said. He liked that. And when she didn't, he resolved to get her back in some small way, like changing shifts without much notice, just to even up the score - which of course was always in his favour. If Debbie thought he'd heard her she might be embarrassed or afraid of what he might say, perhaps, in a way you might be if you don't want somebody to know something about you.

'That isn't it, though – is it?'

'No,' she said.

'What, then?'

'It's power! That's what it's all about. It's not about sex. It's what you can do. It's just control.'

'No it isn't – I don't think so.'

'Yes, you do. That's why you made Murphy fancy me.'

'I didn't. That was just part of the story. Debbie, please.'

'And you…'

'Me?'

'You don't love me.'

'Debbs, I do. I really do.'

'No you don't,' she told me. 'You just needed me to draw him in, to get back at him. You couldn't stand the fact he'd got away with it – even got promoted. You couldn't stand the thought that they'd all hung you out to dry. You had to get your own back. And you needed somebody like me to help you, didn't you? After all, you were never going to get him on your own, now were you?'

'Debbs, that's…'

'What? Not true? Don't lie to me, Sophie. I know this plot as well as you. And now it's over you don't need me any longer – do you?'

I laughed. But it was suddenly no longer funny. Without really noticing, it had come true. Since the murder, we had hardly spoken. I'd been busy writing. She'd – I don't know what she had been doing.

'Come upstairs with me?' I asked her, 'please, for one last time?'

With her it had always fitted into place. It was easy. It had never been easy before. It happened, obviously; that's the story. But I wished it hadn't, yet I wanted more and when I did I then regretted it.

Regretted it?

Regretted it. And needed to erase it. Wash it off and wash my clothes and start again. With her, that simply didn't happen. If I wanted more I got it; there was nothing to regret. She took my hand. I can remember that so clearly– the feel of it: so warm and trusting, like a child. We climbed the stairs. She moved instinctively towards the bathroom. 'No,' I whispered, and I led her to the bedroom. Beneath the floor the music thumped so loudly we could feel it through the mattress. Occasionally shouts and calls would rise above the booming noise like startled birds. We didn't put the light on. We just lay there for a moment in the darkness. I remember thinking, as I started to undress her, that this would be the last time it would be like this. Things had changed. And yet I couldn't see her in the darkness. She was just a shadow. So I closed my eyes and tried to see her there. But inside my head was dark. There were no images. The metaphors I used were all connected with the other senses. What she smelt like; what her skin was like beneath my fingers, on the moist palms of my hand – that's what I remember. The sound her breathing made; the whisper of her breath against me like a feather. And her flavour: the slightly salty flavour of her body as I licked her, quickly, like an ice-cream that was melting in front of me. I felt the fine hairs on her body rising and the muscles tensing. There was nothing, for a moment. Then she came. And I remembered everything.

CHAPTER TWENTY-SIX

Monday June 15th 1981

Up in the early morning, having lain awake for over an hour trying to get back to sleep to no avail. Part of the reason was the fact that I was thinking about the book. It just seemed to be the thing to do while I was lying in the darkness. I sorted several things out, in my head: like the narration, which now seems so obviously to be first-person. It makes so much else about the book much more convincing: the depression, the confusion, the novel as *Bildungsroman*. It seemed something of an epiphany an hour ago at 4am, as did the plan to include some extracts from my diary (like this one). We'll have to wait and see how it goes. Intend to have a go right now, but thought I'd set it all down here before I started to forget. Half and hour later and it doesn't seem so good. But at least I've thought of something else: a novel on the novel-writing process; a novel just like this one; one with all the trials and tribulations of book-writing, based - in other words - on this diary. At 5.12am this sounds promising. No chance to write it down today, though. We're up early, setting off for our week-long holiday. On the motorway we passed through an enormous city. Houses everywhere, and washing on the lines and things stuck to the upstairs windows. Each one was a life, and there were so many of them; there were too many of them. It was frightening. Then we left it all behind. The bus climbed into countryside. The moors were as empty as the sea.

***

Well, we're here at last. Got lost on the way, thanks to Lizzie's navigation. As she's thinnest she had to squeeze in on the double front-seat next to Monica while Will was driving; that was fine, but asking her to read a map wasn't one of Monica's better plans. Ted and Jane were already here when we arrived (they'd come in Ted's car). We unpacked the mini-bus and took our stuff up to our rooms. Debbie and I are in a bunk together; everyone else gets beds.

Tuesday June 16th

Ted and the hostel warden have already had a row. Mr Marron (he's the warden) told Ted he couldn't have us cooking breakfast (like we do back at the unit). He said the staff would have to do it, except he didn't use the word 'staff' – he said 'you' and Ted thought that meant him and he said 'I'm not doing that, I'm in charge you know,' and Mr Marron said 'Not here you're not!' and Ted walked out. Jane cooked us eggs and bacon. Said we'd need it for what we were going to be doing.

Halfway up the hill I knew what she had meant. We set off early, so that Lizzie didn't have her after meal-time supervision and – you've guessed it – half way up the mountain it came back: the eggs and bacon, sausages, the fried bread, everything she'd eaten. Not a pretty sight. After that we struggled to the summit. When we got there, however, Debbie started feeling ill as well.

'Just look at all this!' Will said as we stood at the top and looked at the view. It was ok, I suppose. Most of us were sitting trying desperately to get our breath back after hiking up the final few feet, but we looked up anyway. It was worth it. You could see for miles. This high up the countryside seemed smooth and bare - like a newly shorn lamb. There were no trees to speak of other than small clumps clinging to the hillsides like a group of frightened ladies. It was all so... empty. And that was the problem. Debbie started feeling sick.

'There's too much...' she began.

'There's too much what?' I asked.

'Too much... everything,' she said and held her hands up to her face.

'The space is pushing in on me.'

Her voice was quaking. She was crying.

'I want to go back,' she moaned.

'Go back? Where?' Jane sat down and put an arm around her.

'Back to the hospital,' she cried.

Debbie spent the remainder of the journey peeping from behind her hands. She inched down the hill towards the minibus with her eyes fixed on the floor.

'What was that about?' I said to Will.

'She'll be ok,' he was saying. 'The hospital's become familiar to her, that's all. She's happy there; not happy, but secure. She knows the lanes and trees. She likes the light, or lack of it: being hidden by the trees is good for her, it makes her safe. Here, where the world goes on forever, it is all too big. She feels the hills press in on her from all directions. The emptiness is threatening.'

I didn't really understand what he was saying.

'So, she'll never come and live with me in my dream cottage in the country?'

'No,' he told me.

'But she can't stay in the hospital,' I said.

'You're right: she can't,' he added. 'Hospitals like ours won't be around much longer. They're closing some of them already.'

'Where will everybody go?' I asked.

'Good question, Sophie.'

When we got back to the hostel Ted decided there should be a room inspection: Will for the boys and Monica for the girls, while he discussed some plans he'd got with Jane. Monica didn't seem too enthusiastic, really.

Wednesday 17th

The sunshine here seems different to at home. I mean the hospital. I don't mean home, or do I? I don't know where home is anymore. I can't imagine going back to live at home. The hospital is now my home. These people are my friends. But one day – soon – I'm going to have to leave. It won't be here forever, that's what Will said. I believe him, too. The empty corridors and walls; the gardens overgrown. There aren't the patients anymore to keep the weeds down. I wouldn't want to live there, anyway. Not that I'm ready yet to leave it. Little things keep happening, like thinking – on the loos – of all the people whose bare bums have touched the seat. What were they like? And were they clean? To make sure, I put loads of paper down.

We went into the local town today to do some shopping. Debbie bought her mum something. Patrick and the others talked of going to the pub but Ted made sure they didn't. I bought a new black ribbon for my typewriter.

Thursday 18th

It rained today. We stayed in all morning, it was that bad. There are some books – mainly walking books, although I found one novel by a vet describing treating animals on Yorkshire farms. I read it. It was good. I'd like to be a vet, except for all the dirt. At least it's only animals, though – that's different, somehow. I'd like to live with animals. I'd like to live his life, and write his books: a gentle, country life; a life of church and dog-walks, gentle country-type pursuits; respectable. I'd like to be retired now and potter, pruning roses or else making jam. I don't want to have to do the life that gets you there; I want to go there straight away. The problem is my 'secret' life: the one where I'm in a writer and I write about what's brought me to the brink of suicide. I write about the book we read together. Things like

234

that don't happen in the vet books. Maybe there are two worlds. Maybe I'm the only person with one foot in each of them. So my life is spent in a constant state of schizophrenia, only without the treatment or the voices. There are voices. But they're all my voices, voice: the voice from one world telling me I've sold my soul, that there is no way back to nice things anymore; the other urging me to go on, go forward, keep it up, keep going, whistling the dog and watching wildlife. I suppose that makes me quite a complicated person. I suppose so. But it doesn't seem complicated living like that: just awkward and confusing. Tense and fucking painful.

After lunch we drove to the local cinema. I sat next to Debbie. She indulged me. In the darkness no-one noticed we were holding hands. The fact that no-one noticed, nobody even suspected gave me such a wonderful feeling inside. I'm not sure that I love her anymore – not like I used to do. She doesn't love me – she never loved me anyway, not in the way that I loved her. But she could still do... you know, with me. Like she does with him. I suppose I didn't know that you could do that. I thought that love should always be involved. I thought he loved me, but he didn't. And he didn't even love her, either. We were there, that's all, in our school uniforms. And he was lonely. The film was rotten, anyway: Grease. I don't fancy John Travolta and I hate Olivia Newton-John. You're not the one that I want. I don't want anyone. I just want to be alone.

Friday 19th

Looking out for the last time at the view from our dorm window. There is nothing here: the hills are empty, and the slopes bare; there are hardly any trees and no houses. Sheep across the fell as look as small and still as stones. And the sounds. The noise: birds panicking above, or calling like alarms across the valley; the wind whining over empty fields. It's like being in the middle of the ocean. It's not the countryside I want to spend my life in. It's too hard, like the people. Their voices are cold and grey just like the stone. This afternoon we're leaving and I won't be sorry.

***

On our last day there we all got soaked: thoroughly soaked, soaked through to our skin. Ted – who hadn't really said much all week – decided we should go for one last walk. At about the halfway point it rained. It appeared on the horizon like a dark grey sail, billowed by a fierce wind that had blown up out of nowhere. There was no shelter on the hills. How could there be? We were far out on the sea and being washed by waves of rain. There was no escape. We turned and headed back, but the rain caught up with us before we were even within sight of the hostel. Some of the boys pretended they enjoyed it, taking off their coats and standing with their arms outstretched and faces turned towards the leaden sky. The girls hunched down their shoulders, looked straight at the ground and hurried on.

'Come on you two!' Ted bellowed at the stragglers. Patrick and Jason bounded past us all like a pair of dogs, racing to the mini-bus. Our clothes had all been packed, so we sat and steamed on the journey back. Within a day or two of getting back I'd fallen ill.

***

When you're depressed, you stay depressed. Even when you're ill, you're still depressed. You're ill anyway, of course: depression is an illness. Not like any other illness. Not like a physical disease. It's worse. But when you're ill, you're ill. You. Ill. There is something that the illness is attacking. When you're depressed though, then you *are* depression. There is nothing but depression. That is what you are, forever -depression, desperation, nothing more.

I'd been ill before since coming to hospital and I hardly noticed. This time though I noticed what was happening. I got bored, for one thing. Then on Wednesday morning Jane brought a radio from home. She sat on the end of the bed, smiling, her long dark hair cascading down her shoulders: straight until it reached her neck, then curling broadly like the legs of some antique table. She asked me how I was. She told me how long it would take before I felt ok again. And then she reached down to the floor and lifted up a radio, like someone magicking a rabbit from a hat. I smiled weakly, and she put it on my bedside table.

'You might just feel like listening to something later on,' she said, and closed the door and went downstairs. I fell asleep. But in the afternoon I turned it on.

There was a phone-in: the subject for discussion, teenage problems.

'Our next caller on line one is a girl called Louise, I think. Is that right? Hello Louise.'

'Hello,' said a voice I once knew.

'You're seventeen, I understand?'

'Yes, I am.'

'And what is it you'd like to ask?'

I'd like to ask if... how... why... why would anybody want to hurt themselves? I mean... it's so... I don't know.... it's unnatural...'

'I know what you mean,' A man's voice.

'This is self-harm is it?' asked the woman.

'Yes - it seems destructive. It's the opposite of other instincts. We're all naturally geared up to avoid pain in order to preserve our lives and protect our health. So doing the opposite: deliberately inflicting pain is quite unusual, you're quite right.'

'Am I right in saying it's quite common?' The woman's voice, again.

'Oh yes, and understandable. Sometimes teenage lives might seem completely out of our control. Even if everything else is beyond us, this is something we can do, that we're in charge of – it's a way of taking back control of our own lives.'

'Really?'

'Oh yes: and it can be useful for relieving tension, too. It can be cathartic. In a sense it could be very useful.'

'You're not suggesting this is normal behaviour though, I take it?'

'No, of course not – but understandable; and...well, maybe a normal reaction to an abnormal set of circumstances – some trauma, for example.'

'But it sometimes goes too far?'

'Of course it *can*,' the man went on. 'It can lead to thoughts of self-destruction; it can be linked to guilt and shame. But even then, it's a sign of a desire to wrest control of one's own life back from whatever trauma or misfortune has befallen you. You know, we all do something similar, if we're honest. Any reckless, self-destructive act – hitting the bottle, drugs, affairs, you name it. It's more common than you'd think.'

'But Louise... are you still there?'

'Yes.'

'What makes you want to do that to yourself?' the woman asked.

'I...I can't say,' said the voice. 'I thought he loved me.'

'Who? Is he your boyfriend?' asked the woman.

'In a way,' she said. 'He was. But now he's gone.'

'I'm sorry to hear that. Thank-you for 'phoning, Louise. And on to our next caller please...'

***

'What you listening to?' asked Debbie, cheerfully.

'Oh nothing,' I replied.

'Feeling better?'

'Yes,' I said. 'I am.'

'What you doing now?' she asked, but she could see me, sitting up in bed with a pencil in my hand and paper resting on my knee.

238

'I'm writing.' Stupid.

'Oh!' she said, choosing as always to ignore the irritation in my voice.

'What for?'

'Because I want to. No. Because I have to.'

'Have to?'

'Yes. I have to.'

'Why?'

Good question. Why. Because it's all I can do? Because it's all I want to do? No. It's more than that: I have to write down what has happened. And I have to write down what is going to happen, what I want to happen. I could write down what I wanted. Anything I wanted. I would write it, write my future. On my own.

'I need to write, that's all,' I told her. 'I need to put it down to make some sense of all that's happened, but that's not all I need to do. I need to write; just write: write words. Put them down on paper, one after the other, one by one and add them all together.'

She smiled. Oh God, she smiled and something stirred inside, warm and in the place where everything was always cold. I put the pencil down and held my hand for her to hold. She took it and fell down against my breast and lay there, her warm head through the bed sheets. Long after she had gone downstairs I could feel her head against my breast.

When I woke up it was dark; Debbie was in bed. I didn't know the time, but it was after lights out. I lay there for what seemed like ages. Eventually, the hospital clock chimed midnight. I got up. I went across the landing to the night office.

The door was open. I walked in. The light was on. Ted was sitting at the desk in the corner by the wall. Jane was perching on the corner of the desk. He was leaning forward. As I walked in, he suddenly leaned back in the chair and looked at me.

'Most people knock, Sophie.'

Jane just smiled, and moved away.

'What do you want?'

'I...' I didn't know.

She didn't seem to mind.

'Can't you sleep?'

'I... I'm worried.'

'What about, love?'

Ted had turned back to some papers on the desk. I looked at him, then looked at Jane.

She learnt forward. She almost whispered in his ear. He got up and left the room.

'Sit down Sophie,' Jane invited.

There was only one chair in the night office. It was warm from Ted. My night-dress seemed too thin. The heat against my skin was an intrusion, then just a distraction.

'What's on your mind?' she asked, and smiled, leaning towards me slightly. I looked down at the floor. I tried to think of something. There was nothing in my head though, really: nothing ordinary, like an exam next morning or the dentist or the cane or something. Everything was wrong. Or was it? I wasn't sure.

'Jane?' I said. She seemed to know I wanted to ask her a question.

'Jane... I'm worried. Things are changing.... Louise Anderson - you know...on the radio...' She smiled again, and looked at me.

'I didn't know...' I started.

'No,' she said. 'How could you?' And her eyes were dark and kind; her face was open and expressive. I could say anything I wanted, ask her any question: her expression would remain the same. It would. It was that kind of face. And so I told her what was on my mind, what I'd just thought of. I told her all about us, and the Summer House. I told her all about the writing I was doing, all about my mixed-up feelings and about the girl at school I thought I hated. Finally I took a deep breath and I told her all about the ending I was planning. She looked down briefly and the smile slipped for a moment, then she looked at me again and there was just the faintest hint of sadness.

CHAPTER TWENTY-SEVEN

Chapter twenty-seven already - wow! That's an awful lot of words, that is - a lot of writing: all of it by me; it's all my own, my work. Where will it lead? When will it end? I'm round the bend. I'm mad with words. It's an addiction now. I can't help writing. I sit here and the words pour out of me like pure clear water, cascading down the page in raging torrents, forcing their way into the story somehow, forging their own plots heedless of anything that I might be trying. They take me with them, washing me along in the torrent by a massive current; losing all control and all direction.

'But you can't lose all direction.'

'Yes I can,' I told him.

'You're the author. You are in control. You're supposed to know what's happening.'

'But I can't know everything.'

'No?'

'No, of course not. No-one can know *everything*.'

'No, but you're supposed to know what's happening and you've got to tell us, Sophie.'

'Tell you what?' I said.

'Tell us what we want to know,' he told me. 'What we want to know is what is going to happen to Jane and Ted, for instance. And to Will: maybe there's a party when he leaves? Maybe that's when Ted and Jane are discovered. Or maybe she goes off Ted, gets another job, and leaves the hospital? Tell us, Sophie. Tell us everything. Tell us everything that happened.'

I sat down on a plastic chair and thought about it. The others were all playing in the garden, in the sun; Debbie on the swing, Lizzie making daisy chains and Jason kicking a frayed green tennis ball at Patrick. It was like a family: four kids, the adults, all doing things that ordinary families might do. I stared out of the window, looking at the trees now in full leaf, the fresh green now out of the bud like new-born lambs before the summer sun would burn them. There were birds inside the trees too, hiding. There were nests, and eggs and maybe chicks, and parents coming, going, feeding, flying. Everything was happening, except in here. Inside the classroom, in my head, I thought about the possibilities. I imagined all the things that might still happen. I was sure now I could write them, all of them. But which ones should I choose? Which drawing up of all the loose threads, which grand plan?

'I can't decide,' I told him. 'I just don't know what to do with everyone.'

'You've got to,' he insisted. 'You have to make a choice. Indecision is a decision too, you know. Not deciding is deciding not to; nothing's going to keep you where you are today, now, at this moment. Things change, whatever you decide. You change, too. So do something. There are no right or wrong decisions: just decisions. You make them, and you take a chance on them and then move on. Whatever you decide will be the right decision. It's not a black and white or right or wrong thing. It just 'is', that's all - it happens. And it's all of us it happens to.'

'But how am I know what happens to them all? They're not just my creations. They can think; they make their own decisions. And I can't tell you what they do before they know themselves, can I? Can I? How can I know what these characters will do next? How can anybody know? Does anybody know? Do you know? Do you know what's going to happen before it happens? Does anybody know what's going to happen in the future? Could anybody know?'

'Of course not, Sophie.'

'So, I'm at their mercy. I have to go where the characters take me.'

'But if somebody knew everything about them, every detail of their history, their personality, their hopes and fears, ambitions, likes and dislikes wouldn't they be able to predict what they would do? If they knew everything about us, wouldn't they even have a good idea what we were thinking? Wouldn't they even know before us what we were about to say?'

'Well… no. I don't think that they could…I'm not sure I know that about myself...Not all the time.'

'Of course, there would always be surprises. That's what life's about. But we know when someone's acting out of character; we all recognize when their behaviour is unusual. We know because we know them, we predict them; we decide what's going to happen to them.'

'Do we?'

'Yes, we do. We know what Ted's like for example – he's controlling and aggressive; predatory, even. But that must hide an insecurity.'

'You think so?'

'Yes, he can't be happy. And then Jane...'

'I know about Jane,' I interrupted.

'Do you?' he was saying.

'Well, I like her. And I know that she's worth better.'

'What of Monica?' he asked me.

'Well, I think that Monica is jealous. She feels left out.'

'Good – and Debbie?'

'Debbie's so much more now than she was. She doesn't self-harm any more.'

'And you?'

'And I don't love her.'

'No?'

'No. Not any more. I thought I did. I did. I thought a lot of things.'

'Like?'

'Like I thought that I loved him. I thought he loved me. I thought you had to be in love and if you were, then everything would be ok.'

'Ok,' he said. 'That's very good. We're getting somewhere. Now you need to carry on.'

'But how?' I asked. 'What do I do?'

'You see where what you know will take you. Now you know all this you've got to write the action it entails.'

'How can I do that, though? It's all too late; it's all already happened.'

'It's never too late to become the person that you might have been...'

'I know, I know - George Eliot. But if we all know everything then there's no point reading, is there?' It wouldn't be a change or a surprise. I mean, it would. But then again it wouldn't. Because we wouldn't learn anything new from it.'

'Exactly. And we have to. We all need to know what happens to us and it's you that has to tell us. You're in charge. You are the writer. Write the story. Write what happens. It's up to you what happens. It's up to you what we all do. We're in your hands.'

'You're not,' I said. 'You're in my head.'

'Ok, then in your head. But make it happen, Sophie. Make us move and live.'

But then the unexpected happened. At that moment Ted burst in.

'I'd like a word please Student Nurse,' he said to Will. He stood with the door open, waiting. As he stepped into the corridor Will turned and looked at me.

'Go on,' he said. 'Get writing.'

Ted growled something and then shut the door. Behind the frosted glass I could see movement, moving forwards, fingers pointing, arms gesticulating. And every now and then I could hear voices, too: raised voices. Shards of angry sentences cut through the air; odd phrases came into my mind like things you might catch when you're tuning in a radio.

'Just look, look at this bit here...' Ted shouted.

'And then this!' He started reading. *Ted's long arms were wrapped around her waist. Hers were up around his neck and they were gently swaying to the rhythm of the music. He was smiling down at her and she was looking up at him.*

'The disco – yes that's right, don't you remember?' Will chipped in.

'And then there's this bit,' Ted continued, jabbing at the paper: *But he's bald! said Sophie. Makes no odds, said Debbie. I don't believe it, Sophie went on. You don't want to do you mean, Debbie responded. But I don't know what she sees in him, she said.*

'But that's true Ted, isn't it? That happened.' Will insisted. 'You were dancing with her and, well... we all saw you.'

'And if my wife sees this?' Ted hissed. And briefly it went silent. Then there was a huge explosion.

***

Ted was back in charge now. He'd found out precisely what was going on and he set out to put a stop to it. He objected to my narrative perspective, probably because it wasn't his and he blamed Will because it had been his idea. He said we couldn't carry on - the therapy had not been verified, whatever that might mean. And I knew that he was watching me. It would now not be long before Ted decided that he had to exercise his editorial authority. He had never liked the idea of me writing. But until the next case conference it was still part of my therapy. And anyway, we were nearly at the end. But Will and I were now on borrowed time. How long had I got left? And could I finish it?

'The thing is... he comes in here still wet behind the ears with all this college stuff and starts to interfere...'

And Monica nodded. Ted was sitting at his desk in the nurses' office, reclining in the swivel chair while Monica crouched beside the filing-cabinet, filleting the sheaves of paper balanced on her knee and feeding them into the drawers. The desk was a mess; there was a teetering pile of patients' folders all wrapped in the same brown cardboard covers. There were small, haphazard slips of different coloured paper pressed between the pages like wild-flowers.

'He thinks that he knows better than we do, Monica. How long have you and I been doing this?'

'Oh, too many years for me to trouble to remember.' She was smiling at him as she filed the timesheets on the desk.

'Will you be wanting any of this paperwork completing, Ted?'

The vacancy was influencing her as well. The new post. The promotion. She wanted it. And everybody knew Ted wanted Jane. But Monica had her ways.

'Oh, thanks, Monica. Where would I be without you, eh?' he laughed.

'Oh I don't know, Ted. You're fine. But you're right, you know about these young things coming in and taking over. And Will's not the only one.'

Ted's face changed; the smile on his face dropped like a plate and shattered on the floor. No hiding it. It did. But he hoped Monica hadn't noticed.

'Oh yes Ted,' she went on 'it's true. Experience is what counts. Experience of dealing with the kids and knowing what they're like. You can't teach anyone experience.'

'Er, no you can't.'

Ted was looking down now at the desk. He picked up a handful of the folders and then put them down again. He

247

wanted this to end; he wanted the conversation to come to a natural conclusion. What he wanted was for me to stop the writing. But I wasn't going to.

'Take Rebecca-Jane for instance.'

Rebecca-Jane. Was that her real name?

'Now look...' Ted started.

'She's only been here for a wee while, and she's already thinking of applying for the staff-nurse post. Now let me tell you....'

'I'm afraid...'

'I've been here for fifteen years you know, and if anyone...'

'I don't think we should be discussing this, Monica. It would be improper.'

'You're right, of course Ted. Ted – of course you are. Why, it's your decision, after all.'

'Well it's not just down to me, he stuttered, flattered. He would like it to be though, really. 'There's the Senior Nursing officer you know. And the Health Authority.'

'I know, I know,' she said. 'But we all know that it's *you* they'll want to speak to. You're the one in charge here, after all.'

'I know, but...'

'Ok, ok Ted. I'll be quiet. But we know, you and I, Ted – don't we?'

'Er...' Ted gave a nervous laugh.

'Put down those files a minute Monica,' he continued. 'I want to talk to you about this writing Sophie Western has been doing.'

'Yes, Ted?'

'Well...' he went on, 'I'm not sure it's working...'

'Oh, but Ted...'

'No, I'm not sure that it's leading anywhere; I want it stopped. And I'll need you to speak up for me at next week's case conference.'

'Next week?'

'Yes,' he said. 'The day before the interviews.'

'Oh.'

'Oh.'

'But...'

'No buts, Monica.' And that was that. Or so he thought.

CHAPTER TWENTY-EIGHT

I can't be blamed for what I've done. I know that, now. I can't help it if you don't like what I've written. It's therapy, you know. It's exorcism; all part of the healing process. That's what you've got to do when things go wrong: you've got to get it out of you and get in down on paper. That's what he told me. That's what I've done. You can say anything you want, he said. You can do anything, with anyone. You can say things that you don't believe or things you do but you're too scared to say. You can say things that you don't believe, and you can say things that you do believe but don't want anyone to know; things that you wouldn't really want to own up to. You can say them all and nobody will know. Nobody can tell the difference. It's your characters – not you. No-one knows what you think. So you can say anything. Make them say it, that's all. Make them be your mouthpiece. You can even pre-empt the reaction that you think it might provoke in other people. You can have fun with this. It's wonderful.

You hear something: something gets your interest and you pick it up and run with it; collect it like a jackdaw, put it somewhere, add it to the other things you've got. Then wait. Wait until you see the next thing. Then you get that and you put it with the other things you've got, and gradually the things that you've collected take on their own identity. And that's when you've got a story.

You write it down. You read the things you've written. Then you write some more. Each time another layer gets added; another thought, a new idea, something that connects the other things together in a new way. It's like painting: decorating; sanding down and adding new coats; sanding down and adding, smoothing, deepening and hardening; making the whole thing stronger, strong enough to withstand the knocks and bumps.

Writing is a sprint: you crash out words as quickly as your fingers will allow, trying to keep up with the overloaded wardrobe of ideas as they tumble from your brain, and then you slow down. Stop. Rest. Breathe, and day-dream. Put some distance between you and the things you've written, do the normal things a writer would be doing when she wasn't writing. For example I've done nothing at all today, or next to nothing. And it's taken me until now – nine o'clock p.m. - to do some writing. But now I'm here, sitting in the classroom on my own, I can write anything; I can write all evening. I could go on and on all through the night, because I've had all day to think, to rest, and to create. Doing nothing is what really matters, or at least doing very little. Forget the writers' workshop strictures about writing time and discipline: the discipline is doing nothing. If you've got a writer's mind, then doing nothing is really doing everything you ever need to do to write. It will build and build and burst out when you're ready, when it's ready, when you've got enough material, when you've done enough thinking, when you're ready to begin writing. Doing nothing is the key to everything. Doing nothing - having time to do it in - will mean you can do anything. Time is all you need, time to do nothing; thinking time; down time; time before writing time; staring into space and thinking time, but more than thinking – reflecting, and revisiting, reminding yourself of where it is you're going. Planning the next step of the journey; waiting for the next new rush to come, the next idea; the rising action.

It came more quickly than I thought.

'Miss Western?' Oh God - Ted. 'A word, if you please,' and then that thing he always used to make his index-finger do: point it at your face then curl and flatten it again, writhing on his hand like some poor hooked worm or a maggot.

I went to where he stood, but not too close. But he came closer, so close I could smell his aftershave and underneath, his body odour. He came closer, toe to toe and then leaned forward and he whispered in my ear. It tickled, and I nearly laughed. But I controlled myself. I handed him the papers and he looked at it to check it was all there. He held it up between his finger and his thumb as if it were contagious.

'This has gone on long enough,' he growled. 'It's got to stop.'

'But...'

'No buts...' he raised his voice. And then he looked at me.

'No more writing Sophie,' he whispered softly, dangling the book in front of me.

'But I'm a writer!' I shouted. 'That's what I do – I write. And anyway it's helping and one day I'll publish it and I'll be famous and...'

'Exactly!' he was laughing. 'Self-delusional behaviour, just like I told Monica. You're not a writer, Sophie. This is not a book, not really. This is nothing,' he continued. 'And you're nobody. What's wrong with you is that you think your problem's literary. Well it isn't. It's just chemistry. It's just a problem with the machinery.' He tapped his head. 'The wirings faulty, that's all. And I'll help you fix it.'

'No you won't,' I said. 'There's nothing wrong with it – with me.'

'There you go again,' he smirked. 'Denying it. Why do you think you had to come here?'

'I...I didn't understand the plot?' I said.

'Lost it more like...' Ted mumbled.

'What?'

'You're not an author, Sophie. You're a nobody.'

'That's not true!' I shouted.

'Yes it is,' he said. 'It's true of you, it's true of everybody. Ultimately, we are all just nobody. There's nothing to us. No self, anyway; no mind packed full of great ideas. It's all a game – it's all a trick our brain plays on us, telling us that this is 'you' and this is all the world around you. But there's nothing there. It's gone. It's nothing more than a survival mechanism.'

'What?'

'It's fiction, Sophie.'

'You don't believe that!'

'Oh yes,' he said. 'I do.'

'So what's the point?' I asked. 'What's the point of anything?'

'There isn't one,' he said to me. 'There is no point to anything, or anyone.'

'That isn't true,' I said. 'It can't be.'

'But it is,' he told me darkly. 'And it's time that you accepted it, young lady'.

He looked out of the nurses' office window. It was his turn now to tell a story.

'Look Sophie,' he began. 'Let me ask you something. Have you ever...' he was struggling. 'Have you ever walked through town and seen all the houses and the flats and the apartment blocks all packed together, stuffed like rabbit hutches full of people? Have you ever wondered at the tidal surge of people passing you to go to work or school, or on a journey when you're driving on the motorway and everybody's driving past you in their cars, on their own journey, living their own life – a life not that much different from your own? Why aren't they you, eh? Why aren't they anybody else? What makes you so different from them, eh?'

'They're not here, for one thing.'

'No they're not. And they aren't all called Sophie Western and they don't live in the house where you live and one day they might not get married to the person you get married to; their children won't be called the names your children will be called. The houses that they live in might be bigger, the jobs that they have might be better and their salaries higher. Their lives might even be happier than yours. But their lives could be yours. You aren't that different from them. They aren't that different to you. They could be you. Every one of them. All of them. Which means you could be any one of them.'

'I'm not though!' I protested.

'No, you're not. But just consider why. Think of all the reasons you're not them. Go on. Think of them. What are they? Your name, for one. Who called you that? And why were they your parents? You went to that school because that was where you were. Your friends were the people who just happened to be there. One day you'll marry someone that you just happened to meet somewhere, like everyone does. Just like we all do. We all live near enough identical lives, once you strip away the different clothes we wear and jobs we do. I know some people's lives are worse, and some might even be a little better. But they're not different people. Their lives could be your life. You could just as easily have been them. Look out of your window now. Stand up. Go on. Look down there at all the houses in the town. Look at the windows. Look into the rooms. There's somebody like you standing at the window, looking back.'

I looked out of the window at the trees. And then I saw Ted in reflection take a step back, place his feet apart and tear the sheets in two in one go, going red and grunting as he did so.

***

I was devastated. I had to keep on writing. Will said so. I wanted to. It was important to me. It was helping, really helping; really. I was feeling better; I was noticing things and slowly starting to take an interest in the things and people all around me. It was like waking up after a long cold hibernation. And writing was the summer coming; putting words down on paper, paper filling up and piling high was the days slowly lengthening, and sunlight strengthening and warming, and the sun rising higher in the sky. No-one, not even Ted could stop that happening. How could he stop the world from turning? I had to keep on going. For Will, as much as anyone. But for myself, as well. For me. But how? Then suddenly, a solution was presented to me. That's what happens sometimes when you're stuck for an idea. Something just appears from nowhere. I suppose it's what's called inspiration. Goodness knows where these things come from. From in me, I suppose; but from somewhere that I'm not aware of. Somewhere in my subconscious. Deep, buried; somewhere dark where black thoughts once fermented, problems multiplied and spread throughout my head and now solutions start appearing like new green shoots in spring.

The main item on the agenda at the community meeting that morning was what to do now school had finished for the summer. We discussed all sorts of possibilities. The lady from Rehab had come over too, to tell us all about their classes.

'And you,' Ted looked at me 'had better listen. It's time you started learning some new skills. You won't be here forever, you know.'

'Neither will you.'

'What?'

'I said that's true,' I lied.

'Yes,' he was warming to the idea now. 'I think you need to start a class,' he went on. Perhaps he realised how unfriendly he'd just sounded. Maybe he was suddenly aware of just how nasty he could be. Or maybe Jane had told him. Maybe; maybe not. I don't know. But suddenly it wasn't an instruction but was more like a suggestion.

'It's important that you attend some occupational therapy. It's important that you do something in the morning – that you begin to occupy yourself.'

Something other than writing, of course. That was what he meant. He wasn't going to say it, but he meant it. Inside, I was boiling. I know now what I should have said; and what I should have done. I should have picked up all the torn sheets from in the bin and thrown them at him there and then in front of everyone. I should have stood up to him and argued. Will had, and he had won. But no-one else had done. No-one knew what he had done. No-one knew what he was really like. I should have done something, other than just sit there, listening to the air between us, catching flashes of hidden meaning in the otherwise innocent conversation.

'We also need to think about what you're going to do when you leave school,' he added. 'A career. They'll be able to help you do that. They'll help all of you to do that.'

Meeting closed. Decision made. Will said nothing. I knew why.

There was a long list of rehabilitation classes: painting, pottery and basket weaving, musical appreciation – they had all been crossed out in Ted's handwriting. Those that were left there were vocational, designed to train the patients who would one day be released into the community. I glanced down the activities that Ted had decided should be open to us, things like book-keeping, domestic science, gardening, sewing, woodwork, baking....typing: not even typing - secretarial skills. Lizzie had signed up for cookery; Debbie and the boys were all intent on doing gardening; I quickly put my name down in the space beside the typing classes, hoping Ted would notice the connection.

I already knew exactly how to type. You know I do. I don't need to tell you that. What you maybe don't remember is that my grandfather had once given me a typewriter. I must have been about seven or eight, no older. 'Imperial Good Companion, model T' was scripted round the royal crest. The entire machine was black with round black keys with off-white letters printed in the centre: N spun round to look like Z, a wonky T. The whole thing was encased in a heavy black box which locked. I learned to use it, and I learned to love it. I immersed myself in everything about the process, like the smell of wet ink on the ribbon; the little strips of Tipp-ex paper for typing neat bright white corrections in the shape of the mistaken letter; the sharp crack of the keys like rifle fire, and most of all the words all marching slowly, line by line across and down the clean white paper. He thought that it would be useful for me: I could learn a skill, and then I'd not be short of work. And he was right: it was, especially now. Every evening, every afternoon, every spare moment I'd been using it to recreate the book that I had written. I sat in the classroom on my own and typed the words as fast as I could read them. I could change them. I could write revisions and improve things. Here and there I'd change a word or two, delete a passage, add a paragraph. And no-one knew what I was typing. Not at first at any rate. Will of course had read what I had written; he'd encouraged me to go on writing. As the pile of papers grew it became harder to keep hidden. Then when Will received his warning Ted demanded all the papers. But I still had all the ideas.

CHAPTER TWENTY-NINE

Most of the patients in Rehab were older than we were. In the typing class they sat and licked their lips and pressed the keys down, one by one, then looked up at the page to see what they had done. But I attacked the typewriter with a passion, feeding it sheet after sheet of A4 paper, writing words before they disappeared like warm, moist breath on glass.

There were about twenty desks each facing forwards, with a large white typewriter on top. Someone met me at the door.

'Hi. You new here? I come here every day. Have done for a year,' she said. 'The paper's in the tray just over there. Tipp-ex on the side for if you make a blob. There's stencils if you want them, too, and carbon paper if you need to make a copy.'

She was in her fifties maybe. Short and normal looking, normal sounding; but the eyes gave her away.

'Can I sit... is that anybody's seat?' I asked. I needed to sit at the back. There was a desk on its own in the corner, with a window behind it. I wanted to sit there. I wanted to sit where nobody could see what I was typing.

'No. That's Margery's seat. You can't sit there. That's her seat. She sits there. She always sits there. Always. That's hers.'

'But....' I started to explain. I needed to sit at the back, but the woman wouldn't listen.

'Tell her, Betty. That's her seat, isn't it? Margery's. Her seat. That's why she can't sit there. Can she? You can't sit there. It's not your seat. You've got to sit here. You HAVE to sit here. You MUST sit here. SIT HERE!'

Someone walked across the room, and took her gently by the arm.

'It's doesn't matter, Vicky. Margery's not coming anymore. She's gone. They've closed her ward. Sophie can sit there if she wants to.'

'No!' shouted Vicky and she turned and looked at me with hatred in her eyes.

I was frightened. Frightened by how ordinary the woman seemed at first, and frightened by how quickly she had changed. I felt a fool, too. I'd assumed at first she was the therapist - that this was her typing class. She had seemed so normal. And then something trivial had happened and she'd changed, and now she was stuck in the same mad pattern of behaviour like a broken record. That had once been me. My thoughts had once turned in circles of the same thing, over and over and over again. The pages we were reading; all the tortures and indignities that had been heaped upon Justine were now all being heaped on me. I felt it all as keenly as if I had been her. And I didn't notice what was happening to him, what he was doing. And by then, of course, it was too late.

'You've met Vicky, then?' the woman said. I started.

'It's all right. She won't hurt you. She just likes everything to be the same. Order. Everyone sitting where they always used to sit.'

'I'm sorry... I didn't mean...'

'I know,' she went on. 'But it's difficult for them – the ones that are left behind. Their friends have gone.'

'Where?'

'Back to where they came from?'

'So they're cured?' I asked.

'Yes – some of them,' she answered. 'Anyway – I'm Lizzie by the way.'

Another one! This version though was taller; older - pretty. She had long blonde hair, dyed and she smiled. Her eyes were kind. I smiled back. I sat down at the desk, and turned a piece of paper in the platten. Then at once I began to type.

I am Sophie Western. I am sixteen and a half years old. I live at 38 Larch Drive, Cranford Road, Southey, SH34 6JS, United Kingdom. Telephone number (Tel) 0242 67934. I go to Southey Girls High School. My favourite subjects are:-

Music
English
History and R.E.

Not maths, though; never maths. Not now, not then. But that was not the problem. I didn't know that then. I was never any good at P.E. either: couldn't do it, wasn't picked for teams and dreaded it. Always the outsider, the observer. And then there were the showers; there was Louise Anderson. But even she was not the problem. Wonder what she's doing now, since going on the radio?

I stopped suddenly. This was harder than I thought. I hit the keys as fast as possible with each of my fingers in turn. The letters fired down on the white paper from all directions covering the page in print. The noise was wonderful.

Thekljhkifn\;kdnfakevv\zd ejrbaSJkjbvz;dknf E;KFB |F\GEDFB'F \ZKCB\SJF;K hfcSBD;ksBFehfba;ek bed[ouha[jgbns;kjgb E[UFHw[Obes;Karbg;kjrb v;kdbfasekbvak b;dkfbaek;vbr;kjacbd;jacerbohe[oaehvtgarjbaptvh4q[ivargt9 q4ytv[oma bvjabe;admb\g;

I tried a typing exercise I'd once been taught in school.

'The quick brown fox jumps over the lazy dog.'

I tried again, in capitals.

'THE QUICK BROWN DOG JUMPED OVER THE LAZY DOG.'

I moved the bar at the side of the keyboard down, and typed it twice again, in red this time. With the little ribbon lever in the middle, you could even type without ink. The letters cut into the paper, leaving a faint mark until the last remaining black-red stains had worn off. Little circles from the centre of the 'O's fell onto the floor. I pulled the paper out and tore it up.

There were electric typewriters in here as well. I sat in front of one and switched it on. There was no hard pressing to be done: the lightest touch would send the little golf-ball spinning round to find the corresponding letter and then print it on the paper. If your fingers stayed too long whole lines got printed, just like this one:

HHHHHHHHHHHHHHHHHHHHHHHHHHHHHHHHH
HHHHHHHHHHHHHHHHH

Doesn't H look like a zip? Perhaps it is. Maybe that's the turn, right there. Maybe that's the point at which the plot ends and the truth is suddenly revealed? Right there, that line of typing on the page.

It was no good. There was nothing new to write. No words. Not now that I was well again. And in a few weeks I would be discharged. The book still needed writing, but I'd hit a block. That's what it's like. Joy one day, and despair the next. Sometimes it seems as though it's going well and you can cope; then suddenly it's all disaster and a waste of time.

'Try one of these,' the woman told me, holding up a card with some fictitious correspondence. I looked down at the names and words. I knew them all of course, although at first I couldn't remember where I'd seen the card before. Then the clatter of a typewriter:

Dear Mr Caxton – comma, space-space; carriage return; carriage-return;

Further to your letter of the 7th inst., I have great pleasure in confirming that – subject to agreement to our terms – your book has been accepted for our publication list. We would like to take this opportunity to thank you for showing us your manuscript, and to remind you we are as ever, at your service. Yours etc. Sophie Western. No. Not Sophie Western. Miss S. Western; not just Miss S. Western: Miss S. Western, *secretary*.

They were the ones we used at school. I suddenly remembered I had had a typing lesson on my final day. But Miss Greer had been away, and who was standing in for her – why, Mr Jones of course. And who was sitting at the desk behind me? Who was looking at me, as she always did? And who was smiling, smirking, looking at me, wondering...

'Sir?'

The voice outside my head came as a shock.

'What is it, Louise?'

'Sophie Western fancies you. She does sir: ask her, go on.'

I ripped the paper from the roller and screwed it up as tightly as I could.

***

Next morning at the community meeting, Jane asked us how we had got on. Lizzie was ecstatic, loving every minute of the cookery lessons, regaling us with platefuls of nutritional information, recipes and calories, fat content and other dietary details.

'Did you know,' she was telling everybody 'there's as much fat in a bag of crisps as in a pint of milk?'

'How about you, Sophie? How did you get on?' asked Monica.

'Fine!' I answered.

'Good,' she said.

And people nodded. Jason tried to say something, but Ted had started talking.

'I think it's important, Sophie, that you stick this out,' he interrupted. 'You'll not be here much longer. Soon you'll go back home again. Maybe even back to school, I don't know. But one thing's certain – you will need a skill. Typing is a skill that opens up all sorts of different possibilities.'

I looked down at the floor.

'Well, anyway: as you've got on so well I think you should go over there again today,' he said.

'But...'

'It's ok, Sophie. We'll manage here without you. Won't we, everyone? Debbie – you can stay and ... Patrick, well we'd better have a boy's perspective on the new appointment. Any other business?'

And there wasn't. All the candidates would soon be coming: Jane in her interview suit, Monica in a new dress and the senior Nursing Officer from the hospital to preside over the interviews.

Once the meeting was over I walked on my own to the rehabilitation unit. There was hardly anybody about.

'Market day,' the blonde-haired woman said. 'Short-stay patients always go to town on Wednesday – helps keeps them in touch with reality.'

I sat in my seat at the back of the classroom. The ritual of rolling in a clean, white sheet of typing paper, feeling the rubber platten-roller catch the page and feeding it in and rolling it round until the new sheet stands up stiff and waiting to be printed with the metal letters. If you look closely you can even see the criss-cross pattern of the ribbon, printed through onto the paper, making the letters look a little like a tapestry. There was colour, too. A little lever let you move the ribbon higher, so the letters printed through the red line underneath. The red part of the tape was so well inked that it was almost wet; the black, however had gone to and fro so often, winding back and forth with people typing, it had almost worn to grey. But red was bright and new like blood. It made a splash each time the metal hit. I glanced down at the knife wounds on my wrist, healed now and faded white to scars.

'Here,' the woman said. 'Try writing letters, Sophie. Use the templates if you want, or just invent one. Make sure you lay it out correctly: use the format that I've shown you.'

'Write a letter. Who to?'

'Anyone. Someone you want some answers from. You're writing a book, I hear?'

'Oh God – who doesn't know?'

'Why don't you write a letter to a character in your book.'

I did. It was all I did write that day.

28 Mill Lane
Lowoodfield
WD2 6HY

Dear Will:

The woman told me I should write a letter to a character: to someone in a book. She didn't say which book. She said: 'you choose, it's up to you'. So I chose you. Why should it have to be to someone in a real book? This is not a real book. You know that. Why shouldn't I just write to you? I owe it to you, and I thought I ought to write and thank you after all you've done for me. What will you think when you eventually read what I have written? Where will you be? And what will you be doing? There's a chance, I suppose, that you won't know that the letter is addressed to you. Or will you? Surely no-one else has done what you asked me to do? At least, I must have been the first. Perhaps the last as well. Who knows?

In the end I tore it up and went back to the Unit early. That evening we were going to have a party!

CHAPTER THIRTY

Later on while Jane celebrated her promotion, I took Will into the classroom and I showed him what he'd started. His placement here was nearly over. There was no chance I would finish it before he left. But I wanted him to see that I was still committed. I wanted him to know I hadn't been defeated.

'This is amazing,' he was saying. 'So much better than the first draft.'

He was lying. Parts of it were better, but a lot of it was still a load of rubbish. I waited for him to read up to my new addition.

'How do you manage it?' he asked.

'I don't quite understand,' I told him. 'Book writing seems to be like planting seeds. Little bits of dialogue, scenes of interest, anything gets put down - planted - so that it might grow into something big, substantial, interesting, so that it might link up with other smaller bits and form a whole, so that the individual pieces form a pattern, like a garden slowly taking shape, coming together, joining up to form the bigger picture. At the time of planting what you're doing is unclear; some plants might be in the wrong place. You've simply got to wait and see as it develops.'

And he turned the pages, and I waited. And I waited. And I waited.

Then suddenly, he found it.

'But you can't write that!' he shouted.

'I can. I did.' I looked at him.

'God, Sophie. If Ted sees this he'll go barmy.' But he was smiling now. He liked what he was reading.

'Don't you mind...?' I asked him.

'About this?' He was pointing to page one-hundred-and-seventy.

'No,' I smiled. 'About the job.'

'No, not really,' he replied. 'I suppose I never expected to get it, if I'm honest. It was my first true interview, though. And Ted was so aggressive. It was wonderful experience.'

Monica seemed to be ignoring the result completely, going round the unit pretending that it hadn't happened and she didn't care. The only person with a smile was Jane, and she was always smiling anyway. I was pleased for her, really; she didn't seem to mind if everybody thought the only reason she had got the job was Ted.

***

On Will's final day we held a leaving party for him. Lizzie cooked the food, trying out the recipes that she'd been studying. Jason made the presentation; even Patrick Randle managed to have a normal conversation. Then just before he left, Will made a little speech.

'Look, I don't know what to say,' he started.

'Boring!' someone shouted.

'Ok... I'll try...'

There was a loud cheer.

'It's been a great few months working here,' he started 'really great. I couldn't have had a better placement. I'd like to thank a few people for that now,' he said: 'First Ted, for all his help...'

'...or lack of it,' Debbie whispered.

'and Monica too, for her support...'

266

There was a ripple of applause.

'...and you lot for being such a wonderful bunch of young people...'

There a loud cheer.

'Really... you're the best!' he said. 'And I know some of you have made enormous progress over the last few months and I really hope that will continue, and that you'll get out of here and lead the lives you all deserve... and you deserve the best,' he said.

'He hasn't mentioned Jane,' Debbie whispered. But Jane didn't seem to mind. She was looking at him, smiling as she always did. But this time she was really looking at him; really smiling – beaming at him, looking really happy. Surely...? The more I looked the more I saw... and then he spoke and everything became clear.

'I've got one further small announcement...' he started. 'You won't actually be seeing the last of me,' he told us. 'And I'm still going to be able to hear all about you.' There were some puzzled noises from around the room, and a strange and slightly frightened look from Ted.

Will looked at Jane and held out his hand. She walked over to him with her head down shyly, smiling, almost laughing and then reached out and took his hand in hers. There was an enormous cheer. People started jumping up and down. I was hugging Debbie, dancing. Why were we so happy for them? I don't know. It doesn't matter. When I looked again though, Ted had disappeared.

Next morning, Will said his farewells. He had a present for us all – a little something, as he said, because he was a student and he had no money. Debbie got a comb – 'save her borrowing yours, Soph.' Pat received a key-ring; Jason got an Airfix model kit and Lizzie got a mirror. 'And this,' he said 'is for you Sophie,' he said, handing me a bag with something heavy in it. I took a cardboard box out of the bag. It was as heavy as a book. At first I wasn't sure what he had given me. But then I saw the writing on the side: A4, cream, laid – one ream.

'Paper! Oh, Will – thanks!' And then I kissed him.

'Watch her Jane,' someone called out. 'She'll do anything for a box of typing paper.'

Once the motorcycle noise had died away, I went down to the classroom. It was Saturday. No lessons. I was on my own. I got a pair of scissors to cut the sellotape that held the box lid down, and took out the first few sheets of clean white paper. I rolled one slowly in the platten with all the care of someone doing something for the final time. And then I started typing...

At first, the clatter of the typewriter in the empty room was deafening. The noise was random. Tap tap tap-t-tap-tap-tap as fingers hit the keys, then the sharp crack of the metal like a rifle, cutting letters on the page, and adding others, making words and sentences and paragraphs. It was impossible to imagine anything of any order coming out of such a random noise. But slowly, paper started moving up and up the roller. Pages started filling up with words. The noise began to settle. There seemed to be a rhythm in the typing. I rolled another sheet of paper in the platten. I put my fingers on the keys. And went on typing...

This is not a real book; not really. A real book tells a story. That's what proper books do, anyway. That's what they are; that's what they're for; that's what they do and I should know. I've been reading them for long enough - first of all at school and then between appointments at the psychiatric surgery. There was nothing else for me to do. I wasn't going back to school – not after what had happened to me - and I wasn't getting any better, either. I could hardly walk the streets in winter. And the library was always warm and dry. I went inside and hid behind the stacks of books...

And now there is another book to add to the library shelves. My book. The book that tells my story. My therapy: writing therapy. It might have taken twenty years to finish, but it's done now. It's completed. I have written myself a future. I've become the author of my life, controller of events. I've written my own destiny.

It needed time, that's all. Time to understand; time for what had happened Time to unravel slowly in the dark recesses of my mind, to straighten out. Time for the solutions to appear; time for me to take it all apart and put it back together in a different order. Slowly all the pieces of the jigsaw of my life began to make a picture. I began to see exactly what had happened. I started to explain things. And I found the words; it took a long time, but at last I had the answers to the questions Dr Grimshaw and the others had been asking.

But by then, however, there was no-one left to tell. Where had they gone? Where are they now?

A short time later I was finally discharged from Cranford Hospital. I never did go back to school. I moved away from Southey. And I hid my time in hospital from everyone I knew. For years I didn't even put it on my application form for jobs. If I had done, they wouldn't have been worth the effort to complete. I lied about my leaving dates at school. And no-one seemed to notice. No-one seemed to care. So I kept quiet. I kept my head down; life went on – a life I hadn't wanted and I nearly didn't have. I got a job; I met new people, and I got promoted. Then suddenly, the other day, I happened to be sent back to my home town for a training course: 'Understanding the Past – A New Approach to Source Material' it was called. The local Archivist was running it. I could have been sent anywhere in the country for a course like that; but I was sent here. Maybe someone in the company had got a sense of humour.

For weeks before the conference, each night I had been back there in my dreams. So by the time I got there and got off the train and walked past the old Child Guidance Clinic to the market place, it all seemed so familiar. There were three white taxis waiting in a row. The front one had its doors wide open, but the driver was sitting smoking in the car behind. I got in. The leather seats were hot. Eventually he wandered up and threw his fag into the gutter.

'Where to, love?' he asked.

Instead of telling him to take me to the conference hotel, I asked him for the hospital, the Cranford Psychiatric Hospital. The loony-bin; the Funny Farm. I hadn't planned to. But I heard the words as if they had been spoken by another person

'Where?' he said.

'Cranford Psychiatric Hospital,' I repeated. 'It's on the Sutton road, right out of town. You drive up the hill about a mile and…'

'I know where it is love,' he interrupted. 'Or at any rate, where it was.'

He got in and eyed me in the rear-view mirror. He seemed to be in no great hurry to begin the journey. Instead of starting up the engine he looked down and started counting coins into a coin dispenser. And now and then he raised his head and he was scrutinising me again, narrowing his dark eyes and looking at me for some clue; some flicker of emotion, some expression on my face or some reaction which might tell him what to think or say, some clue to tell him how he should react; some small thing that would tell him whether he knew more than I did, and if so, whether he could use this knowledge to his own advantage.

My appearance, though, confused him. I was smartly dressed; I wore a suit. He couldn't work me out. And I was carrying a briefcase. I looked down at a print out with directions to the conference and waited. He was going to have to make the next move. I didn't want to ask him what the problem was. I wanted him to tell me.

'What do want to go there for?' he asked at last.

I didn't answer. I pretended to be searching in my handbag.

He didn't bother asking me again. Instead, he started up the engine. As he put the car in gear and drove off a sudden panic gripped me. He turned left out of the railway station concourse, the indicator ticking in the rhythm of my heart. As he waited for an opening in the traffic, I decided to get out. But then he suddenly pulled off into the road.

It was too late now. I sat back, clasped my handbag to my chest and looked out of the window. We drove out of the town and up the long hill, past factory units where I remembered there had once been open fields. On the way I caught him glancing in his mirror at me. When I caught his eye he looked away. I looked out of the window for the landmarks that I once knew, but most of them had disappeared.

As we climbed the hill I was surprised to see the trees, still standing, if a little thinner; then, as we approached, the entrance to the hospital between the tall stone gate posts. The iron gates still hung there, rusted open. The tiny dolls-house cottage where the charge-nurse from the mens' ward had once lived was tucked behind the pillar. But the drive now curved instead of leading straight up to the hospital's front doors. And smaller side-roads sprouted off like branches left and right. Each cul-de-sac was lined with small, neat houses tightly packed around the narrow tarmac ribbon. There were hundreds of them: hundreds and hundreds of little yellow houses, all with tiny gardens, neat mown lawns and bright white plastic window frames. I got out of the taxi and I looked around.

'Wait here for me, please.'

In the distance I could see where the adolescent unit had once stood. But I couldn't find a way of reaching it. All the roads seemed too small and to lead nowhere. It was like a maze. The broad, central driveway had been lopped off like a diseased elm. A stump, a few yards from the main road, was all that remained. And instead of leading straight into the heart of the estate it curved and curled. Wandering around was like climbing a tree: seeing the branch that you wanted, but seeing no way forward for the tangle of the leaves and branches right in front of you.

I walked back to the main road. The engine of the taxi was still running.

'How long has this been here?' I asked the driver. He paused and looked at me before he answered. Something about him seemed familiar.

There was no-one else about. As I walked back up the drive I felt self-conscious. All the houses were so tightly packed together. Upstairs the windows were all open. People were about. Was that them, watching? Was that the downstairs curtains twitching?

This time I turned right instead of left. I needed to go left but couldn't see a way of making progress. So I went right, then right again, then left. Then nothing. Another dead end. I retraced my steps and took a different right turn this time, then another and another. I was going further and further away from where the unit might be but at least I felt that I was getting somewhere. Then suddenly, in front of me there was the field where we had played our rounders match. The little iron railings round the edge were still there too, and the area was curtained off on two sides by new trees. I walked into the middle of the field and for a moment thought I saw the big bright rehab building with its flat roof and the strange white ventilation box on top. Perhaps they had converted it to flats? But when I turned my head it wasn't there and in its place a row of larger houses stood and faced the field.

As I walked back to the taxi I passed street signs with familiar names: Netherfield Drive and Shandy Crescent; Brooklyn Close; and Pemberley - all names of the wards in the old hospital. Names that I'd forgotten, but now recognised again; names I'd never thought about until seeing them screwed to walls or fixed to picket fences. I wondered if the people living there knew the origin of their addresses. But there was nobody to tell. Back at the entrance was the small green bus shelter where I'd waited with my suitcase on the sunny August afternoon I'd been discharged. And next to that, the small red pillar-box where I had posted letters to my grandmother in order to prevent them being franked with 'Cranford Hospital'. I turned right and walked along the main road, past the taxi. The adolescent unit had been nearest to the road and I thought that I could see a few of the tall trees that had once stood in the garden. It had been a big house, once home to the hospital administrator. It would have made a spacious dwelling if converted. Surely they'd not demolished it and built these pretty-pretty houses on the rubble?

When I finally located where it once had been I stopped. I peered through a thin fence into somebody's back garden. There was a blue swing on the lawn and somebody had placed a paddling pool on a tiny square of patio. A loose hose was filling it with water, and a little girl was screaming as she ran off after dipping hands and toes into the icy water. There was a smaller child – a boy - pedalling a bright red, plastic car. The morning sun was warm. Collared doves cooed in the trees. I walked back along the main road to the entrance, where the taxi was still waiting.

'So,' the driver said when I got in. 'What was your business there, then?'

'Oh, I used to know the place' I told him, 'years ago: when it was a hospital.'

'Really?' he replied, suspiciously.

'Yes,' I said, defiantly. 'I did.'

'Work there, did you?' he went on.

'In a way, yes.' I said. 'I did.'

He eyed me through the rear-view mirror.

'What kind o' job was that then, love?' he asked.

'Oh Author,' I replied, and smiled. 'I wrote a book about it.'

273